THE INFINITE SERIES: BOOK 1

NICOLE
CORINE DYER

Infinite

Printed and bound in the United State of America

ISBN-10:0-9970212-0-9
ISBN-13:978-0-9970212-0-2

First Edition First Printing

Editing by Beth Hemmerich
Editing by Jennifer Tovar at Gypsy Heart Editing
Cover Design by Michelle Preast
Formatting by Stacey Blake at Champagne Formats

Dedication

To my children, Deegan and Shane. It's never too late to follow your dreams.

Prologue

Tall bookshelves lined the walls with stained glass windows settled above them. The frigid night air seeped through the broken windows and filled the room with a sense of dread. There was no joy left here. The once happy furnishings from a family long ago were now plagued with fear and sorrow as muffled screams could be heard coming from outside of the old library.

Candlelight flickered across thousands of books. Some were haphazardly stacked in the shelves, while others were aflame in the fireplace. A small stack of tattered tomes were piled next to the roaring flames, ready to be sacrificed.

A large black gothic throne sat in the middle of the far end of the room with five, tall backed chairs on each side. It was adorned with gold trim and jewel incrusted legs. Silhouettes of weapons and statues were cast all around, and broken shards of stained glass littered the wooden floor.

The sweeping of cloaks sounded in the room as each figure took a seat in the tall black chairs, forming a half circle. Their identities were hidden beneath low hoods, only their hands were visible.

"Are preparations being made?" a smooth voice asked as he sat in his black and gold throne.

"Yes, we are analyzing each detail," a thick voice replied.

With a nod, the first hooded figure reached into his cloak and revealed a gun. A loud pop echoed throughout the room as the second man fell out of his seat and on to the floor. His hood fell back to reveal the face of a young blond man with a fresh wound in the middle of his forehead.

"Analyzing, indeed," the leader growled in disgust. He turned his attention to the seats that surrounded him. "Weed out the traitors. We need to be fully prepared. One mistake will cause us to fail."

Breaking the silence, another figure rose. "What was Henry's crime?" His voice cracked with uncertainty.

"He was going to make our plans public, from what I am told. True or not, it had to be dealt with," the smooth voice said. "Each piece of the puzzle is important."

The man sat back down nervously and refrained from drawing more attention to himself. Whispers filled the room as the leader with the gun rose to his feet.

"We cannot afford any error. Do you understand? We have to calculate everything! If I suspect any treachery, you will die." His voice was chilling and a few members shifted nervously. No one dared to question his authority. His hooded gaze steadily crossed all ten figures. "I have a job for you all."

The air grew still and no one dared move. If expectations were not met, their life would end. Mistakes were not allowed in such fragile times. "I want a recruit from the Domus."

"That will be almost impossible," a young voice to his left spoke. "The Warriors are the most loyal to the Gods."

"As if I didn't already know that, Max," the man growled. "We need spies. We need a true Warrior to train you for battle."

"We are perfectly capable," Max spoke quietly.

The man on the throne laughed causing Max to shift nervously in his chair. Everyone's attention was turned to the poor cowering man who had the nerve to challenge the leader of them all.

"You are no where near their skill," the massive man proclaimed as he sat down in his throne. "Recruit who you can. If you reveal our intentions to the wrong person, you will be taken care of."

Max shifted. "But-"

"Meeting adjourned."

Chapter I

Ryan

Loud music blared throughout the camp. The sound echoed in his ears as he ran through the never-ending sand pile that is Iraq. They were having a party and celebratory gunfire popped in every direction.

It was too close for comfort for Ryan.

It was not a difficult mission, but he remained cautious as he made his way around the small town. He continued to move through the dark as lights flashed when bombs would go off all around him.

"Must be some party," he whispered. Blood trickled down his eye, making it even more difficult for him see in the dark. "Dammit."

Ryan stopped running to lean against the nearest stone wall. His gear was slashed across the front from a scuffle with a very angry militant.

Ryan looked around the broken buildings and shook his

head. War had destroyed this small town and was taken over by the corrupt. Rubble littered the streets and makeshift roofs out of large pieces of cloth flapped in the wind.

He made his way slowly over to the tented area that housed the militants.

His boots kicked up dirt and he cursed to himself. He hid behind a pile of rubble when a jeep drove down the narrow street, and a searchlight pointed in his direction. He lay completely flat on his back on the dirt ground. The jeep came to a halt and Ryan heard the doors open and close.

He slowly reached for the knife strapped to his thigh and grasped the handle, ready to defend himself. No one came though.

"Get some rest and prepare for tomorrow," a man said.

Ryan heard house doors shut, before he peaked over the pile and found no one around. The jeep sat empty with its keys in the ignition. He contemplated stealing it and going for a joy ride, but his brain told him otherwise.

He rolled over and pushed himself up, before he took off in a sprint towards the tents. Another jeep was about to cross in front of him, and he ducked into an abandoned home.

Ryan took off his helmet and wiped the blood out of his face the best he could then looked down at his hand. He noticed dark hair mixed in with it and realized the knife must have got up under his helmet. "Thanks for the haircut," he muttered. He could not afford to lose focus right now.

He lost Damian and Cato during the knife fight. They continued on without him to ambush their target when Ryan waved them on. They knew he could handle one man on his own. However, the terrorist was more experienced than Ryan believed him to be and his vest and helmet suffered the price.

With a deep breath and one last swipe at his head, Ryan strapped his helmet back on and ran after his companions. He hated Iraq. It was hot, and everything looked the same as it did two thousand years ago. Hell, they were still fighting each other as they did back then. Religion would be the death of mankind and also its savior.

As he reached the tents, Ryan noticed a smear of blood on a nearby truck. The good news was at least it was easier for him to see here. The bad news though, was he had no idea where his team was. He shuffled over to the truck. A small amount of panic raced through his heart when he saw the blood was fresh, but he continued on.

A soft, metallic clang came from a nearby tent, and Ryan thought it was probably a can being kicked. He crouched low with his gun ready to fire and searched each tent as he went by. Each one contained tables, chairs, weapons, and were dark inside.

After searching five tents, he noticed the sixth had a dim light on. He cautiously walked around to the front of the tent.

Two people were inside of the tent judging by the shadows he saw creeping along the ground. Ryan made his way towards the possible threat—steeling his composure the closer he came to the entrance. Adrenaline washed through his body priming him for another fight.

Now at the entrance, his gun up and at the ready, Ryan breached the entrance quickly with his finger on the trigger. Nothing.

There was no one he could see as he continued inside. He could feel the presence of someone else though. There was a table and two chairs sitting in the middle of the room and boxes of weapons were stacked on each other throughout the tent. A small lamp was lit on the table and flickered slightly.

Ryan turned back towards the entrance, momentarily dropping his guard and found himself face to face with two men in full black gear. Both of their guns were pointed at his head when the taller one spoke, "Well, well. What do we have here?"

"Looks like someone is lost," the other man spoke.

Ryan rolled his eyes, let his gun hang across his shoulder and hit the taller one over the head. "I swear, Cato. I am going to shoot you the next time you sneak up on me."

"You're just pissed I could," Cato said.

Ryan wiped the blood out of his eye. "I am perfectly fine kicking your ass head on rather than behind your back."

"All right children, play nicely. What the hell happened to you, Ryan?" The second man sounded amused. He unbuckled Ryan's helmet and tossed it over his shoulder casually. He shook his head at Ryan as he examined the cut, annoyance plastered all over his face.

"It's nothing, Damian, I just got cut by the Kung-Fu terrorist." Ryan stood still and waited for Damian to assess that he was fine. He constantly felt bad for making Damian worry about him. Ryan was careless and passionate, whereas Damian was the safe one, always analyzing situations instead of running straight in to battle. Ryan looked into Damian's brown eyes and silently told him to quit worrying. "I'm fine, Mom."

With a sigh, Damian shook his head. "You owe me three thousand dollars you know."

"Come on, that was just a joke. No party involved should take that bet seriously," Ryan protested.

"Yeah, unless the party that won is named Ryan. Pay up." Damian held out his hand.

Ryan glared at Damian, took a roll of cash out of his pocket, and tossed it to him.

Damian caught it easily and examined the bills. He stuffed it in his pocket and patted it lightly as he winked at Ryan.

"Cheater. I am going to assume you got him." They were after a terrorist leader, a less known one, but an up and comer. The world was full of people that wanted to make a name for themselves and these days that tended to mean hurting others for no real reason, in his opinion.

This mission, like many others, dealt with assassination and Ryan was not a fan. Assassination missions were long-range and his expertise is up front and personal.

"Of course we did." Cato rolled his eyes. He walked to a chair, sat down and propped his feet up on a table. The empty bullet shells on the tabletop chimed together, and a few fell silently to the dirt. "Honestly, I don't know why an alarm hasn't sounded yet. These people have no sense of security."

"Don't get too comfortable. We need to get back to the Domus and report to Ahmose. Maybe after we tell him how easy it was he will give us an actual challenge." Damian walked over to Ryan's helmet, picked it up and held it out to him. Dirt clung to the inside of his helmet from his sweat and blood.

Ryan took it and placed it back on his head. "I wouldn't bet on it. The Jesse dream team is far more equipped." His words dripped with sarcasm.

"Everyone knows where the talent lies. Don't worry about them." Cato never agreed with Ryan on much except Jesse and his gang of miscreants.

Otherwise, Ryan and Cato didn't have much in common. They both were fighters and have known each other for a long time, but sadly they had nothing in common. Damian was the buffer between the two of them, and it was a full-time job.

Damian walked over to the table and picked up a bullet shell. He tossed it in the air and Cato held out his hand and caught it.

"It amazes me how they gather all this equipment. It isn't hard to follow the weapon trails and honestly the US government has enough technology. Perhaps they just don't care?" Cato tossed the bullet back in the air and Damian let it drop to the ground.

"Don't talk like that. We don't know what the mortals are thinking." Damian had a soft spot for the Americans, and as hard as Ryan tried to figure it out, he could not. In his opinion, every country had its secrets and failures and could all be blamed for something. It was utterly pointless to blame one country for all of the world's problems.

"I'm just saying it could save us the trouble of having to chase after these idiots."

"Please, Cato, can we not talk about politics and the problems with modern society this very minute? Honestly, it's getting old." At Cato's disappointed look, Ryan pulled his sleeve up and checked his watch.

"What's wrong?" Damian raised his head.

"It's just getting late and I'm wondering where the heck security is. Seriously, either they didn't like this guy, or they suck at their job. Either way, this is feeling like a waste of time and I want to leave."

"Fine, let's go then, no need to stay any longer," Cato responded.

"No," Damian added. "You know the drill. We have to make sure they find the body which will sound the alarm."

"Which will allow the Americans to find out where they are. Yeah, I get it. Come on, they will find it and the alarm will go off." Cato spun a shell around and flicked it off the table. One after the other, bullet shells fell to the ground until the table was empty.

Sirens started to blare all around them.

"About damn time," Ryan muttered.

Cato hopped up and stretched his arms. "All right lets get going. I got a double padded bed calling my name."

Ryan opened his mouth to talk, but Damian held up his hand and cut him off. "Don't worry Ryan, we all know someone or something will be calling your name."

"Got to suck the fun out of it, don't you?" Ryan teased. "You know me too well. It's becoming a problem."

"I am fairly certain you are the problem, Ryan. You share too much information that we really have no desire to know," Cato said.

"Someone has to teach you about the birds and the bees, you little cutie pie, you." He squeezed Cato's cheeks and puckered his lips.

"Get off." Cato knocked his arms off and rubbed his face. Ryan laughed and turned to see Damian chuckle behind his hand.

Ryan casually reached inside his jacket and pulled out a small leather sack. He loosened the strands and pulled out a small white crystal, about the size of a quarter, and tossed it in the air. "Domus," he muttered, calling out the name of their home.

A glowing blue circle formed where Ryan threw the crystal, wide enough for three people to walk through comfortably. It showed their destination in a clouded mist filled with bookshelves that lined the walls and a roaring fireplace straight ahead.

"Ready fellas?" Damian advanced on the portal.

Loud voices could be heard in the distance and they could see lights shining throughout the camp through the crack in the tent's entrance. The alarm seemed to blare even louder and the three looked at each other, rather pleased with themselves.

"Unless we want a Columbian neck tie, definitely." Ryan glanced at Cato and grinned.

He returned the sack into his jacket and the three of them walked together through the portal. As Cato took the last step into the Domus, the portal shrunk up and disappeared like a flame being blown out. The crystal flicked up in the air and turned to ash.

Inside the Domus was like being inside a museum, but it was still home. Everything was silent and the transition from chaos to peacefulness was a welcomed relief.

They entered the parlor, a large sitting room filled with bookshelves that harbored the history of the their people.

Shadows were cast on the floor as the moon shown through the tall arched windows. Each window reached from floor to ceiling. Ryan felt the desire to walk on the large balcony and fall asleep in the calm of the night. He longed for peace and tranquility.

The soft ocean breeze came through the open windows and made the long red drapes tickle the white marble floor. Waves crashed against the rocks below, and Ryan began to feel tired from the relaxing symphony.

The ocean always reminded him of his home and every time the Domus was stationed next to an ocean he felt a longing to visit his homeland, but there was a sadness there that he could not bear to face.

The parlor was the separating point for the male and female

dormitories. It had four staircases on each side of the room that led up and down to the two other stories of the Domus.

The men were to the left of the windows—the women were to the right. Down the hallways was an endless line of paintings of famous historical figures. Each painting was exactly the same size and shape and lined up perfectly with one another.

"So much for the welcoming committee." Ryan turned to his team and bowed dramatically. "Now if you gentlemen will excuse me, I seek mind altering substances and the warm embrace of a willing participant."

Damian chuckled lightly. "Have fun."

"You know me, I always do." He righted himself and took off his helmet. "Have a good evening boys."

Ryan left his feigned happiness with his friends and slowed his pace when he was out of sight. Melancholy threatened to take over, but he decided to try and celebrate his never-ending existence.

Chapter II

Ryan

Ryan waited hours for her to fall asleep. Emma's long, blonde hair was spread out along her pillow and her eyes moved under her eyelids as she breathed evenly—always a good sign for deep sleep.

She looked at peace and he momentarily felt guilty for sneaking out every time he came to visit her. He had to remind himself this was nothing but a fling, and she hopefully knew that too.

After last nights' mission he stopped by his room and showed up at her door with a bottle of whiskey in hand. There was no need to take his gear off while he was in his room. For some reason, she seemed to like it when he was dressed for battle. Then again, she always welcomed him into her room when he showed up, battle gear or no battle gear.

She knew he was not the monogamous type, but he suspected her feelings for him were growing. No matter how much she talked about a future with him, he felt nothing for her. Ryan would probably have to stop these late night visits for a few months. He didn't want to deal with a lovesick woman living in the same castle as him.

Gently, he got up off her red satin sheets and looked around for his clothes and gear. He was used to making sure his things ended up together. It made for an easier getaway later.

As he dressed he looked outside towards the ocean. The sun was coming up, and he was nowhere near tired now.

Ryan didn't bother putting on his protective gear as he started to tiptoe his way towards the door with it in hand. Emma's room was cluttered with massive amounts of clothing, shoes, and other various woman things.

He looked back at her just to make sure she was still asleep, opened the door and closed it gently behind him.

He ran his hand through his shaggy black hair. He felt a sudden relief to be out of the gossip queen's bedchambers that was decorated more like a modern teenagers room. The posters and magazines of American celebrities seemed to glare down at him as he slept. It was unnerving.

The morning sun began to light up the long corridor through the tall windows and reflected off the white marble floors. The torches that lined the walls were unlit, yet the brush strokes on the paintings could be seen clearly.

A long time ago an enchantment was cast upon the Domus in order to keep any possible enemies from being able to attack it. It's location changes every day to ensure that. It also allowed the Warriors to experience and see what they were risking their lives for. Hiding away in Urbs, the city for Immortals, would make them lose sight of the purpose of their existence.

The ocean view from last night was the same. They obviously got back after the change of location. The water lacked the smell of salt and with the amount of humidity clinging the air—his guess was they were in the Caribbean, perhaps around the Virgin Islands. The water was bluer than the sky and the sand was white and clean.

Ryan never cared for the Caribbean. He preferred oceans to smell of salt and if possible, with a hint of food cooking permeating the air. There were some positives to the Caribbean though. It was a good vacation spot and he hoped to enjoy it today.

He left the female dormitory area and crossed through the parlor to the male dormitories.

Cato and Damian's rooms were on either side of his. They were lucky enough to get the ocean view nearest the parlor. His team was most likely fast asleep. Ryan had other plans. He always woke up earlier than most to go train and sleep deprivation was never an issue for him.

He opened his door and the refreshing sight of mess welcomed him. Clothes and books lay all over the floor, and his untidy bed was beckoning for him to come. Swords, daggers, guns of all kinds, and many other forms of weaponry lined the walls of his room. It was like an armory with a bed and a small collection of books.

Ryan threw his gear on the black leather loveseat and shimmied off his clothes. He opened the armoire doors of his dresser and quickly put on gray sweatpants and a white cotton shirt after he laced on his tennis shoes. As he left his room, he popped in his headphones and jogged towards the training arena.

The training arena was massive, easily as big as a football field. Weapons lined the walls and were separated by type. Guns were located to his left, swords and daggers to his right. Gear of all kinds lined the wall by the doors. Men sizes were by the door that led to the male dorms and women sizes were by the door that led to the female dorms directly across the room.

Like the rest of the castle, this room was bright white and organized—the difference is that it is completely enclosed with no windows. It was a playground for killers.

As he walked inside, he realized a woman sat cross-legged in the middle of the white floor with her eyes closed. She wore all white clothing and her long, wavy, blonde hair laid over her shoulders.

Julia. Her name danced around his mind.

As the door clicked shut, she opened her eyes. "How did last night go?"

"Smooth, easy, boring, all the above."

"Oh, really?" She slowly stood up and walked to him. Ryan cleared his throat and refrained from going to her. She was so close now that he could smell her jasmine perfume. She looked deep into his eyes and his breath caught in his throat. Out of nowhere she smacked the cut on his forehead, causing him to flinch.

"Uh, ouch." He pouted dramatically.

"Poor baby." Julia rolled her eyes and walked away from him. Ryan could not help but watch her hips move and quickly refocused his attention on the swords across the room. He had to avoid her, so he crossed over to them. Ryan took down a Dao sword, a slightly curved single-edged blade with a black hilt. Not his favorite, but it definitely got the job done. It was extremely sad that swords were obsolete for the most part. Damn technology.

He gently put it back in its place and decided he was more in the mood to throw knives. At least knives were still a somewhat useful skill. He picked up a few practice blades and faced a target that hung near the swords.

He planted his feet and stared at the black target. Countless puncture holes faded out the white lines on the board and no one seemed to bother to get a new one. Neither did Ryan for that matter.

Ryan threw the knife and hit a perfect bull's-eye. He really didn't need much training anymore and hoped the mortals would finally invent something new for him to master. After all, being born many years ago allowed more than enough time to master many things.

He turned towards the next target and hit another bull's-eye. One after another he hit all ten targets perfectly. He sighed and turned to throw another knife at the first target when his heart skipped a beat.

Julia stood in front of the target. The knife slipped out of his hand and struck the floor in front of his foot.

"Don't have too much fun."

"Shit, Julia," he grunted. He was extremely happy he noticed her before he let the blade fly. Julia laughed and walked towards him with an amused smirk on her lips.

Armed with a white cloth, she leaned in towards him and pressed it against his head. He was so deep in thought he didn't notice the blood that ran down his face.

"Sorry," she cooed.

"I nearly killed you."

"Don't be so dramatic." She smirked. "I meant I am sorry for reopening your cut."

He shook his head slightly, took a deep breath and closed his eyes. "I think you like hurting me."

She cocked her head and dropped her hand. "What do you

mean?"

"Nothing. Forget it."

She pressed hard on his cut and he flinched. Julia bit her lip, obviously amused. "So sorry."

His eyebrow rose. "I'm sure."

"Do you have to be such an ass?"

"You like it." He winked.

"You are disgusting, Ryan."

"I'm aware."

Julia pulled him gently towards the first-aid kit that hung on the wall and opened it. She pulled out a few butterfly bandages and put them over the cut. His eyes never left her face as she concentrated on putting him back together. Regardless of her tough exterior, she was gentle with him now and the urge to pull her near engrossed him.

What was wrong with him? He never felt this way about her until recently and there was no explanation as to why he was feeling this way now.

He studied her face. Her eyes were as blue as the Caribbean ocean and her lips were full and red. Her features were angelic and her body was what a mortal would call an hourglass figure.

"Why are you staring at me?"

His attention was brought back to the present, while she looked at him in confusion. Ryan definitely felt like an idiot and that was a rarity.

"Uh…"

Thankfully at this moment the door burst open. Cato and Damian ran inside, and their disheveled appearance made it clear they had just woken up—Cato was only in his boxers.

They ran towards him. Cato glanced between Ryan and Julia, his face grim and annoyed.

"Figured you'd be here. Get ready. We have orders," Damian said hurriedly. He bounced on his heels. Obviously, he was eager to get going.

"Calm down, what's the rush?"

"The rush is that we have one hour to get some girl out of trouble, otherwise she's dead," Cato answered. "Go get your gear on, we're headed back to Iraq."

Ryan groaned. He really hated Iraq. "Figures."

He looked back at Julia, who was already headed towards the female dorms and his face flushed. Without a word, he walked out the doors with Cato and Damian at his heels. He desperately wanted to look back at her but forced himself forward.

"What did you do?" Cato asked, as the doors closed behind them, walking briskly to catch up with him.

"What are you talking about?" he snapped.

Cato yanked Ryan by the arm and pushed him against the wall. Ryan felt the urge to punch him, but refrained. "Julia looked upset. Don't mess with my sister, Ryan. I know how you are so don't even think about it."

"No need to get jealous, buttercup."

"I'm serious, Ryan."

Ryan yanked his arm out of Cato's grasp and laughed.

"Don't worry, Cato. I am in no way, shape or form, interested in your sister." It was not a complete lie. He honestly didn't want to get involved with her. He knew he would only end up hurting her. "Now, can we please get on with this mission? I need to shoot something."

Anna

AC/DC blared inside the Humvee. Anna sat on the passenger side and gazed out of the window. Sand. Always sand everywhere. It was late in the afternoon and the sun glared down on them. They were transporting ammunition to a camp and were only ten miles out. She was anxious to get there.

The vehicle left a dust trail behind them from the dirt road. They were the lead vehicle in their convoy. She stared out of the windows—large hills surrounded the area, which didn't ease her tension.

Anna had a bad feeling in the pit of her stomach and nervously picked at her fatigues. Ever since she was little, she picked at her clothes. Every foster parent she had complained about having to buy new pants all the time, because she looked like they put her in ragged clothes.

She took off her helmet and wiped her brow quickly. No matter how long she was here she just could not get used to this heat. It was worse than California, in her opinion. A strand of her black hair was loose from her bun, and she tucked it back behind her ear.

She placed her helmet back on her head and looked to her left at Nathan. He was in foster care with her and they joined the Marine Corps as soon as they were both able. They'd been only friends growing up, but as of recently they had decided to become a couple.

It took all of her willpower to hide it from their superiors.

Every night she wished she could fall asleep in his arms and show affection openly, but she feared being transferred.

Nathan must have felt her gaze and turned to look back at her, the smile she loved was on his lips.

"Morales, quit looking at Sanchez and keep your eyes on the road."

"Shut up, Dan," Nathan muttered.

Anna sat back and felt uncomfortable. She was very shy by nature and when it came to Nathan, her heart raced when people seemed to notice their relationship.

"I mean it, man," Dan said nervously, "you're swerving."

"Quit being a girl." Nathan looked at Anna. "No offense."

She forced a smile and looked ahead. They were about five miles away now. Nathan was swerving, and she reached out nervously and grabbed his arm. Nathan looked down at her hand and whispered, "It's okay, babe."

She quickly let go of his arm and felt her cheeks turn red. Thank God she had dark skin, otherwise it would have been noticeable.

"I think I saw something." Dan looked out the back left window. He gripped his gun and searched.

Anna followed his gaze. She squinted her eyes and saw a flash in the hills. "Maybe it's some discarded metal?"

Dan shook his head. "I don't think so."

"You are the most paranoid person I know, Dan." Nathan laughed. "We have been driving this road for months now and nothing has ever happened."

"I swear I saw something," Dan protested.

"Whatever." Nathan reached over and squeezed Anna's hand. She tried to pull away, but he held onto her. "It's okay."

"Yeah," Dan said, "I know you two are doing the nasty."

Nathan let go of Anna's hand and swung at the back seat, hitting Dan on his helmet. "Dude, shut up," Nathan exclaimed.

An explosion went off in the front of the vehicle, and they came to an instant halt. Her body lurched forward and smacked her head against the dashboard.

The noise from the bomb pierced her ears, and she could not hear anything. She stared ahead, but her body would not move. She remained in the Humvee until Nathan shook her.

The front was destroyed and they had to get out. They were sitting ducks. She pushed with all her strength to open the door, but it would not budge. She turned to see Nathan crawl out of his side, turning around to drag her out by her vest.

Anna landed hard on the ground and jumped up. She looked around at the chaos, her hands instantly finding her gun. Dan was on his radio, Nathan had his firearm ready, while they crouched down by the destroyed vehicle. The rest of the convoy stopped and mirrored them.

She was terrified and stared at her surroundings. Nathan fearlessly shot at any targets he could find. Militants surrounded them. Dan talked on his radio, and Anna looked around for anyone she needed to take down.

Bullets ricocheted off the Humvee. She watched their backs in case the enemy came up from behind them, but she saw nothing.

"Stay here!" Nathan yelled. Anna's attention was drawn to him and their eyes connected for a split second. He kissed her lightly on the lips and disappeared into the storm.

Anna stayed in her spot and shot at the bastards, trying to cover Nathan as best as she could. Dan remained at her side, his gun firing around the back of the Humvee. Anna forced her eyes in the opposite direction of Nathan.

Dan knocked her over as he fell on top of her. Anna pushed his body off and looked down at his bullet-riddled body. His eyes were wide open and a militant lay dead five feet away from them.

Did he just sacrifice himself for me?

She didn't have time to process what she just witnessed. Dan was gone, Nathan was nowhere to be seen, and she feared what would happen next.

She closed Dan's eyes and kissed him on the cheek. He was one of their good friends, and her heart started to ache until the scene came back in focus. She took Dan's spot and shot at the enemy.

Bullets whizzed through the air and every so often cries were heard.

Click.

"Dammit!" she hissed. She popped out the empty clip and went to grab another in her jacket.

"Drop it," said a thickly accented voice. Panic rose in her chest. She felt a gun touch the back of her helmet. She dropped her weapon and held up her hands. All the while, gunshots still went off around her and bodies of her fellow Marines littered the ground.

The man kicked her square in the shoulders, and she fell on her stomach where she lied flat on the ground. The man stepped over her, bound her wrists together, ripped off her helmet and violently pulled her up. Half standing, half being dragged, another man gagged her with a dirty cloth and pulled her towards a nearby hill.

She knew what was going to happen and she had no way to stop it. These men didn't give female military personnel an easy death. She would be abused in the worst ways. Her heart felt like it was going to jump out of her chest from fear.

How did she not see them coming up behind her? Where was Nathan?

So many questions came to mind and she could not answer any of them.

A sharp blow hit the back of her head and she blacked out.

She was in California with Nathan. They sat on the beach, their toes wiggling in the sand. Her frayed jean shorts and tight black tank top were speckled with sand. Nathan wore his board shorts and no shirt. He was so distracting with his shirt off.

The sun started to set and nearly touched the water.

The sky was beautiful. Full of orange, yellow, and purple that weaved their way through one another.

Anna looked over at Nathan and smiled. "I think I love you," she blurted out.

His silence scared her and she looked ahead. The sound of the waves hitting the shore soothed her.

Maybe he wouldn't bring it up and let it go. She hoped that was the case.

Nathan grabbed her chin gently and made her look at him. His eyes were calm and she felt like butterflies were taking off inside of her stomach.

His fingers stroked her cheek, his voice calm and steady as he declared, "I know. I love you too."

He pressed his lips firmly against hers. She tackled him in the sand and her world felt complete.

Her sight started to come back into focus as the militants yelled at her to stand up. There were three of them that she could see. Every time she tried to look around she was hit. Blood and sweat trickled down her neck.

The way up the hill was so difficult that her legs kept collapsing under her. Her body suffered more blows.

The gunshots behind her died down and suddenly the fight seemed over. She heard occasional single gunshots behind her and each time she jumped in fear for her friends' fate.

These men didn't seem nervous or in a hurry to get her somewhere—it was a clue that she was the only living one from the convoy, and all hope left her.

As they reached the top of the hill, she could see a small hole with ammo boxes strewn about inside.

Kill me God, was the only thought she had.

As she closed her eyes and prayed, she heard three gunshots go off. Was she dead? Could she hope for anything more?

She slowly opened her eyes and looked down at her body. There were no bullet holes and she was still standing upright. The three militants lay lifeless around her.

Nathan. Her heart raced as she looked around. After a few minutes went by she was still alone and for a split second she thought God had intervened. Then she realized that was insane.

Suddenly, she saw three figures, in all black gear, running up the hill towards her. Their faces were covered, except for their eyes, their guns held at the ready in search of other people.

She panicked and tried to run.

They caught up to her. Her binding was yanked on and she stopped in her tracks. Two of them remained ready to fire, while the third let his gun hang by its strap and pulled her between the other two. She was flanked on both sides, but that didn't stop her attempt to fight them off.

Their gear was unrecognizable and for all she knew, they were the enemy too.

The man took off her gag and her instinct kicked in as she bit down on his hand, hard.

A lot of curse words came behind the man's masked mouth, and he pointed at her almost as if he was about to say something. She knew he was going to strike her, but instead he growled and kicked sand as he paced.

"Damian, please grab this woman before I loose a finger," the man said.

The one named Damian walked towards her and pulled down the cloth that covered the bottom of his face off. His brown eyes were kind and she calmed down some, but kept her guard up.

His gun drop to his side and he held out his hands. He acted like she was a stray puppy he didn't want to scare away.

"It's okay, miss. We are here to save you." His tone was amused and he looked like he wanted to laugh. "I am very found of my fingers as well, so could you please not bite me?"

The first man looked at Damian and pulled off his cloth mask as well.

"Not funny! I'm pretty sure she drew blood." He glared at her. "Just grab the cannibal and let's get out of here."

"Where is the rest of the convoy?" she demanded.

The three men exchanged looks before Damian calmly put his hand on her arm. "Let's just get you out of here okay? Then we'll talk."

"No," she said firmly. She tried to wiggle out of her bindings and failed miserably. She only pulled them tighter and the pain increased on her wrists. "Tell me where they are, now!"

The third man, still on guard, glanced over at them. "Ryan, Damian, hurry the hell up!"

Ryan walked up to Anna. His eyes were strikingly blue, and had he not looked like he wanted to smack her, she would have thought he was extremely handsome. "Sorry, but we really need to get out of here."

Ryan reached into his pocket and to her left Damian asked, "What's your name?"

She tore her focus from Ryan and looked at Damian. "Anna." As she answered she felt a pinch on her neck. Her attention was brought back to the smug grin on Ryan's face.

"Sorry Anna." He held up a syringe. She felt her body go limp and arms wrapped around her as she fell into darkness.

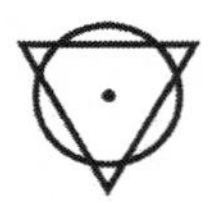

Ryan

Ryan was the last one to step out of the portal and into the parlor. Damian carried a knocked-out Anna to the nearest couch and gently laid her down. Her black hair was a mess and her lip was cut, otherwise, she looked to be fine.

"Cato, go get Ahmose. I'm interested to know what is so special about the little mortal," he said. It wasn't that Ryan was cold blooded, but when you have lived for so long, death really doesn't bother you anymore. It is part of life—inevitable and common. The attack on the Americans was nothing, but a typical act of war and loss of life.

Cato ran up stairs and Ryan turned to Damian. "That chick is crazy," he stated.

Damian crouched down to examine her at a respectful distance for injuries. He looked up sharply and glared. "You do realize she was attacked, captured, and watched her comrades die, right?"

"Who hasn't?"

“I swear, Ryan, you’re an empty shell. Show a little pity when she wakes up at least. It’s going to be hard enough on her without you cracking jokes and being insensitive.” His voice was firm and Ryan raised his eyebrow. Damian rarely got like this. Usually, he kept quiet and let Ryan make a jerk of himself in front of others. Ryan’s superiority over Damian had slowly chipped away over the years, and Damian no longer feared what he said to Ryan.

With a salute, he walked over to the couch opposite Anna and fell into it. He had brought her helmet from the fight and tossed it on top of the coffee table. It was a dirty mess and stained with specks of blood on the outside.

He unclipped his helmet, tossed it on the seat next to him along with his gun, and watched Damian curiously. He seemed to have an interest in the girl. Ryan had to admit, Hispanic women tended to have a certain attractiveness about them that made them stick out from other women. They were hardheaded, fiery, and had full curves. Good gods did they have curves. Anna was a natural beauty. He could still felt the sting of her teeth in his skin, so he was not overly enthralled with her at the moment though.

“What?” Damian looked at him. He took his helmet off and his gun from around his shoulder and laid them on the coffee table between them. He then cut off her bindings with his pocketknife.

“She’s cute. I’ll have to introduce myself properly when she wakes up.” Ryan put his hands behind his head and leaned back against the couch. He looked Anna up and down and Damian’s shoulders tensed. “Perhaps I should ask her to dinner and a walk around the castle. Hey, if she’s lucky, I may even give her a tour of my bedroom.”

"Don't talk about her like one of your conquests, Ryan."

"So you do fancy the girl." He grinned.

"How could I? I just met her."

"Sometimes one look is all it takes." Ryan sighed. "I don't blame you. She really is a very attractive young woman. Even with blood dripping down her forehead."

Damian turned to her and wiped her head with his long black sleeve. She laid still and in a peaceful sleep. Ryan envied her.

Cato briskly walked in with Ahmose behind him. Ahmose was a tall, bald man and his dark skin masked the many scars etched over his body. If Ryan had to describe him, he would say he looked like a body builder, and he was the one man Ryan feared.

"Well, hello there. You're looking particularly shiny today," Ryan mused. "Didn't interrupt your weekly waxing, did we?"

"Ha, Ryan, very amusing." Ahmose rolled his eyes and subconsciously rubbed his head. "This is Anna Sanchez, correct?"

"Yes," Cato replied, "confirmed at the site."

"Good. Wake her up please, Damian."

Ryan sat up quickly.

"First, why the hell did we risk our lives for her? I mean no offense, but it didn't look like she was much use down there," he said with a quick glance at Damian.

The three of them looked at Ahmose and waited for an answer. "Very well. The reason you were sent to acquire Miss Sanchez is because she is to be chosen."

Ryan's mouth fell open slightly and he stood up. "Whoa, you're telling me, this girl, who froze up and got herself captured by the freaking terrorists, gets honored with immortality? You've got to be joking boss."

"It's no joke," Ahmose said firmly. His tension was obvious and Ryan sat down again. "You know very well how difficult it is in this day and age to choose women. The sexism of militaries and countries alike make it nearly impossible to recruit. Miss Sanchez shows promise. So we will offer it and hope she accepts."

"Accepts what?"

Ryan's eyes flew to a conscious Anna lying on the couch where she remained still and awkward. She looked nervously at Damian, who was closest to her and back to Ahmose. Blood started to trickle down her forehead again, and Damian tried to wipe it away. She swatted at his hand and he cleared his throat.

"Just cleaning you up, Miss Sanchez."

She glared at him with her deep brown eyes before turning her attention back to Ahmose.

"Take it away, Captain." Ryan used his best game show host voice.

Ahmose walked slowly over to Anna, who looked like she was ready to bolt. He didn't blame her. Like Damian said, she had definitely been through a lot today. So Ryan kept his mouth shut and waited.

"Anna, can I get you anything? Water or perhaps something to eat? I know the effects of the drug upsets your stomach," Ahmose said calmly. Despite his powerful presence, Ahmose excelled in patience and understanding.

She slowly sat up and reached for her head as if she were barely aware of her wound. "Where am I? Where is everyone? What am I supposed to accept?"

"You're okay now, Anna, we promise. It was a very coordinated attack and it happened so quickly that our team was unable to assist," Damian answered quickly.

She studied Damian like a bug she contemplated squashing.

"I am not okay. What happened to them? Are there any survivors?" She looked between the four of them and yelled, "Answer me!"

"We ran up to the convoys, looking for you, and when we got there the jarheads were all deceased. We took out all the militants and heard your captors yelling at you. So we climbed onto one of the transport trucks and killed them. The rest you know." Ryan didn't feel the need to go into details about the event. It was all she needed to know and by the look on her face, she could not handle any more than that.

She breathed heavily and shook her head repeatedly. He could see the news begin to sink in and it was making her hysterical and inconsolable. All four of them looked uncomfortable as she ran her hands through her hair and pulled. Her cries were unbearable. This was not the grief of the loss of friends. It was as if she lost family in the literal sense.

Ryan's heart went out to her in that moment. He experienced this feeling on more than one occasion. Nothing could be said to heal this moment, nothing but feeling every ounce of this pain until she became numb to it.

After a few moments, she gained control of herself. Her tearstained eyes pleaded for answers. "Why me? Why did you come for me?"

"You are special, Anna. You have promise and talents that we wish to see at its fullest potential," stated Ahmose. "We are a group called Immortals. We are chosen by the Gods to fight for the betterment of humanity and wish for you to join our ranks."

Anna blinked and stared at Ahmose like he just ate his shirt. Ryan wanted to laugh but cleared his throat instead. When he was chosen, it was not something that seemed impossible. His people's lives and beliefs were based on the impossible. However, these days anything unbelievable would be seen as insane or a lie.

"This has to be a joke."

"No, Anna, it is not. We are serious and want to offer you the chance to live forever," Ahmose said. His face was solemn and firm.

She looked at Damian. "No survivors?"

"None."

"Fine." She sighed in defeat.

Ryan felt like he was the one in shock now. Most people had to at least think about joining their ranks. Leaving their loved ones behind was the main reason for a person not to accept the honor. Anna had no problem with it, and a young woman like this had to have people in her life.

"Excellent." Ahmose smiled and clapped his hands together. "I'll have one of our females show you to your room."

With that, he walked out of the parlor plunging the room into an awkward silence. Ryan clicked his tongue out of boredom and Cato turned to stare at him. Neither one of them said a word.

Anna finally broke the silence. "So, you're all chosen or whatever it is?" The drugs must have worn off sooner than he thought.

"No, Damian and I are chosen. We were mortal once. Cato over here is a reborn." She looked confused. "Just a term we use for Immortals that are born from Immortal parents."

"Then how do reborns grow if they are Immortal? Doesn't that mean they can't change or grow old or whatever?"

"Simple, if it is a boy, physically they grow as a mortal would until they reach the point when their father stopped physically aging and the same if it's a girl with her mother," said Cato.

"So at what point do their kids stop growing if their parents have been around forever?" Anna asked.

"It all depends on how old their chosen family members were when they became Immortal. My father was twenty-eight when he was chosen. So I grew as a normal mortal would until my twenty-eighth year and ceased to age physically after." Cato explained the best he could, "My children with another Immortal, if it were a boy, would grow to be twenty-eight just as me and my father are. A ripple effect for all generations."

"So do you force your children to fight?" She continued with her questions.

"No we aren't barbarians." Ryan laughed. "Reborns can either join the ranks of Immortal Warriors or live forever in peace, but once one is chosen, one must serve the Gods for any amount of time as a Warrior."

Her body language made it obvious she was still on edge. "And what does he mean chosen by the Gods? Which Gods exactly?"

"All of them. The Gods were created by the minds of mortals. When a God of a certain religion needs help to protect their people, they call on us. We're slaves to the cause," Ryan said bluntly. He had to have this conversation multiple times and all three of them repeated the identical answers. It was always the same questions.

"But God created us, not the other way around."

Ryan sighed. "Hate to break it to you, but man created the Gods. They have all the power you believe them to have and all the weaknesses as well."

"Then where did we come from?" she asked.

"Ever hear of the big bang theory?" Cato chimed in.

"Anyway," Ryan said ignoring Cato, "mortals handed themselves over to their Gods and in return the Gods do what they can to keep the mortals safe."

"I see." She scrunched her eyebrows together. "This is all weird. An hour ago I was a Marine, and now I am going to be some Immortal Warrior."

"It's a fairly quick process I must say. Usually people take forever to decide," Cato replied. He pushed Ryan's gear to the side and sat next to him. He took off his helmet and revealed his high and tight brown hair. A long, thin scar stretched down the right side of his face.

"Well, I don't have anyone now. There's nothing for me out there so why not join? Besides, I still think I'm dreaming or dead." She said no more about the subject. "Can Immortals die?"

"Of course. We don't get diseases or grow old, otherwise, we are fair game," Cato said lazily.

They sat there again with nothing to say. Damian ended up on the couch with Anna, but she was as far away from him as possible.

Ryan tapped on his helmet with his fingers. Damian and Cato slowly looked at him, at the same time. He cleared his throat and started to tap his foot. His friends were obviously annoyed, but he continued on.

"Ryan, I'm going to kill you," Damian blurted out. Anna glanced at him briefly and Damian shrunk into the couch.

Footsteps interrupted them, and they all turned towards Julia as she walked in the room. Ryan inhaled slowly and tried to stare at the portraits instead. He did, however, notice she was wearing a short white dress that revealed every one of her curves.

Cato stood up. Relief covered his face. "Anna, this is Julia. Julia, Anna," he introduced.

"Hello, Anna." Julia smiled warmly and briskly walked over to Anna. She held out her hand for the girl to take. "Let's get you cleaned up, hon."

Anna truly seemed to calm down. Julia had that effect on people. She was as nonthreatening as they came, and it aided to her success in battle. Anna took her hand, slowly rose from the couch, and looked around the room as they walked.

Ryan watched Damian closely as the women headed to the female dormitories.

He'd watched Anna leave and turned quickly to look at Ryan. Damian could not be more obvious if he tried. Ryan was not going to mention it again, last thing he wanted was his best friend to fall in love and leave him truly alone.

Chapter III

Ryan

Ryan snuck out of Emma's room. His guilt had set in after last night. She had admitted her feelings for him grew and all he did was kiss her to shut her up. Now that he thought about it, kissing her could have been taken as a sign of it being mutual.

Ryan had a bad reputation, but he really didn't like to hurt women. He just could not help it. They all knew him and knew how he was, so he tried to convince himself that they should know better.

There are few women who actually made him want to be monogamous, and that had not happened in many years. It usually ended with them dying, or they left him because he would not give up his Warrior's lifestyle.

After he changed into workout clothes in his room, he found his way to the training arena. Sleep still evaded him and he could not relax. What better way was there to blow off steam than to hit something?

He opened the doors and stopped abruptly. There she was, the beautiful blonde of his dreams, and he needed to avoid her as much as possible. Ryan slowly took a breath and turned around to leave.

"Hello, Ryan. We must stop meeting here like this."

He closed his eyes and turned back around. "Hello, Julia," he said indifferently.

"Where are you going?" She cocked her head to the side.

"Just assumed you wanted to be alone." He shrugged. He crossed his arms and leaned against the wall.

Be calm, his mind yelled at him.

Julia made him nervous, but he never showed it. He could not afford to fall in love and tried very hard to stay away from her. She was the perfect woman—beautiful, smart, funny, and extremely dangerous. Not only because she was the best female Warrior they had, but also because she was Cato's sister. The last thing he needed was part of his team wanting to kill him.

"Assuming is idiotic."

"So is staying when you're obviously unwanted," he growled.

"You're wanted everywhere, Ryan, and by everyone." She smirked. "That is no secret."

He didn't have anything to say to that. People in the Domus talked a lot about him being with multiple people and part of him didn't want Julia to know about it. It was stupid of him to think she would not catch wind of it, but maybe it was best that she did. He purposely made his reputation the way it was so marriage was not a possibility in any woman's mind.

There was only one person he felt a true desire for, and it was the one person he could never have. "I'll go find a warmer climate then. It feels a little cold and lifeless in here."

Her glare gave him chills. Those intense blue eyes mirrored

the ocean nearby. As she began to stand up and walk toward him, his pulse raced. If he didn't have years of practicing self-control, he would be a shaking mess. Her very presence made his stomach flip and put his nerves on edge.

She was now face to face with him—her eyes never once left his. Her gaze pulled him in and Ryan was doing everything in his power not to kiss her.

She leaned toward him slowly—her lip's parted and suddenly Ryan was on the floor. She'd caught him by surprise and quickly swiped his legs out from under him with her own.

That escalated fast.

"Don't ever talk to me like that."

Ryan grinned and propped himself up on one elbow. "Going to have to try harder than that for me to fall for you."

That seemed to make her angry.

She tried to kick him, but he caught her leg, twisted her around, and she fell to the ground. He sat precariously on her back as she pushed herself up. She bucked him off making him land on his side.

Julia put him in a chokehold and Ryan stood up with her on his back. With momentum, he bent forward and flipped her over. She landed on the mats with a soft thud.

"You want to play with the big boys?" Ryan grinned as he stood over her. To his surprise, she was calm. Her leg swung around and hit the back of his knees again collapsing his legs and forcing him onto his back.

One word came to mind about her—perfection. She quickly straddled him and pulled out her small knife, lightly pressing it to his throat.

"From what I hear you're not a big boy."

"Only one way to find out." He winked.

"You couldn't handle a woman like me. Keep messing with those girls of yours. Break some more hearts."

"Let me break yours then," he whispered. Her smile was amazing and breathtaking, but he truly didn't want to hurt her. She had to dislike him in order for him to protect her from his idiocy.

He moved his hands up her thighs, and the knife came closer to his neck.

"Try it. I dare you."

He put his hands on her waist and ran them up her sides as he pulled her lightly down towards him. For a brief second of joy, he thought she was giving in, and then he felt her fist connect with his jaw. *She is definitely stronger than she looks.*

She leaned down and whispered in his ear, "Want to try that again?"

"Depends, are you going to kiss it and make it better?"

"It truly is amazing how full of yourself you are, Ryan." She shook her head, stood up and threw her knife across the room at a target. To his surprise, she held out her hand and helped him up. "You're lucky you are my brother's friend. Otherwise, I wouldn't have a problem killing you."

"You, ma'am, are very violent. Attacking men for no reason, how do you ever expect to find a decent husband with such an attitude?" he mused.

"Easy, find someone completely opposite of you." He detected a smirk about to play across her lips, but she hid it well.

Ryan looked appalled and grasped his chest. "Are you saying you want an ugly, untalented, uneducated, skinny, weakling with no sense of humor? Now Julia, you don't have to set your standards so low. I know I am intimidating and amazing, but I could learn to love you."

Her arms crossed and she looked him up and down. "Idiot."

"Easy with the foreplay."

"You're disgusting."

"You love it."

Julia started to walk towards the door.

He didn't want her to leave and was disappointed he had pushed her to do so. Wasn't that his goal?

"Can I tell you something?" he asked. Julia stopped in her tracks and she turned to face him.

Ryan could not imagine telling anyone what he truly wanted. Not even Damian, and especially not Cato. Yet he felt a strong urge to reveal all his feelings to her. It was easy to lose himself with her. He constantly had to remind himself to be a jerk.

"Sure." Her anger seemed to subside. He could not believe he was going to say this to her out loud.

Ryan stared at the floor. He felt weak and vulnerable. He forced himself to look at her, and his breath caught in his lungs. Those stunning blue eyes were the same color as his.

Ryan would never understand why they acted so distant from one another. Their bipolar relationship always went up and down in a matter of minutes around each other. Sometimes he felt she may be interested in him and other times Julia acted as cold as Ryan did. It was annoying and confusing, which may explain his attraction to her. She didn't give in easily. He had always heard you want what you cannot have and there was definitely truth to that.

"I really think I want-"

The doors opened and instantly his demeanor turned cold. Jesse and the dream team burst through the doors. Ryan felt an intensely strong urge to throw something at them. Julia and he were constantly being interrupted and the pattern was becoming obnoxious.

He stared at the three men walking into the training arena. Jesse, who never seemed to wear a shirt that fit right, was ahead of the crew. He was built like a house and had the same short-cropped hair as Cato. Ryan feared that if he tried to pick something up, his shirt would rip open and reveal his pasty-white skin.

Aden walked in behind him. He had the same black, shaggy hair as Ryan. He was thoroughly convinced Aden copied everything he did. They had similar hair, clothes and were fond of the same women. Except, Ryan was much more muscular then him, which had to count for something.

Then there was Caleb. Quiet and the only one Ryan could stand for more than five minutes. His curly, brown hair bounced as he walked and his dark eyes darted around the room. His Star of David necklace hung down against his chest as it always did.

Aden glared at him as he looked between Ryan and Julia. Ryan raised an eyebrow and stood at her side. Not that being a dick was out of character for Aden, but he looked oddly mad at Ryan for no apparent reason.

"Surprised to see you here with such foul company, Julia," Aden spat.

"Surprised you're up before noon." Ryan smiled. "He is proof that evolution can go in reverse," he muttered to Julia. If he didn't know better he'd say he saw a small smile on her lips.

"You're so clever, Ryan. Your wit never ceases to amaze," Aden said.

"No need to point out the obvious." Ryan looked at the three. Aden must have been in a particularly fowl mood. Usually the tension had to be built up between them first, but right now he seemed overly aggressive.

"Since this place is already occupied, we will leave you two alone," Jesse spoke up.

Aden glared at Jesse and then looked at Ryan. "One day I am going to rip that stupid grin off your face."

"Sounds particularly unpleasant. To do that though, you would actually have to win a fight with me. Aren't your bones still healing from the last time you tried?" he asked. Ryan and Aden had a tendency to fight often, and it usually ended in Ryan breaking a part of Aden's body.

"Let's see what happens?" Aden walked forward. Caleb caught him by the shoulders. For such a small man, it was quite impressive he could hold back Aden.

Ryan stepped towards him, his fists clenched.

"Now, now, boys. Not in front of a lady or have you lost manners throughout the ages?" Julia smiled brilliantly at Aden, turned in front of Ryan and placed her hand on his chest. She spoke so only he could hear. "Do me a favor and don't make me question my poor judgment of you."

Ryan looked into her eyes and melted—he could not deny her that. He never backed down from a fight, but she seemed to sincerely want them to calm down. "You heard the lady, Aden. Manners matter."

Even though everything in his body screamed to beat some manners into the idiot, Ryan just stood there and waited. The pit of his stomach dropped, and his face felt red. Impulse was much better than the constraint he was practicing.

"I see." Aden's eyes shot daggers at him. "Julia, when you decide to be with a real man, come see me. You deserve better than the Immortal Whore."

Ryan lost his control and started at Aden. His fists were

curled, ready to connect with Aden's face until Caleb and Julia pulled him back. "Julia, let me go. I don't want to hurt you," he said between clenched teeth.

"I know you don't and that's why I'm going to stay right were I am." She struggled against him. "Calm down."

If it were just Caleb, Ryan would have thrown him to the ground and had a clear shot at Aden. Jesse stood back, indifferent and with no care as to what was going on. There was no way to get past Julia without harming her, so he took deep breathes to calm himself.

Aden stood there highly amused. "I cannot wait until you die."

At that, Jesse pulled Aden violently by the shirt collar and out the doors. Ryan could hear them yelling at each other, but he was unable to make out what was being said.

Caleb let go of Ryan when he calmed down and silently walked out the doors without another word.

Ryan smoothed out his shirt and hit the nearest punching bag. They stood in silence and Ryan almost forgot Julia was there. He flinched as she cautiously placed her hand on his shoulder, and he glanced back at her.

"What the hell did he mean by that?" Ryan asked.

Ryan became very aware of how close she was to him. "I have no idea."

Chapter IV

Ryan

Ryan set the bar back on the bench rack and sat up. "Whew."

Damian leaned on the bar and Ryan turned around to face him. "So, you really tried getting with Julia?"

He threw a towel in Ryan's face, and he dabbed the sweat off his brow. "Not really, I was just messing with her. She took it a little personal."

"That woman will kill you."

"Probably."

"Cato will too." Damian laughed.

"Probably."

Ryan stood up and threw the towel back at Damian. "Gross."

He grabbed a forty-pound dumbbell and started doing arm curls. Damian started to jump rope, and they were silent for a few minutes. Ryan had a hard time trying to figure out the Julia situation. He didn't want to think about it anymore.

They decided to come to the weight room and blow off some steam. It sat on the third level of the Domus, and had to be reached by going through the male's side of the castle. It was to the left of Ahmose's office, which was rather annoying when he blared his polka music. Today, however, they didn't have to suffer.

The weight room had a multitude of different exercise machines. They were repeatedly getting the newest and latest equipment the mortals could come up with. Some of it was amazing, but others Ryan did not understand. He could not for the life of him understand the point of a giant blow up ball you bounce around on.

Ryan sometimes got a headache in this room. The walls were completely mirrored—even the door. The black floors were the only sanity he could find. He had to concentrate on them otherwise he got dizzy.

"So was Aden threatening you or what?" Damian spoke between breaths.

"From the sounds of it." Ryan switched arms. "There's not much the little worm can do to me though."

Ryan grunted and set the weights back on their rack. He grabbed his water bottle by the door and drained it. Aden's last words started to eat at Ryan. Should he be cautious from this point on or was it just a generalized assumption he would someday be killed?

"Probably just jealous of you," Damian mumbled as he started doing push-ups. "He likes Julia and she shut him down the other day."

"No way."

"Yeah, Cato told me." He laughed.

A small amount of pain hit his gut. Was that jealousy?

"Whatever." Ryan stripped his shirt off and wore only his black shorts and shoes. "Nothing happened and nothing will."

"I don't know." Damian grinned. "Seems like you are interested in her to me."

"Not in the least."

Damian dropped to the ground and rolled over to start doing sit-ups. "Where's Cato?"

Ryan was thankful for the change of subject. "I think he is out riding. He wanted to break in those horses."

Ryan got down next to Damian and started doing sit-ups as well. He went faster than Damian and looked to see if he noticed. He did and Damian started to speed up. They went as long as they could until Ryan sprawled out on the floor and breathed deeply.

"Dammit."

"Pathetic." Damian grinned.

"Suck it." Ryan laughed.

They stretched after they were done with their work out. Something still weighed on Ryan's mind about what Aden said. People do not just say things like that out of jealousy or generalizing the future. Something was wrong and he needed to find out what Aden was up to.

"What?" Damian looked up after he stretched his legs.

"What?"

"Why do you look like someone stole your pudding?"

Ryan's arm crossed over his chest and he pulled to stretch it. "Don't joke about that. I'll have nightmares."

Damian rolled his eyes. "Okay, but still, what's up?"

"Aden."

"Get off it."

"He looked serious. I wonder what is going on with him."

Ryan sat on the bench press. "I just have a bad feeling in my gut."

Damian sat on the floor with his knees up and his arms at rest on them. "Would you like to spy on him?"

"I think that would be wise." Ryan hung his head and closed his eyes. There was something wrong going on and his instinct was usually correct. Aden was always aggressive when it came to Ryan though. They had never gotten along and fighting was a usual occurrence.

"Are you serious?" Damian lay back and covered his eyes. "Nothing is going on with that idiot except the lack of brain cells."

"When have I ever steered you wrong?" Ryan was somewhat annoyed.

"Never," Damian exasperated.

"Exactly."

"Remember when you stuck his face in horse manure?" Damian laughed.

Ryan grinned. "He called me piece of crap. He brought it on himself."

"Then you asked, 'How do I taste?'" Damian grinned. "Or that time you broke his arm for talking about your mother?"

Ryan felt like a bully, but Aden had always asked for it. The only difference between them was that Aden was not as strong or as well trained. "He should not have called my mother a rotting whore."

"Agreed."

There was one thing you didn't do, and that was insult Ryan's mother. She made sure he was as successful in his life as possible and would have given her life for him if it came to it. He respected his mother in life and in death. She was a constant reminder of how he became more than just a man. "He should not take things so personal."

Damian laughed. "Right, because breaking his arm was not taking it personal? Why do you think he hates you so much?"

"Who knows why?" Ryan shrugged. "Whatever, if he is up to something, we will find out."

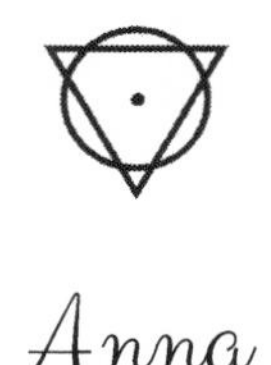

Anna

Anna paced around her new room. Her fatigues were washed and hung up in her armoire. They were a constant reminder of what she lost, but she could not bear to get rid of them.

It was her first day of training and she was wearing black sweatpants and a gray top.

There was a picture in her hand. It was Nathan and her smiling, sitting on a park bench back home. She carried it in her jacket everyday in Iraq and was relieved it was still with her.

After crying the first two days, the third day came around, and she was numb. After a week, she gained acceptance and was finally ready for her new life. She could not change that Nathan was gone forever or that her friends were as well. They sacrificed themselves for their country and were the bravest men and women she ever knew.

Julia had told her that Ryan and Damian made sure their bodies were found by the Americans and would receive a proper burial at home. That made her feel more at ease. She was unable to attend Nathan's funeral, if he even had one. Julia said it would cause too much emotional stress if she went. She threw countless fits about it, but apparently it was against the rules to visit the mortal world without the proper time of morning one's old life. Ryan gave his word that the number of bodies recovered were all accounted for except hers.

Julia walked her around and showed her everything about the Domus. It helped keep her mind off things, even if it was only for a little while. It was like a giant beautiful museum.

It reminded her of the old Greek and Roman palaces with white walls and floors and airy surroundings. She felt like she was in a fairy tale, but instead of princesses and princes it was a bunch of people that like to fight put together in a massive castle. The towering windows were almost overwhelming. Her favorite part was the huge, perfect garden in the middle of the castle. If she walked out of her room, she could look through the small arched windows and see the garden down below.

Julia said it could house up to one thousand people but only a few hundred lived in it. Most of the Warriors had retired due to the lack of long-term missions and now live in the city of Urbs.

The only room with modern electronics was the game room. Anna wanted to go in there desperately, but it was probably better for her sanity to stay away from things that reminded her of her past. Here technology didn't consume these people—it was odd. She grew up in a generation of phone addicts.

She put the photo on the mirror of her vanity. The happy faces seemed like a dream. She sat on the chair in front of the mirror and stared at her empty room.

It came basic for recruits and obviously was not lived in for quite some time. She had a fireplace and only an armoire for a closet. A small vanity sat beside her white bed, made of a dark wood and had wooden floors to match. The walls were white and Julia said she could have the Domus workers paint it any color. Her room was bare and Julia begged her to go shopping. She was in no mood to decorate though.

She looked behind her and out towards the city the Domus was currently in. She had no idea where they were. It was a small town and a mountain towered above them.

Julia was Anna's saint. Apparently, she'd helped many newcomers to this life. Even though Julia was born into it rather than chosen, she seemed very understanding of how difficult it was to adapt.

Anna was going to train with Julia and her team today. Women taught women, and men taught men. A bit sexist, but she was used to it. She didn't mind though. The men who saved her were an interesting bunch and in all honesty, they were a little overwhelming.

She turned around to look at her reflection. Her cut lip turned into a small scar, a constant reminder of who she once was and how it came to be there.

"Quit thinking of that life, it's gone for good now," she told herself. "He's gone and there is nothing you can do about it."

Instead, she forced herself to think of what happened after she was saved. Ryan was funny, in a brotherly way, though she found herself wanting to hit him more than anything. According to Julia, it was a common feeling among many Immortals here. From what she heard, that was what most siblings wanted to do to each other anyway so it made sense she wanted to smack him upside the head.

She could see why most women wanted him. He had that Zac Efron mixed with Channing Tatum thing going on. Ryan was cocky though and that was really unattractive.

Cato, Julia's brother, is the total opposite of Julia She has long blonde hair, which made Anna jealous, and Cato's hair was brown with a high and tight haircut. She would have never guessed they were siblings, but they both seemed stubborn and level headed.

Then there was Damian. He seemed kind and very calm. His hair was as shaggy as Ryan's but much lighter. They both had the same tanned white skin and were almost identical in height. He was much leaner than Ryan, in a runner sort of way, where as Ryan was a few protein shakes away from being a body builder. Those three boys definitely have different personalities. She wondered how they possibly got along.

Her thoughts wandered to Damian.

If she didn't know better, she would have thought he liked her. The way he took care of her and always asked if she needed anything, made it obvious. Or, maybe he was just being friendly? It was hard to say, but she felt secure with him. She needed to feel safe right now.

A knock at the door startled her. Julia walked in wearing white shorts and a shirt. White was her usual color Anna noticed. This girl needed a little more black in her life.

"Ready?" Julia grinned.

Anna nodded and walked out of her room with Julia. The fresh breeze hit her face through the small windows and she saw a bird fly by. The torches that lined the walls were unlit and she started to count them as they walked in silence.

"I'm nervous," she spoke up.

"Don't be. Today we are just going to see what we are working with. Don't get upset if you can't do some things either. The best rewards in life come when you're patient." At that moment Ryan and Damian walked by and judging by their sweat-drenched clothes hanging over their shoulders, they'd just worked out.

Anna tried not to look at their bare chests that gleamed in the sunlight, but she could have sworn Julia locked eyes with Ryan. Anna glanced back at them and saw Damian quickly turn to gaze ahead of him.

This place made her feel like she was in high school with all this secret admirer crap going on.

She shook her head and continued to follow Julia. Anna was thankful that she didn't mind the silence between them. In her experience, girls hated being quiet and this was a welcome change.

Along the way, Anna looked at all the portraits that hung on the walls. There were so many it was insane. She was never good at history, but if she had to guess, these were famous dead people. There were men with helmets and women in super fluffy dresses. Then there were men who looked as if they didn't know about personal hygiene and women that looked like men. So many different races and heritages, it was like a group of random histories on the wall.

"You're always so intrigued with them," Julia said.

"Huh?"

"The paintings—you study them."

Anna was impressed that Julia noticed.

Julia smiled softly and stopped in front of a portrait. It was a young woman with short, black hair, cut like a boys, and doe eyes. She was dressed like a man from around the fourteen hundreds or somewhere in the knight and shinning armor days.

"This is Jehanne d'Arc or Jehanne la Pucelle. You are about to meet her."

Anna cocked her head. "That sounds familiar, for some reason."

"More commonly known as Joan of Arc." She smiled warmly. "Now known as Colette."

Anna would never get used to this Immortal thing. All of these people were well-known dead people at some point. "So that's literally her, on a mission or what?"

"No, she was born Jehanne d'Arc and was chosen. She will continually remain the ripe age of nineteen." She almost looked sad about that. In a way, the whole thing was rather depressing, never growing old and being young forever.

Okay, maybe it wasn't such a bad deal but having to see all your loved ones die had to be tough.

"Were you anyone super famous?"

Her expression faltered slightly. "Yes, we all have been at some point. Some day you will be too." She grinned.

"This is still freaking weird." She shook her head and continued down the hallway.

"You'll get used to it, I promise."

I doubt it, she thought to herself.

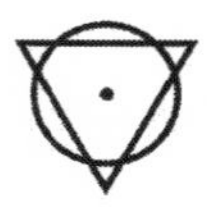

Julia

Julia held the door open for Anna, and both women entered the training arena. Julia grinned as she turned towards her and saw how impressed Anna looked. "Huge, isn't it?"

Anna just nodded her head and walked in cautiously, ready for something to happen.

Next to the practice dummies stood Colette and Grace. The two women turned around and watched Anna walk in. They accessed her every movement with the utmost interest.

"Anna, this is Colette," Julia introduced. Anna smiled and studied Colette with obvious curiosity. Perhaps she should have waited to share the information about Colette. "And this is Grace."

Grace had red hair and bright green eyes. She was taller than Colette, and her presence was more demanding. Julia may have technically been older than Grace—however, Grace had been a Warrior longer than her. Her mother's old teammates welcomed her with open arms when she died.

"Hey, what's up?" Anna held her hand out. Julia could not help but smile. Colette and Grace were proper and poised women.

"Nothing." Grace raised an eyebrow and walked around Anna as she looked the girl up and down. "She looks in shape enough."

Colette grabbed Anna's arms and squeezed them. She moved her hands down both of Anna's legs as well. "Some muscle."

Anna looked as awkward as could be. She was being compliant and stood there as the women dissected every inch of her. They even went as far as examining her teeth and nails.

"Cut these down," Colette instructed. Anna nodded and looked over her shoulder to Julia—her face pleaded for intervention.

"Don't worry, ladies, I'll get her fully prepared. Let's get on with it," Julia said warmly.

"First, I want you to stretch. Go to the mats over there." Grace pointed to her right.

As Anna walked over to the mats and bent to touch her toes, Grace and Colette stood in front of Julia.

"They must be desperate," Colette muttered. "Her figure is curvy and her bust is distracting."

"She's better equipped for this than you think, I promise you that," said Julia. "Besides, what do her curves and breasts have to do with her skill."

"It's a distraction," she muttered.

"To what?" Julia laughed.

"Men." She glared. "It will distract the male Warriors and cause potential fatalities."

"That is ridiculous." Julia scoffed.

"Enough." Grace sighed.

"She will do fine," Julia assured her.

Grace nodded in agreement. "Some potential there, we just have to find a way to bring it out of her. She reminds me of a little girl I once trained." She winked at Julia.

Grace had trained Julia to become a Warrior when her mother died. She wanted desperately to be on the team with the women who knew her mother best. Grace was like a second mother to her in many ways. She looked out for her, gave her advice, and took care of her when she needed it.

Anna was now doing arm circles before moving on to trunk twists.

"Give her time." Julia looked at Colette, her eyes pleading for her acceptance.

"We have all the time in the world." Colette sighed. "We are going to need it."

Anna looked anxiously at the three women and stood in place. Julia was the first to walk over to her, Colette and Grace followed. "All right, let's start you out running today. We will see what your stamina is, and if we need to build it up or not. Though I doubt it, you Marines can go far with heavy gear, from what I am told."

"I guess," Anna agreed.

"Just make laps around the gym and don't overexert yourself. Don't sprint," said Colette.

Grace held up the timer hung around her neck and locked eyes with Anna. "Go."

As Anna jogged, the three women watched her from the center of the arena. Every movement was important, and her form was studied. Anything less than perfect was not acceptable and Julia knew Anna would pass with flying colors. Though Colette seemed to hope otherwise.

"Thirty minutes down. I wonder how much longer she'll go." Grace pointed at her watch.

"My guess is ten minutes," Colette muttered.

"No, her breathing is still even and her body isn't giving way yet. She's got more in her." Julia was amused. She was not sure why Colette seemed to have it out for Anna, but she did, and it was obvious.

Colette crossed her arms and glared at Anna as she ran. Julia and Grace simultaneously looked at Colette.

"What is your problem?" Grace asked.

"She's weak. Not physically, but mentally and it's an insult to all Immortals to even have her here." Colette cringed.

"Quit it, Colette. She's one of us now whether you like it or not." Julia sighed. "So stop treating her like a disease because she needs us to survive."

"Sadly." Colette was bitter.

Julia rolled her eyes and Grace checked her timer. Julia was not happy with Colette's answer, but there was nothing else she could do. Anna would have to prove herself and quickly.

A good amount of time went by before Julia could tell Anna

was getting tired. Her breath came out quicker and her sweat made her shirt cling to her chest. Julia was impressed that she lasted this long.

Anna's knees wobbled and she came to a stop. She put her hands up and behind her head and took in deep breaths in through her nose and out of her mouth.

"An hour and forty-five minutes," whispered Grace. A small smile rested on her lips until the tension in Colette became apparent. "Beat your hour and ten minutes, Colette."

"That's enough for today, get her cleaned up and see you tomorrow," Colette spat. She walked out of the training arena as fast as she could without a second glance back.

"She is a terror today." Julia sighed.

Grace kissed Julia's cheek and smoothed down her hair. "I would blame PMS if I were you." She smiled and followed to catch up with Colette.

Julia turned back to Anna. "Not bad, Marine."

She still breathed heavily yet managed a sarcastic laugh. "Thanks. They didn't seem to think so."

"Ignore Colette."

"She seems to have it out for me."

"No way, I just think she dislikes you." Julia shrugged.

"What's the difference?" Anna asked. "Any idea why?"

"Not a clue." Julia put her hand on Anna's back and directed her towards the door. "Grace was impressed. She doesn't show emotions very much so don't take offense to that."

"I'll keep that in mind."

"Good," said Julia, "let's get you to a shower. You smell."

Chapter V

Ryan

It was tour day in the Domus for prospective reborn Warriors. Ryan loved when they did this. Damian, Cato, and Ryan took bets on who would join and who would not be able to pass the test. More often than not, Ryan won. Many citizens in Urbs were living to eat not eating to live, and their lack of stamina was a problem.

Ryan had his arm around Janett. She was a reborn and had barely reached her Immortal age twenty years back. Her long black hair, light brown skin, and plump red lips instantly drew Ryan to her. She was the daughter of a council member, and Ryan was assigned as her tour guide today.

"Over here is the dining hall. Most of us just stay in our rooms and have our meals delivered, though." Ryan pointed towards the doors of the large cafeteria and led her away from it.

"Aren't we going to look at it?" she asked.

"No, ma'am."

She grinned, and she put her arm around his waist. This was going well. “Is there anything else on the third level?”

“Ahmose’s office and the weight room, but what you really need to see is the dormitories.”

She giggled and rest her other hand on his chest. “I would absolutely love to see were the best Warrior in Urbs lays his head every night.”

“Most definitely not every night, but I understand the appeal.” *Poor impressionable girl*, he thought.

They walked down the left staircase and turned towards the male dormitories. “Oh, what’s that room?”

He looked down the hallway and saw she was pointing to the parlor. There was nothing particularly interesting about it. Ryan sighed, and they walked in the opposite direction of his room. “This is the parlor. We typically leave the Domus in here for our missions. Don’t ask me why, we just do.”

“Come on, tell me why.” She giggled.

That was super annoying. “It’s sort of the designated meeting area. The crystals that transport us around the world are connected to this room.”

“So all these paintings are people from the past?” She gazed around. “Like, famous Warriors?”

“Yes.” He nodded. “I have a few different ones around here. Most do.”

She squeezed his side. “Because you are the most important?”

What an idiot. “Because I have been different people in my lifetime. I was an emperor, king, and general. I’ve played many roles.”

“Oh.” She let go of him and sat down on the nearest couch. She patted the seat next to her, and he lazily sat down. “So, what else can you show me?"

Desperation was unattractive, but she was young and he understood it. Desperate or not, he was not an idiot. When a gorgeous girl wants you, you do not deny her.

"Well-"

Her lips interrupted him as they pressed roughly against his mouth. She jumped on top of his lap and straddled him. Ryan would have laughed at her boldness—instead he slipped his hand under the back of her shirt and pulled her closer to him. Her body shook with nerves and he tried not to grin.

She nipped his lip as she moved her hand down his chest making him groan. His eyes opened and she looked pleased with herself. "You are a good kisser."

"I know," he growled and gripped the back of her hair. Her back arched as he kissed her neck slowly until his lips found hers again. Slowly she started to unbutton her shirt off.

"Are we interrupting?"

Ryan calmly turned his head towards the entrance. Julia stood there with her tour member. He was a short, bulky kid with shoulder-length brown hair and pale skin. She looked as if she wanted to stab him in the groin.

"You sure are." He rolled his eyes. The girl quickly jumped off his lap and awkwardly walked towards the balcony and out of sight. "Thanks, Miss Buzzkill."

"No problem." Julia glared at him. "You do realize you could be punished severely for that, don't you?"

"How so?"

"She is underage."

"No, she turned her Immortal age already." He sat up and leaned his elbows on his knees.

"Is that part of the tour?" the young boy asked and Ryan

laughed when he heard the kid's deep man-like voice.

"Sure is kid." He grinned. "Have at it."

The boy put his arm around Julia, which she swatted off. "It is most definitely not part of the tour."

If looks could kill, Ryan would be dead and buried.

"This is the parlor." Damian's voice echoed through the hallway. "There are multiple important manuscripts in here that tell the history of each of us. Spells are kept under lock and key in the hea-"

Damian turned into the parlor and stopped dead in his tracks. A very tall and muscular boy followed behind him. He towered over Damian, and his dark skin stood out next to the pure white marble walls.

He must have sensed the tension in the room, because his mouth remained shut. His tour member looked bored and ready to leave. Damian gave the worst tours. He had a tendency to make it a history lesson.

"Damian." Julia grabbed his elbow and led him over to Ryan. "You're moronic friend decided to get to know his tour member a little too well instead of actually giving her a tour."

Damian looked between Julia and Ryan with pure dread. He was stuck between a rock and a hard place and looked uncomfortable being dragged in the middle of this awkward situation. "I am not his caretaker."

"Yes, you are," she growled. "That is all you do—take care of him."

"Umm." Damian's eyes got wide for a second as he looked at Ryan. He was begging for help. "Bad, Ryan, bad."

"Don't get your panties in a twist, Julia." Ryan crossed his ankle over his knee. "There's no need to be jealous."

She let go of Damian and pulled Ryan up by his shirt. He

was much taller than her, but that didn't stop his fear of her wrath. She yanked him against her body and she stood on the tip of her toes to growl, "Speak to me like that again and I will turn you into a eunuch."

She kissed his cheek then pushed him backwards and onto the couch. He refrained from making a comment—the need to protect his private parts was too great.

When she was gone with her tour member, Ryan turned to Damian and inhaled. "She's terrifying."

"Want a suggestion?" Damian started to leave the room with the man-child. "Buy a cup."

Chapter VI

Damian

Damian and Ryan crouched low against the wall in the Domus. They were both dressed in black sweatpants and cotton shirts. They wore only socks, to be quieter, as they followed Aden around the castle. The rain drizzled against the roof, which helped silence their footsteps. All the windows were closed to protect the paintings and the echoes of thunder rang through hallways.

So far, Aden had eaten in the dining room and took a nap in the parlor. Damian started to doubt Aden was up to something. This was a waste of time—however, for Ryan's sake, he kept his mouth shut. He would need to come to that conclusion on his own.

Now Aden was on his way to the female dormitories. Damian was behind Ryan and followed his instructions. He waved him forward—Damian ran past Ryan and hid in a doorway. He really hoped no one decided to come out of their room and blow their cover.

Ryan went past him and hid in another doorway in front of Damian. They watched Aden walk further down the hallway and then he stopped in front of a door.

Damian looked over to Ryan, who looked as if something smelled or he was disgusted.

He realized whose room it was. Damian ran over to Ryan and got uncomfortably close, next to him. "Why is he there?"

Ryan pressed his finger against his lips. Damian rolled his eyes and leaned around Ryan to look at Aden. He messed with his hair and straightened his clothes. Damian's face probably matched Ryan's at this point, both of them disgusted and annoyed.

Aden knocked on the door and waited for a few seconds. Julia opened her door, but remained standing inside her room. He was thankful Aden was not being invited in. Ryan would lose it.

Julia was breathtaking and Damian understood Aden's liking for her, but he pitied him at the same time. Julia would never give him the time of day, and he was glad he saw her as nothing but a sister. Not one single Warrior ever got a chance with her.

"Let's get closer," Ryan whispered.

Damian tried to protest, but Ryan had already left the doorway and ran along the hallway towards Julia's room. They had no cover unless they hid inside the doorframes or by the occasional tall cabinets that held mementos.

Neither Julia nor Aden seemed to notice, as they managed to sneak almost in front of her room, hiding behind a large cabinet filled with Egyptian jewelry. Damian flattened himself as much as he could against the wall, and Ryan knelt down and peaked around the side.

"I would be honored if you would allow me to take you out to dinner," said Aden.

Damian looked at Ryan, who pretended to throw up. He smiled and backhanded Ryan on the head. Ryan feigned offense until he heard Julia answer Aden's request.

"I don't think that is a good idea," Julia replied. "I do appreciate the offer."

She turned back to her room, when Aden grabbed her hand gently. Ryan looked severely annoyed and ready to fight. Damian caught him by the shoulder and held him back.

"Its just dinner, Julia, not marriage." Aden kissed her hand. "Dinner. That is all."

Julia looked torn. Damian had no idea what was going on in her mind, and it looked as if neither did she.

"Okay," she finally agreed. "Just dinner."

Aden smiled wide. "Eight o'clock?"

Julia nodded and Aden kissed her hand once more before she retreated back into her room. Aden chuckled to himself. Damian was in absolute shock. How in the hell did he pull that off?

Damian felt Ryan leave his side and watched in horror, as he prepared to attack Aden. He quickly grabbed Ryan while Aden had his back turned, put his hand over his mouth and pulled him back and out of sight. Ryan tried to break his grip but he didn't let go until Aden was long gone. Damian finally let go and faced an infuriated Ryan.

"What are you doing?" Ryan demanded.

Damian took a deep breath. "What is your problem, Ryan? Why were you going to attack him?"

Mixed emotions washed over his face. "That is Cato's sister and she doesn't want to go on a date with him. We have to defend her."

"Pathetic excuse, Ryan." Damian pushed him towards the direction Aden was going. "Let's keep following him until you realize the guy isn't up to anything, okay?"

Ryan rolled his eyes in annoyance. They caught up with Aden, who was now in a deep conversation with Caleb, in the parlor. The two of them stood on either side of the doorframe that led into the room and listened patiently. Damian occasionally peaked around the side.

"I will not do it," Caleb gritted through his teeth. Damian had never seen Caleb like this. He was always so calm and collected. "It is wrong. Why can't you see that?"

"Stop living in the past and just come to terms with it," Aden pleaded. "You are like my annoying little brother and I do not want anything to happen to you."

"I will not," Caleb repeated. His hair was drenched and stuck to his forehead. "Don't force me to turn you in."

Aden grabbed Caleb by the shirt. "Take time to think about it. I cannot protect you forever."

"You need to take the time and figure out why it is wrong." Caleb was infuriated and Damian's interest was peaked. Ryan seemed glued to the conversation and didn't even blink. Caleb shoved away Aden's grip on his shirt. "As far as I am concerned, you are dead to me."

"I'm begging you, Caleb." Aden sighed. "Jesse is on board. I have plans for Julia and I know it will work."

"Julia will never go for it." Caleb shook his head and laughed. "I'm surprised you even succeeded in getting a date with her."

Aden seemed to take offense to that. "Why?"

Caleb laughed. "She's pretty much the Virgin Queen of the Domus."

"That will change." Aden seemed so sure. Damian was a little annoyed by that comment.

With that being said, Ryan walked into the parlor before Damian could try to restrain him. Didn't stop him from gritting his teeth and hissing, "Ryan!"

"What's up, boys?" Ryan grinned. "Wonderful weather, isn't it?"

Damian smacked his head with his hand and sighed. He casually walked around the corner and into the room as well. "Hey, guys."

Aden and Caleb exchanged looks. He could sense the fear in them and tried to act normal. He wanted to punch Aden in the face and smack Ryan for being nosey.

"What are you two doing here?" Caleb asked. Damian could tell he forced his nonchalant attitude.

"Just walking around." Ryan fell onto the couch and faced Aden. "So, who's virginity are you going to take, Aden? She must be desperate."

"Were you eavesdropping?"

"Just caught that part," Ryan assured him. He didn't hide his obvious disgust and anger for Aden. Ryan glared at Aden, almost challenging him with his eyes to start a fight as he gave him a look of absolute hatred. Damian crossed his arms and leaned against the bookshelves. He would not stop Ryan anymore.

Aden looked pleased at this point. "For your information, I am having dinner with Julia tonight."

"Oh, are you?" Ryan seemed genuinely excited for him. "That's great."

Aden and Caleb looked at each other nervously. Damian waited for the storm to begin.

"It is?" Aden treaded carefully.

"Oh, yeah." Ryan grinned. "It is so nice of her to do charity work."

Aden crossed his arms and Damian saw the fumes starting to rise from him. "She is going because she wants to."

"Right." Ryan laughed. "Because Julia has been on how many dates? Like I said, charity."

"Farther then you have ever gotten."

"I have no interest in her, Aden." Ryan laughed.

"I've seen the way you look at her." Aden smirked.

"Oh?" Ryan grinned. "Is that the only reason you are interested in her? I mean you always copy everything I do so it makes sense."

"No, I-"

"And I am sure she would not appreciate you taking claim over her purity in such a crude manner." Ryan shrugged. "She's not going to give herself to you willingly. Should I tell Cato you plan to take away his sister's virginity forcefully?"

Caleb grabbed onto Aden, but his grip was shrugged off. Aden lurched forward and grabbed hold of Ryan's hair and yanked him off the couch.

Ryan calmly grabbed Aden's thumb on the hand that held his hair and bent it back hard. Damian closed his eyes when he heard the bone snap. Ryan uppercut Aden in the jaw and he fell back against the couch.

Ryan's fists rained down on Aden's face with no restraint. Caleb jumped to intervene, and Damian grudgingly decided to pull Ryan off Aden. Before Caleb got a grip on him, Aden's fist connected with the side of Ryan's head with a loud smack and Ryan staggered for a moment. Damian almost lost his balance as he held onto him and Caleb finally got Aden in his grasp.

"Enough!" Caleb demanded.

Aden glared at Ryan, who had a large smile spread across his face as blood trickled down his head. "Have fun explaining your messed up face and why it got that way on your date, you little prick."

Julia

Julia heard a knock on her door and checked her appearance in the mirror again. Her hair was in curls and pulled back into a low loose bun.

What was she thinking, going on a date with Aden of all people! Sure, he was attractive and sweet to her, yet her brother despised him. Her heart was not in this, but the way he looked at her made her feel pity for him. Was this terrible of her?

He was handsome, but Julia could not force herself to think of him that way. There was something about him that she was not attracted to. As she walked to the door, she smoothed out her white cocktail dress and reached for the handle. Aden stood there with a single rose in his hand and dressed in black slacks and shirt.

He handed her the rose, which she took with a smile. His face looked horribly bruised. She had to force herself not to reach out to him. His eye was blackened, his lip was busted, and there was a cut under his right eye. "What happened?"

Aden's smile faltered and he held his arm out for her. "Ask Ryan about that."

Julia shook her head, took his offered arm and they walked

down the hallway and out of the Domus. It was settled on Bora Bora Island and the castle somehow floated on top of the water. It still amazed Julia how the mortals could not see the massive structure and how the Domus seemed to have a mind of its own.

A boat waited for them at the bottom of the stairs that led out of the Domus, which Aden helped her climb in to. The sun started to set and the teal water begun to turn a dark blue mixed with purple.

There were a few clouds in the sky with multiple colors mixed together. Purple, blue, and yellow were so perfectly blended that it was a gorgeous symphony of color. *This is real beauty*, she thought.

Tropical huts were held up by wood poles in the ocean, which made it seem as if they floated on the water. A long wooden bridge connected the houses to each other, like a walk-way. Lights outside of the huts started to come on and twinkled in the water.

A mountain sat peacefully to her right, and a blanket of green covered the jagged heap. They rowed in between it and the huts, away from the Domus and out of sight of the mortals. She could make out a small platform that floated in the distance and turned to face him. "Like it?" he asked.

She turned back around, and they came upon a dark, wooden table and chairs that seemed to hover above the water. Tiki torches were lit all around it and a glowing light came from under the table. Nervously, she rolled the rose's stem between her fingers.

They pulled up to their personal dining area and Aden tied the boat to a torch. She took his hand and stepped out of the boat and onto the glass flooring. He pulled out a chair for her, and she sat down nervously. Julia looked down at the glass platform and she could see assortments of fish, clear as day, as they swam under the platform.

On the table, she was surprised to see her favorite meal—goat cheese and olive stuffed chicken breasts with balsamic butter pan sauce and a side of asparagus. She looked up at him, and his smile was contagious. "How did you know what I like?"

"Grace." He shrugged and sat down opposite of her. "I got threatened with my life if I don't get you home at eleven, by the way."

He poured white wine into her glass, then his and she instantly felt like this was a horrible decision. Perhaps he would get the wrong impression from her. She was not interested in him romantically and he was being so sweet. Guilt started to set in and she had no idea how to let him down easily.

"All of this is lovely, Aden." She smiled sweetly.

"What's wrong?" Was she being that obvious?

"This is the most romantic thing a man has done for me." She sighed and folded her hands on her lap. "I just think this means something differently to you than it does me."

Aden grabbed his glass and emptied it in one long swallow. He looked mildly amused by her and rested his elbows on the table. "Does it now?"

She was horribly confused. "I believe so."

"Julia." He grinned. "You are a beautiful woman and yes, I wish you felt the same about me as I do you. This is just my attempt for you to get to know me and to show you this is what you deserve from a man. See it as a date if you wish or just a nice dinner with a friend." They looked at each other for a moment and she felt his sincerity might be lacking. However, Julia felt more at ease and picked up her silverware, cut into the chicken and took the first bite. It was just like her mother used to make.

It was delicious and Aden was obviously pleased by the look on her face.

They both ate their dinner and made small talk. More wine was poured and liquid courage had set in for both of them. Aden was apparently very into rock music, and a sport called wake boarding. She didn't understand the appeal in strapping your feet to a single piece of wood and gliding across the water, but to each their own.

"Could you imagine a world with no war, Julia?" Aden stared at the island. "No conflict or fighting. Religion is the main cause in most cases and also for power, but still, it's all about beliefs."

"I suppose." Julia shrugged. *That was a random thought.* "I would never change my beliefs though. Neither would anyone really."

"This is true." Aden nodded. "It would be wonderful though, wouldn't it?"

"No war?" She laughed. "Keep dreaming. It's human nature to destroy ourselves."

Aden grinned. "Couldn't be more true."

"Besides, the Immortals would be rendered obsolete." She studied the fish that swam under her feet. "Then we would cease to exist."

"Answer me something?"

"What?" She sipped on her wine.

Aden chugged his wine down and gently set the glass back on the table. "If there was a way to get rid of all the evils in the world, even if innocent people were to die in the process, would you help make it a reality?"

Julia thought about it. Few dying for the greater good is what the Immortals were all about, but not at the expense of innocent lives. "Absolutely not."

Aden looked disappointed. He tried to pour more wine into his glass only to realize the bottle was empty and Julia started to giggle.

Aden seemed to be more relaxed and stared out into the ocean as he laughed at her silliness. "It's nice seeing you loosen up, Julia."

"It's a rarity, I assure you." She grinned. "So tell me, what exactly happened between you and Ryan?"

Aden cleared his throat and sat up straight. This was obviously a subject he wished to avoid.

"The usual. We argued and fought and of course he took it too far."

"What provoked him?" she asked.

"More like what provoked me." Aden looked ashamed. Suddenly his demeanor changed. "He said it was pointless to take you out because you are..." He trailed off and her eyes squinted.

"Because I am what?"

Aden bit his lip. "That you were the Virgin Queen of the Domus and that you weren't worth wasting a perfectly good dinner on."

Julia felt anger wash all over her, but her face remained calm. She would not let Aden see how much this upset her. Ryan was going to get a piece of her mind. How could she possible believe, even for a moment, that Ryan was a decent person deep down? "Ryan is a child and is very mistaken about me."

"Oh really?" Aden smirked. His interest in her seemed to peak, and she grew weary about his intentions. Ryan was a jerk—she made no mistake about that, but he was not that terrible, especially to her. Something just didn't seem right.

"So tell me..." She leaned forward and traced the lip of her glass with her finger. “Why did you feel the need to tell him about our dinner?”

Aden started to look uncomfortable. Julia could sense she was being lied to and she intended to get the truth. He picked at the asparagus left on his plate and crossed his legs. She watched him squirm and she rather enjoyed the view of his discomfort. Her loyalties to her brother and his team were far greater than a man she somewhat knew.

“I was excited,” he stated simply.

“So instead of telling Caleb or Jesse, you decided to tell someone you hate?” she inquired. He seemed nervous as she sat back in her chair with a sweet smile on her lips. “That’s rather unconventional.”

“He was eavesdropping on me and Caleb.”

“I thought you told him because you were excited.”

“I did.”

“Well, which is it?” She tilted her head to the side.

“Okay, fine.” He sighed. “I rubbed it in his face that you picked me over him.”

She closed her eyes and took a deep breath. Her annoyance level was at its peak. “This was a very lovely evening, Aden, but I better get home.”

Chapter VII

Anna

ANNA WALKED NERVOUSLY INTO the training arena. Today she would be tested to see if she were capable of becoming an Immortal. If she failed, her memory would be wiped clean of their existence and she would be dumped in the middle of Iraq for the Americans to find. She really didn't want to fail.

Julia briskly walked up to her and pulled Anna into a tight embrace. "Are you ready?" She grinned.

How could one person be so optimistic?

"No," she admitted, "but do I have a choice?"

"I have faith in you." She smiled sweetly. If she let Julia down, she would have felt like the scum of the Earth. "Just relax and follow your instincts. Don't overthink anything."

"Easier said then done." She sighed.

Julia rested her hand against Anna's cheek. She imagined this is what having a mother would feel like. She could feel Julia was proud and fully confident of her abilities. Even though they looked to be the same age, she saw Julia as her elder. "You will do amazing."

Grace and Colette sat in chairs that lined the wall against the guns. They quietly talked with one another and Colette pointed at her. She instantly felt her nerves going nuts.

Members in the Council of Command were here to evaluate her performance. They were her age of course, but most of them looked like tooth picks and others were muscular and scarred.

"I'm going to freak the heck out." Anna took a deep breath.

Julia looked over at the Council and laughed. "Most of them have never been in a single confrontation in their life. They know nothing of real battle Anna, so do not worry."

Anna sort of guessed that already, but what did she know of this world? Nothing. Exactly.

"Then how did they get on the Council?"

"Politics," Julia whispered. "Money makes things happen."

True story, thought Anna.

"Are we ready to begin, ladies?" A tall thin man stood up out of his chair and checked his pocket watch. He looked like he was from the Victorian era or something. *Get with the times, buddy*, went through Anna's mind.

"Yes." Julia hugged Anna one more time and made her way over to sit with Grace and Colette.

Anna stood by herself in the middle of the room. She hated the attention. They all looked at her like they expected her to do something. Julia smiled brightly while Colette looked bored out of her mind.

"Miss Sanchez, your test will be administered through a computer simulation." She wondered how that was going to work but didn't ask any questions.

"Okay," she muttered.

"This helmet," he said as he held up an ordinary military helmet with goggles on the front, "will depict a scene. It is a mission simulation."

Another man stood up. He was one of the scary, scarred men who looked like he could kill a lion with his bare hands. "Your mission will be to assassinate a king. He will be highly protected and you must get in without being caught. If you are caught or killed, you fail."

He handed Julia a picture of a man and the helmet. Julia got up to give it to her and Anna tried very hard not to laugh when she saw a picture of Damian. Was this a joke? "Damian is a king?"

Julia grinned. "Of course not. He did, however, help develop the simulation and made himself the target. He thought it would be indecent to pick an actual mortal to kill."

Anna sighed. She really didn't want to shoot Damian. Anna grabbed the helmet and put it on. She could not see anything. Suddenly, a gun was being thrust into her hands, and she held on for dear life. This was going to be awkward. "What if I shoot someone?"

"It's a fake gun programed for the simulation. You will be led around this room although it will feel as if you are somewhere else," a man chimed in. *Who was that?*

The goggles turned on and she was surprised at the detail of the simulation. She truly felt as if she were somewhere else. It was sort of creepy. She was in a huge, run-down house with torn furniture, broken glass and holes in the walls. She expected Jason to pop up with a machete at some point.

She held the gun at the ready to shoot. Anna quietly shuffled along the bottom level and tried to avoid the broken glass.

She was successful, for the most part, but heard small crunches come from the bottom of her feet.

This is like the world's best video game. They should market this thing.

She saw a shadow about to come around the corner of the living room. She pressed her back against the dirty wall and grabbed the knife that was strapped to her leg. How did that get there?

She gripped it tight and as soon as the figure stepped past the wall, she swung her arm fast and stabbed the man in the chest. He fell down hard, and she turned around the corner with her gun held steady. No one was there. She looked down at the man and cocked her head.

It had no face, just a blank canvas, which made this simulation even creepier.

She picked up no-face by the legs and dragged him toward a gapping hole in the middle of the kitchen. She looked down and saw an empty basement area and kicked the body into it. There was no noise from the fall and the body just disappeared.

Anna heard multiple people come in through the front door and ducked down into a crouched position. There was a door leading to a bathroom that was in direct view of the kitchen and she made her way to it. She tried to open the door quietly, but the hinges squeaked so much she had to resort to squeezing herself in.

If this were real, she would have thrown up. The toilet was black from decay, and the floors looked like someone dumped everything that was in their vacuum on it for an entire year. The bathtub looked to have dried bloodstains on it, but she decided not to think about it too much.

She looked out into the kitchen and saw three men sit

around the worn and broken table. They started to polish guns, and laugh about something that sat in front of them. A young woman sat tied to one of the chairs and as she begun to cry one of the men slapped her across the face.

Anna forgot about it being fake when anger started to rise in her. She wanted to hurt these men and was about to come out of her spot until she saw Damian. She snapped back to reality and remembered this was not real. There was no way in hell Damian would hurt a woman.

Damian slapped the girl and started to laugh. She recognized the other men as other Warriors she had seen around the Domus, but she didn't really know them. So she felt somewhat at ease about having to shoot their fake selves.

Anna got low and pointed her gun at Damian's back, right between his shoulder blades. He was the target—he must be taken out before anyone else, even if that meant the end of her life. That was the mission and she would succeed.

She squeezed the trigger and Damian collapsed to the ground and shuddered on the dirty floor. She fired two more shots almost instantly after the first and the other two men fell to the floor. Blood started to seep from their wounds and onto the filthy floor.

Anna walked up to the bodies and looked down at one of the fake men. He was still alive, so she shot him in the head for good measure. She half expected something to happen, some sort of twist to make it harder, but she realized this was programmed for realism. No super human would burst through the room and beat her senseless and Damian would not come magically back alive to kill her.

She beat the simulation successfully. *This was easy, almost too easy*. Anna looked at the girl Damian had hit. She sat there as if she were put on pause with the look of shook plastered on her face.

She reached out to the girl but the helmet she wore was pulled off and came face-to-face with an overly excited Julia. She jumped and hugged Anna, who now faced the male dorm hallway and laughed. "That was great!"

"You saw it?" Anna's cheeks reddened.

"Of course." She pointed to a large screen that now hung across the room. "That was done so gracefully and professionally that you even impressed Colette. Most people don't realize the bathroom is there and try to hide around the refrigerator and have to actually wrestle with the enemy."

Anna felt extremely pleased with herself. The looks on the council's faces were priceless. Some were shocked, others looked satisfied, and the pocket watch guy was utterly baffled. Colette nodded her approval and left the room with an amused Grace. Anna felt a sigh of relief. She was made for this life. She just had to be.

Chapter VIII

Ryan

He calmly walked up to the arena that held the untamable horse. Men have tried and failed to ride this magnificent beast all day and none had prevailed.

He put his hand out to touch his muzzle. "Ready yourself, my friend." He grinned.

He studied the beautiful black horse and noticed the horse was afraid of his shadow. No one else seemed to have realized this, but him. Every rider had failed, and he was determined not to. Failure was not an option, ever.

Slowly, he reached out and grabbed the beast's reins. The skittish horse pulled away from him until he led the horse into the sun. With his shadow behind him, the steed calmed down.

The entire crowd was in silence. He could only hear the horse's breath.

With ease, he climbed upon his new friend. He could feel the power of the horse below him radiate through his entire body.

He grinned and took off out of the arena. He became the first to ride the untamable horse. He grew an instant bond with the steed and claimed him as his own in that very moment.

The speed was intoxicating and he pushed the horse harder. Before they got any further, he turned the horse around and reentered the arena. He would not want to miss the praise he would receive.

As he entered the arena, he could not contain his smile. He found the entire crowd, including his father, down in the arena, cheering and yelling him on.

Ryan woke with a start and out of breath. He ran his hands through his hair, rubbed his face, and let his hands drop down to his sides. Sweat drenched his brow and chest and he kicked off the hot blankets that covered him. As he sat up the dream begin to fade from reality and he felt more at ease. He hated those dreams.

He was being haunted in his sleep and there was no way for him to escape. The dreams started up a few months back and he had no reason as to why. Karma perhaps? Guilt? He didn't know.

He swung his legs over the edge of his bed and took deep breaths. The sun was not even close to being up and he heard the roar of New York City outside of his window. He hated when the change came here. It was noisy and polluted, and the people were like angry robots.

His door opened and Ryan put his head in his hands. "If I woke you, I'm sorry," he said.

"Dreams again?" Damian asked.

"Depressingly, yes."

Damian crossed over to the loveseat near the bed wearing only sweatpants. He sat down with his elbows on his knees.

"Ryan, you really need to talk to someone."

"Well, good morning to you too."

"I'm serious, it's not healthy." Damian gazed at him. "You yelled this time."

"Don't know why." He shrugged. "I was just riding a horse."

Damian sighed. "I'm worried."

"Let me worry about me." Ryan stood up and pulled jeans on over his briefs.

"Honestly, why haven't you figured it out by now?" Damian sighed. "I'm always going to worry about you."

"That's not healthy."

"Shut up." Damian looked tense.

Ryan pulled a plain white shirt on over his head and ruffled his hair. He stretched his arms out in the air and yawned. "So tell me, did you come in here to calm my nightmares or is there an ulterior motive?"

"Perhaps a little of both." Damian stood up and crossed over to Ryan. "I've noticed something."

Ryan walked away from Damian and over to his small fridge. In an attempt to avoid his friend, Ryan reached in and pulled out a bottle of water. "What do you mean?"

Damian followed him and grabbed the water out of his hand. He was not going to let this go. "Julia."

Oh crap, he thought. "I honestly have no idea what you're talking about." He grabbed another water. As he closed the fridge, he looked Damian in the eyes and got the stare down of the century. Was it so obvious? All these years, he was able to hide his affections, until now, and he needed to get a hold on it.

"Don't lie to me. I know when you are lying," Damian pushed. "Admit it."

"I have nothing to admit."

"Gonna go down swinging I see."

This conversation needed to stop. "Perhaps if you were more specific."

"Okay, how about this—you're in love with Julia, but won't admit it," Damian spat. "Specific enough?"

He just stood there and stared at Damian. Ryan forced a convincing chuckle and smacked Damian's shoulder. "The fact that you think I could love one woman is funny in itself. Julia? That's just damn hilarious."

He maintained his amused expression and walked back over to his bed. He chugged the water and tossed it in the trash next to his nightstand. Ryan started to put his shoes on while Damian just stood there and stared at him.

"What?"

"Don't insult my intelligence, Ryan. You know I can't stand it."

"I'm not." Ryan sighed.

"You are."

"Look," Ryan said as he and Damian locked eyes, "she's good looking, which I've barely noticed. That's it. I promise."

Damian, obviously annoyed, raised and dropped his arms in exasperation. "Just admit it."

"I'll admit it when you admit you like Anna."

Damian stared at him in disbelief, turned and walked out of his room without another word.

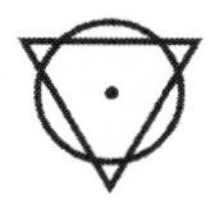

Ryan

"Tell me why we have to go to Urbs instead of just the girls?" Ryan groaned. They stepped out of the Domus with Julia's, Jesse's, and his team. Ahmose followed behind them as they continued down the steps.

"I told you. I wanted to be there for Anna's ceremony," Damian snapped. Their previous conversation seemed to linger between them.

"Then why is Jesse and his team here?"

Damian looked in front at the other men. They were dressed in their all white ceremonial gear with only a sword at their side. "According to Cato, they simply wanted to get out of the Domus."

Ryan shrugged and gazed out at Urbs, City of the Immortals. It was as if they stepped into a melting pot of the past. They were in the part of the city that looked like a scene from ancient Rome. White columns and marble towered over them. It was an odd site since the old structures were modernized with glass windows and furniture.

Statues of famous Romans and Greeks lined the street in a triumphant spectacle as if to say they were superior to everyone else. Most of the city was very modest with their culture. However, Romans were not known for their modesty.

Urbs was an island that existed in its own world. It was about the size of New York City, and although it lacked the pollution, they were rather similar. Urbs was made up of all races and ethnicities. The Gods made it in the mirror image of Earth, but lacked the oceans that separated the lands from one another.

The Domus was currently stationed in what would be considered Europe. Although the Gods had begun to create the Immortals in Africa, it was the Greeks who formed the idea of a city away from Earth and because of that, the Greek culture was the heart of the city.

Ahmose waved them over to join the others. Anna looked very nervous and shifted her ceremonial gear over and over. Ryan guessed it felt stiff from being new.

The girls all wore their hair the same, in tight buns, and he could not help but admire their strong, yet beautiful profiles. Ryan wanted to tell Anna it would be fine, but kept his mouth shut. Damian didn't need to get the wrong impression.

"We are the only ones from the Domus, so everyone be on your best behavior. Be professional and act like the soldiers I know you are," Ahmose ordered.

Everyone nodded and they automatically got in lines of three. Ahmose alone at the head, followed buy Ryan's team, then Julia's, and lastly Jesse's.

They all kept their composure and almost marched as they went. Ahmose felt it was important to show the strength of being an Immortal Warrior, as if they were exceptional to the families that choose not to serve anymore. Ryan believed they were superior.

They passed shops that made breads, candies, weapons, clothing and more. Ryan longed to visit the bookstores, and the smell of fresh bread was intoxicating.

As they walked along the stone roads to the Great Temple, where Anna would be made into an Immortal, Ryan briefly saw children run around in the corner of his eye. They stopped playing with their wooden swords to watch the group go by. Their little fingers pointed and waved at them with excitement.

Adults watched as well and held both hands over their

heart. It was a sign of respect to those who serve the purpose of them all. The very thought of being a bystander gave Ryan the chills.

The crowd parted for them along the way and Ryan could not wait to get this over with. They walked up the steps to the Great Temple where many people gathered outside to wait and witness the ascension. It is a tradition to welcome and show respect to those to dedicated their lives for the greater good.

The Great Temple was a round coliseum-shaped building with stone seats that lined half of the space. It could fit up to one thousand people. The temple was big and a wide circle remained open in the ceiling to provide airflow.

The tall doors were already open—the Council Of Command waited for them inside, dressed in ceremonial gear as well. Most of them had never been in a single fight. *The life of a reborn must be boring.*

Ryan had been asked on many occasions to join the council, but his place was with his team and to do the job he promised to do. Politics were no longer part of his life, and he had no desire to return to the drama.

Statues of all the Gods known to creation sat on the opposite side of the seats in arched wall niches—each about two feet tall. In the center of the room there was a silver chalice half full of wine on a plain wooden table. It was not much to look at and the cup had no significance. The substance that would be in it was the important part of the process.

Ahmose led Anna to the center of the room and stood in front of the chalice. The teams formed a circle around them and simultaneously took out their swords. With the hilt of the sword in their left hand and the blade in their right—they formed a circle of steel around Anna and Ahmose.

The small amount of chatter instantly became silenced by their presence and Anna looked extremely nervous. All eyes were on her and her gaze shifted around the room. Ryan tried not to smile when Damian's and her eyes met. She seemed to relax and a smile tugged at the corner of her mouth.

Ahmose broke the silence. "Adrianna Marie Sanchez, do you hereby swear yourself to the life of the Immortals? To protect mankind as the Gods see fit, no matter the cost? To sacrifice everything for the greater good and to never abandon those around you?"

To Ryan's surprise, Anna spoke with confidence, "I so do swear."

Ahmose grabbed the chalice from the table and walked up to Damian. Damian squeezed the edge of the blade tightly, his blood dripping down to the floor. Ahmose held the cup under the blade, and caught Damien's blood in it.

He went all around the circle. The chalice was filled with their Immortal blood and he ended with Caleb. The cut on Ryan's hand throbbed, but no one showed any sign of pain. It was their duty to show their strength to the civilians even though it stung like hell.

Ahmose returned in front of Anna, placed the chalice on the table, and took out his own blade. He cut his own right hand, along with Anna's, and dripped their blood into the cup together.

"In wine is truth, in blood is life. Drink the blood of your brethren and forever become infinite." Ahmose held out the cup to Anna.

She stared into the cup with a look of disgust on her face. Even with obvious revulsion, she took it into her hands. Ryan had to admit—drinking wine mixed with blood was a disgusting thought. However, Anna put the cup to her lips and drank every last drop.

It only took a few seconds for the transformation to start. Blue flames crawled out of the chalice and surrounded Anna. The flames danced and licked around her body until she was swallowed in a sea of blue fire.

It was not a painful process. In fact, the flames chilled your entire body. Ryan remembered the sensation well. It was like an ice-cold bath that you fell into, but could not get out until the transformation was over. The feeling took your breath away, but no scream would come from your frozen lips.

Finally, the blue flames returned to the chalice as if being sucked back through a vacuum. Ahmose smiled proudly. "Welcome to the Immortals."

The ceremony was over. Each team returned their swords into their scabbards and everyone in the Great Temple stood up and placed both hands over their hearts. Anna looked relieved, and her smile was contagious. Julia looked like a proud mother and exchanged words with Grace.

Ahmose led Anna out to the steps to present her to the crowd. Her composure was regal. The teams followed out in lines, just as they had come in.

As they went outside they were met with loud cheers of joy and roses petals were tossed in the air. It was a celebration for Anna alone.

Everyone clapped and smiled at Anna, who looked embarrassed at the attention. Hands reached out hoping they would touch the new Immortal. It was believed to be good luck for her newfound purity.

Many of the chosen Immortals were no longer around, but their families had survived. It was very rare to be chosen anymore, as most of the citizens were reborns. They never saw a fight in their lives and were awarded Immortal purely by chance of their parents. Ryan was always impressed when a reborn Immortal decided to become a Warrior.

Ahmose leaned towards her and whispered something to her, and she quickly put both hands over her heart. Ryan started to chuckle at her surprised expression, but Damian nudged him. "Stop."

Loud pops burst throughout the crowd. At first, Ryan thought it was celebratory gunshots until he heard the screams of terrified bystanders. His eyes darted through the crowd—he saw people run in terror from ten men dressed completely in black gear and cloaks. Their hoods covered their faces and they had scabbards at their sides.

They calmly walked towards the Great Temple and began to shoot at the teams. They were the obvious targets to take out first. No civilian had a reason to carry weaponry and the Warriors were the only defense in the city.

A grenade landed near Anna and Ahmose—Ryan grabbed it and tossed it quickly in the air. The explosion was loud and they were showered with specks of fire and shrapnel.

Jesse's team jumped quickly into battle and began to fight with the enemy. The sound of clashing steel and screams filled the air. For a second, Ryan thought Aden had been killed, but his arm had received a blow from the enemy and blood trickled down his white gear.

Julia's team and Anna ran quickly down the steps to clear the crowd far from the area. They tried to push the crowd back and were yelling something to the citizens, but Ryan could not understand what they were saying. It was chaos below.

Bombs went off all around as Ryan, Damian, and Cato

jumped into the fight.

The Warriors were at a disadvantage. The enemy had guns and swords, whereas the Warriors were only equipped with ceremonial swords. Shots fired into the crowd and Ryan saw a blonde woman clutching a bloodied man who lay on the ground as the crowd surrounded them.

Ryan ran swiftly towards the large cloaked figure that seemed in charge, unsheathed his sword and brought it down hard on the man. He was blocked by the man's sword and Ryan swung the blade quickly. No matter how fast he was—the man matched his movements.

Ryan was shocked at the skill he possessed as continued on in battle. He ducked a swing and rounded quickly on the man bringing his sword down swiftly on his opponents arm.

He connected. The man held his blood-drenched robes and took off in a run.

"Retreat!" his husky voice roared through the crowd. Ryan started to chase him but stopped. He looked around for his friends and saw the rest of the cloaked figures were retreating as well.

The cloaked figures ran into the thick crowd and managed to disappear. Buildings were on fire and stone rubble littered the ground. The sheer chaos of it all left the teams in shock. Bodies lay within the area—victims of the bombs and gunfire. Families and friends knelt down by the bodies and looked around pleading for anyone to help. There was no help for the mutilated remains.

Ryan wanted to chase after the men. He wanted to kill every last one of them, but they were gone.

Healers began to show up to help the wounded and gather the dead after the threat was gone. The teams came together below the Great Temple. Damian had a cut on his cheek and Aden bled from the back of his leg and arm. Julia and Grace had blood all over themselves. Ryan was momentarily worried until it was clear that it was not their own.

Ahmose held his bloody sword to his side and breathed deeply. "Come."

They all walked slowly towards a crumpled figure that gasped for breath and clutched his stomach on the steps of the Great Temple. Ryan glared up at the figure and lost control.

He climbed that stairs to the man and hit him hard in his face and stomach—he went to town on that battered figure. Cato and Damian's hands grasped his body, straining to pull him away. "You bastard!" Ryan yelled.

They could not constrain him. Pure rage built in Ryan after he saw all the innocent lives lost. He wanted to kill this man. He would kill this man. He wanted to make him suffer, and his instinct told him to attack.

"Ryan, enough!" Damian said harshly. He pulled Ryan up by his vest and slammed him against a nearby column. Ryan almost swung at Damian just so he could continue his attack.

It was not until Julia and Caleb helped push him back that Ryan began to calm down. He took deep breaths, and Damian finally released him. Ryan punched the column and his knuckles started to bleed. He welcomed the painful feeling and punched it one more time leaving a bloody mark on the column.

Ahmose ignored Ryan's actions. His guess was Ahmose wished he could do the same thing to this scum but had to refrain from such behavior. Ahmose leaned down over the figure and pulled his hood back. The man was in his twenties with short brown hair, and his face was drenched in his own blood. "Who are you?" Ahmose asked.

The man had the nerve to laugh and started to cough. Blood trickled out of his mouth and seeped through the front of his cloak. "You will find out soon. I promise you that." His bloody grin infuriated Ryan. He wanted nothing more than to kill him. How could he laugh about anything right now?

The man's cough worsened and his blood quickened out of his body. He started to shake then his eyes grew wide. His body was going into shock. Ahmose pressed his hand against the man's wound. Ryan instantly wanted to hit Ahmose. Why was he trying to save this little disease?

"Get someone! We need him alive. We have to interrogate him." Ahmose looked to Colette, who ran off to find someone.

The man laughed and pointed at Ryan. "You better watch out. They are coming for you." Then with one last deep breath the man was gone, his eyes still open with a blank stare fixed on Ryan.

Ryan stood still and could not think or even breathe. His heart began to race and he could not figure out why.

Looking defeated, Ahmose rose up and tossed a crystal in the air. "Domus."

The portal opened and he turned to face the teams. "Everyone, back to the Domus. I will follow after I speak with the Council." He turned and walked away without another word.

They all made their way into the portal and appeared in the parlor.

"We could have walked," Ryan mumbled.

"He wanted us out of the situation, Ryan." Aden purposely bumped into him.

Ryan was about to retaliate until he started to feel weak and dropped to his knees. He felt so tired. Damian and Cato pulled him up by his arms and dragged him to the couch.

Julia ran up to him and knelt down to his level. Her eyes grew wide and he could see fear in them. Everyone seemed panicked and worried and he could not figure out why.

"Ryan, you idiot!"

"That's uncalled for." He followed her eyes down to his stomach and saw a wide gash along his left side. His robe quickly turned from white to red and he laughed at himself for not knowing he was wounded. "Well that's problematic."

Julia ignored him and with a worried look on her face she turned to Damian, who was busy pushing his hands hard against the gash. In seconds his hands turned red and Ryan did nothing but watch with interest.

"Don't move, Ryan," Damian croaked. The look on his face gave away that his injury was severe. It was not something he was used to. Usually he walked away with minor injury, but he knew this was different.

Ryan slowly looked at Julia, his eyes growing heavy. "Julia," he muttered. Black began to cloud his vision and before he fell unconscious, he thought he heard Julia call out his name.

Chapter IX

Ryan

Where was he? He could not remember. His consciousness went in and out. All he could see was darkness and then light. He was on comfortable pillows. They felt nice. He wanted to sink farther back into them and disappear.

Darkness.

"Is he better?" Damian sounded panicked and Ryan thought he heard a door click shut. Poor Damian. Always worried.

"We aren't sure, it was deep. He lost a lot of blood." Julia sounded tired. Her voice was close. "How did he not know he was hurt?"

"Adrenaline? Shock? Who knows?"

"Stupidity? Lack of self-preservation?" Snickered Cato.

"Shut it," Julia growled.

Was she worried? *This is a dream, only a dream. It had to be.*

"He really has been careless lately, Julia. You have to admit it," said Damian.

Be quiet Damian. You need to calm down.

"Like I would know. It's not like I fight with you guys on a daily basis."

Damian backtracked. "Okay, calm down. I'm telling you then, he has been reckless. If you could talk to him-"

"No."

"Maybe if you just-"

"No! He is selfish and ignorant and..." she paused. "Maybe this will be the lesson he needs."

"Doubtful." Cato chuckled.

Ryan wanted to punch dream Cato, even though he had a point.

"I didn't mean to make you angry." Damian sighed.

"I'm sorry," Julia whispered. This was a vivid dream. "I'm just stressed."

The light was coming back.

"I think he is coming around," said Damian.

"Ryan?" Julia put her hand on his head and smoothed back his hair. It felt good. "Ryan, are you awake?"

He opened his eyes slowly. Everything was in a fog. The bright light blinded him and he rubbed his eyes. Ryan could make out figures around him. The closest was Julia. She sat on the edge of the bed and leaned towards him.

Everything started to come into focus, but was still a bit fuzzy around the edges. He tried to sit up and felt four hands push him back down. "I'm fine."

Damian and Julia would not release his hold on him. Damian shook his head. "You're not. You almost died. Lay back and rest."

"I'm serious guys, I don't feel anything."

"That would be because you're high as a kite from the pain

meds." Cato smirked.

"Cato, charming as ever," he muttered. Ryan turned his head to stare at Julia. There were bags under her eyes. The three of them were still in their bloody ceremonial robes. "What happened?"

"When you were fighting one of the cloaked guys, they stabbed you. You lost a ton of blood and nearly died," Cato summed up.

"Sounds about right," said Ryan

"Sensitivity isn't your strong suite, is it, Cato?" Damian looked back at him. Cato shrugged and took a seat near the door. Ryan was okay with his blunt attitude. If he ever needed the truth without it being sugar coated, he came to Cato.

The healers quarters were equipped with every medicine and machine known to man that helped save lives on a daily basis. The white room was far too clean and bright for his taste, and he wanted to get out of here. He felt like he was being quarantined.

"Why should I be sensitive?" Cato added, "The idiot runs into a fight like a bat out of hell. Not thinking or giving a damn about where we are or himself."

So this wasn't a dream. Great.

"Can you please save this conversation for when he is, oh I don't know, not on the verge of death?" Julia hissed.

Ryan smirked when he saw Cato and Damian look at the ground in shame.

Pain filled his entire side and he reached for the wound out of instinct. Even if he barely touched the wound, it hurt like hell. His head fell back, and he stared at the ceiling. Ryan breathed deeply and closed his eyes—he didn't want to look pathetic in front of Julia.

He noticed Julia flinched when he gasped in pain and Damian looked as if he wanted to do something, but could not figure out what. They acted as if he were glass about to shatter. They really needed to calm down. He was fine and alive.

"How long have I been out?" Ryan tried to be nonchalant.

"A day or so. They had to give you a blood transfusion," Damian replied. "None of us would leave your side."

"Why Cato, how sweet of you." Ryan grinned.

Cato rolled his eyes and stared at the ceiling.

"So," Ryan went on, "any idea who those guys are?"

Damian shook his head. "No idea. Ahmose has yet to return."

Ryan figured as much. This was a unique problem.

There had never been an attack in Urbs before. It was unthinkable and unrealistic. Why would they attack one another? If you wanted to die naturally, the Gods allowed you to. If you wanted to live peacefully with your family, forever, they allowed it without punishment. In no shape or form were any of them forced to live the life of an Immortal. "It's our own people that did this." Ryan winced.

Julia shook her head. "There is no way any Immortal would do that. We care for each other. We are all family."

"Only Immortals can enter Urbs, Julia. You know that." Ryan grimaced. She was in denial and he could not blame her.

"It would explain their fighting technique," Cato added.

"Not to toot my own horn, but no mortal could even come close to killing me." He almost made Julia smile. "And here I lay useless."

"So what else is new?" She rolled her eyes. No matter how much Ryan thought he had Julia figured out, she always surprised him.

They stared at each other for a moment until Damian cleared his throat. "Well, now that I know you are up and awake and still an arrogant ass, I think I better get some sleep." He looked to Cato.

Damian started to walk out of the door and smacked Cato upside the head. "Ouch, uh yeah, me too. You kids be good." Cato glared at Ryan, pointed his fingers to his eyes and then back at Ryan.

They both left hurriedly, and Julia seemed amused and tired all at once. Ryan had to admit, he was glad to be alone with her. "Not trying to seem ungrateful, but why have you been here this entire time?"

"You're my brother's friend." She sat back in her chair and looked at the floor. "Also, I was worried about you. I couldn't imagine what I would do if you died."

He was taken back. Does she really mean that?

"Julia..." He reached for her hand and she willingly gave it to him. His heart raced, and the monitor beeps quickened, "Well that's embarrassing."

She laughed and leaned forward again. His heart raced more and he pulled her hand to his cheek. She traced her fingers along his jaw line and his lips with the lightest touch that sent his nerves on end.

"If it makes you feel better," she whispered, "my heart is pounding too."

She leaned in towards him and their lips almost touched. *This cannot happen*, he thought as he urged himself to calm down.

He cupped her face gently and pushed her back away from him. He looked deep into her eyes. "Julia?"

"Yes?" Her lips quivered.

"I can't." The monitor beeps returned to a steady pace. He managed to look as bored as possible.

She stood up straight and stared down at him in disbelief. "Why not?"

The hurt in her voice made him hate himself even more. "I don't want you—plain and simple."

With that, she turned to walk out of the room. She stopped at the doorway and turned around, her eyes started to tear up. "You are cruel!" Then she walked away.

Julia

Julia walked briskly away from the healers quarters. "Quit crying," she told herself out loud.

Ryan was an idiot and a waste of life. He was perfectly fine with being with other women, why not her? What disgusted him?

She wiped the tears away just in time as she turned a corner and ran straight into Damian.

"Whoa." He turned around and smiled. After he saw her face he seemed instantly worried. "Are you okay? What happened?"

He was confused—after all, when he left her and Ryan alone they were both in good moods.

"Nothing whatsoever. Your friend has made that very clear." She moved around Damian and started down the hallway.

"Hold on, Julia." He caught up with her. He looked genuinely concerned. "What did he do?"

She laughed and walked faster. Damian almost jogged to keep up. "Amazing how Ryan's friend blames him instead of the girl. That says a lot about him."

"Tell me, please."

"Let's see, where to start? He makes me think there is something between us and then says he doesn't want me." Julia choked back tears. "After having a stupid crush on him since I could remember, I never would have thought he would hurt me this badly. I should have just listened to myself and stayed away. Apparently there is something so wrong with me that not even Ryan wants me."

"I highly doubt that."

"Why?" she growled. "He sleeps with anyone and everyone. Just not me."

"Maybe he feels you are out of his league?"

"I practically threw myself at him. I was so worried he was going to die that I decided not to waste another second hiding my affections." She felt like an idiot. He could not possibly return her feelings. He had no feelings.

Damian looked shocked and was rendered speechless. Instantly, he pulled her into a huge, awkward hug, and she patted his back for some reason.

"Let me talk to him, Julia. He is an idiot, I give you that, but don't give up." He grabbed her shoulders and looked deep into her eyes. Poor Damian. He was always in the shadow of such a crude person. He deserved to be the famous and loved one.

"Whatever you want to do, go ahead. I am not going to beg for him though." She moved away slowly. "I will talk to you later, Damian."

As she walked to the female dormitory, she could not help but wonder why she didn't fall for Damian instead. He was the decent one.

Damian

"Are you simply a moron or are you trying to be the dumbest man on Earth?"

"Well, hello to you too, Damian." Ryan smirked.

"I'm serious, Ryan. You two obviously like each other and yet you are purposely messing it up." Damian was angry. He didn't know what to do with Ryan. A sudden urge to punch something rose inside—however, that was not him. He always felt guilty when he created a mess for the servants to clean up or fix.

"You don't understand, Damian. You never will."

"You're right. I don't understand." Damian's voice rose and he came closer to Ryan. "I don't understand how a man could not want a woman like that."

Ryan would not look at him—instead, he ran his hand back and forth on the blanket. Damian wanted to smack him, and if Ryan were not injured he would have.

"I just-"

"No," Damian interrupted. "There is no excuse. She is the perfect woman. Not only is she beautiful and strong, she is smart and funny."

"You think I don't know this?" he whispered. Ryan picked at the loose strings on the blanket. Damian was tempted to rip it out of his grasp.

"If you know it, then get your head out of your ass and be

with the girl." Damian felt his cheeks get hot. He was sick of seeing his friend alone and ruining his life. Ryan needed to find happiness, and he had just pushed it away.

"Can we please not talk about this, Damian?" Ryan groaned. "I feel like hell and I don't want to be fighting right now, especially with you."

"No, we are talking about this," Damian pushed on. He was not going to let this go.

"No, we are not, Damian." Ryan's expression grew tired. "Do not get involved with my love life."

"What love life? You avoid love like the plague."

"Then let me avoid it and move on. I am happy the way I am and you have no say in how I live." Ryan was beginning to grow angry.

"You like her," Damian urged.

"Stop."

"Be with the girl, Ryan," Damian growled.

"I can't, Damian!" Ryan yelled. He grasped his wound obviously in pain. "I can't be with her because I can't lose her."

His mouth gapped. Damian was not accustomed to Ryan being afraid of something. Ryan had many wives in his lifetime—he could not understand what was so different. "Why would you lose her?"

"What if she died? What if she had to be with someone on a mission? What if she realized I am no good for her and left me?"

Ryan's eyes were sad and Damian felt terrible inside. He should have known that this was why Ryan pushed everyone away. Ryan's life consisted of continuous loss.

"You can't live alone, Ryan, it is not okay."

"What's not okay is losing the people I love all the time. I can't do it anymore, Damian. She is the light in a world of darkness, and if I have her and I lose her..." Ryan took a moment to calm down. "I can't do it again. I lost everyone I loved when I was chosen and many people after. Losing her is unthinkable."

Damian stood there and stared into the eyes of his best friend. He could think of nothing to say.

Chapter X

Julia

THE FAMILIAR SALTY OCEAN BREEZE filled the air. The Domus was permanently stationed in Urbs since the attack, and the busy city refreshed Julia. Comforting smells of food and unusual aromas filled the air—her nose was overpowered by the smells of home.

It had been two weeks since the attack, and Julia decided it was time to take Anna out into the city. They both needed the distraction.

They walked down the roads of the North American side of town. Julia loved it here. It embodied Urbs with the many mixes of races and cultures. The shops were extremely interesting as well.

There were cowboy taverns and Indian hookah bars. There were even places for hippies from the sixties. One of the more popular places was a restaurant and bar for United States military from any point in time of its existence. She wanted to show

Anna it, but thought it might bring back bad memories.

"How about we get you some nice dresses? Just for everyday wear." She cocked her head. Anna looked at her like she was insane—she could not help but laugh. "Work with me. I know every girl, deep down, wishes to wear lovely things."

"The only girls who wear dresses in California are actually comfortable with their bodies and conceited."

"I highly doubt that." Julia brushed her off. "Even so, I know you have always wanted to wear one. Even the biggest tomboy has some desire."

"Not me." *What a stubborn girl Anna is.*

Julia continued to walk down the stone roads and looked inside each shop. "I doubt that, as well, so humor me."

Anna sighed and walked by her side. "Fine."

There was a pastry shop to their left that had amazing cakes, some were a few feet high and there were doughnuts of every color. "Want some?"

Anna looked at the shop with interest. "Maybe later."

"All right, off to dresses we go, then." She smiled wide. Anna rolled her eyes but didn't complain.

Usually, Julia went with her team everywhere. However, Anna had no team as of now, and she wanted her to feel welcomed. Grace understood, but Colette kept walking away without a word when Anna was mentioned. Your team is your family and right now Anna had no one. Ahmose was too busy to select a team for her and few recruits showed enough promise to create a team.

It was a beautiful day and the sun shown bright. They could see the Great Temple and noticed workers on their way to rebuild it the best they could.

"That's looking better," Anna observed. Some of the workers walked next to them and Anna looked away.

"They have had years of experience," Julia acknowledged. The workers stopped to look at them and started to whisper to one another.

Anna quickly glanced away, and Julia could not blame her. Despite the crowd, they were noticeable with swords strapped to their backs and guns in holsters at their sides. It was a dead giveaway who they were and some of the citizens were nervous to be around them, since the attack.

"Here we are," she exclaimed. Julia found the shop she was looking for called Muumuu. It reminded her of a log cabin on the outside and sat next to a tall apartment area and a music store. She directed Anna through the wooden door and into the dress shop—Julia could not help but be excited. "Let's see."

She looked Anna up and down like a Barbie doll—ready to make her new project a success. Dresses covered the entire store. There were no decorations—there was no room for them. There was just rows of clothes racks filled with gorgeous dresses of every color and style. They had dresses from designers in New York, L.A., and London. This was basically the style hub of the world.

"Be gentle," Anna muttered.

"Don't worry, you are in good hands." She winked.

A tall, dark-skinned woman came out from behind the counter. Her smile was bright and her dreadlocks barely touched her shoulders. The tight cream dress she wore was rather short and looked great with her black heels. Julia was envious. "Welcome, Warriors, my name is Zarah." She looked pleasantly surprised.

"Hello." Julia smiled. "We are here for this lovely lady. She is new to anything feminine."

Zarah looked Anna up and down. "Beautiful black hair and amazing curves." She ran her hands down Anna's back and Julia was mildly amused. Anna looked as uncomfortable as she did when Colette and Grace accessed her, especially when the woman grabbed her waist and buttocks.

"These Latinas are blessed, aren't they?" Julia grinned.

Zarah nodded and held up her hands. "I have just the things you need."

The woman walked briskly around and grabbed dresses from different spots as if she knew exactly where each one was. When she was done, she handed the large pile to Julia.

She held the dresses up to Anna one at a time. The first was a tight blue dress, simple and somewhat short. "This one." She handed it to Zarah, who put it in a bag.

Dress after dress, Julia put it against Anna's body and determined their adoption. She reached the end of the pile, and Anna looked relieved. Julia chose a flowing white dress with a matching beaded band across the breast and black sundress with no straps.

"Don't you want me to try them on?" Anna asked.

"Why do you think she was frisking you?" Julia whispered lowly as Zarah returned the denied dresses. "How much do we owe you, Zarah?"

"Nothing," she declared as she handed the bag to Anna. "A gift to the new Warrior."

"Oh no, I can't accep-" Anna started.

"Thank you very much," Julia interrupted. She placed her hands over her heart and ushered Anna out. "Never deny gifts, it's an insult."

Anna nodded and held on to her bag. Julia felt pleased with the selections and could not wait for Anna to wear them in public.

Horses trotted by as they left the shop. Soon a tavern caught her eye. "How about a drink?"

Anna grinned. "Most definitely."

The two of them crossed the busy street and tried not to bump into pedestrians. The tavern was called Moonshine. The name suited itself.

The tavern was built with wood and looked exactly like it came out of an old cowboy movie. It had the swinging door in the front and even the sign below Moonshine said Saloon. Julia looked at Anna, who seemed to have gotten a kick out of the place.

"Hee-haw," Anna muttered.

Julia pushed the wooden doors open to discover the inside matched the outside. Wooden tables and western decor filled the room. The tavern was moderately busy, but thankfully not overcrowded.

"Jesus, what Eastwood movie did they steal this stuff from?" Anna asked.

"Urbs is a city full of history and different types of people and times." Julia smiled. "It helps us relate to the world we no longer belong to and find comfort in what we came from."

"Hey, girls, over here." Julia looked to her left to see Damian and Ryan sitting at a table in the corner.

"How the..." She raised an eyebrow in question then walked over to the boys with Anna and took a seat across from them. "Were you following us?"

Damian shrugged and Ryan responded, "Of course. Dress shopping didn't seem very exciting, so we stopped in for a drink."

"Why were you following us, may I ask?" Julia glared.

Damian shifted awkwardly in his chair. "Just wanted to see

what you ladies were up to."

"As much fun as being around men all day every day is, female companionship sounds pretty nice right about now." Ryan kicked out a chair for Anna, who sat down across from Damian.

"Not getting enough in the Domus, I see." Julia snickered. "Tell me, how is Emma doing these days?"

Mid drink of his beer, Ryan choked. "Couldn't tell you. Haven't seen her in a while."

"Just leaving her high and dry like everyone else?" Julia glared.

"Nope." He took another drink. "I just ignore the ones that are desperate for my attention."

Julia rolled her eyes, and the server came over to them. "My name is Chao. What can I get you ladies?" He was small for a man and had tanned skin with a long black ponytail.

"They will have two beers as well," Ryan spoke up.

Julia shot daggers at him. As Chao walked briskly away, she turned on him. "Let me make this perfectly clear, Ryan, stay far from me."

"Why?"

"Are you serious?" Her fists were clenched, and he looked as if nothing had happened between them.

She opened her mouth, ready to let him have it when she heard the doors open. She turned her attention to the four young men who came in to the tavern and sat down at a nearby table. They laughed and had black scabbards strapped to their side.

Glancing back at the boys, she could sense their tension. "What is it?"

Ryan bent over the table, the others followed suit. "Do those scabbards look familiar to you?"

Julia slowly turned around. Her heart stopped. "It can't be.

That would be foolish of them to come alone."

They all sat still and tried to eavesdrop on their conversation. Julia's heart raced and her annoyance with Ryan somehow disappeared.

"I still can't believe those idiots are permanently here. It's not like their presence will do any good." The strikingly blond one laughed loudly and kicked his dirty boots up on the table.

"They will be dealt with, John. The General wants all of them gone. They are the most loyal to the Gods." The bald one grinned and patted John on the back.

"Seems a shame, wasting all that talent." The bigger one grimaced. His ebony skin made it hard to see his features in the low lighting. It was baffling how loud they were being while talking. Everyone in the saloon could hear them speaking and the room filled with unease.

The fourth spoke quietly, "They are as bad as the Gods and when we slaughter them all, we will finally be free of this hell."

Julia stared at Ryan, and he stared back. She could tell Ryan was ready to pounce and she shook her head at him. He had little to no self-control, and he was in no shape to fight right now.

"We don't have to wait for long," the bald one spoke again, "these four over here will do for now."

Julia felt her body slam against the floor moments before the air was knocked out of her lungs. Ryan had jumped across the table and tackled her to the ground as the sound of gunshots blasted throughout the tavern. Patrons began to scream and run out of the bar, but the four men were not interested in them—it was just the eight of them now.

Ryan yanked her up off the ground and dragged her behind a thick beam that held up the second floor. She took a deep breath and pulled out her gun. Standing side by side, Ryan leaned forward slightly and nodded.

Julia followed his gaze and noticed Damian and Anna were behind another beam to her right.

"Stay here," he whispered. She grabbed his shirt when he started to leave the beam.

"No." She was not about to play the damsel in distress.

He glared at her, his sword in his right hand and gun in his left. What an odd combination. He groaned and bumped the back of his head against the wood. "Please."

She stared at him briefly. She could feel the bullets knock against the thick wood beam. Before she could say anything, he leaned down and kissed her lightly on the lips.

She stood in shock before realizing that he ran from the beam and disappeared. Her eyes drifted over towards Anna. Damian was going as well and she had tossed her bag of dresses across the room.

Julia heard swords clatter and the gunshots died down. Anna looked nervous, and she should be. She was too new to be up against skilled fighters like this.

Julia took a deep breath and ran from her beam to Anna's. She dared a glance at the boys who were taking on two men each and were starting to become out matched. She took one roll on the ground and popped up behind Anna. "Get your gun ready. The boys are distracting them. You're a good shot so aim to wound, not kill."

Anna nodded, and both women bent around the beam on either side. She could tell Ryan's wound was still bothering him. He'd kept popping the stitches over and over since it happened. If he kept at it, the wound would never heal. He moved slower then normal and blood started to seep through his white shirt.

Somehow he used his gun as a shield, blocking blows from

one man while he slashed his sword at the other.

Damian was pushed against the wall. "Oh no!" Anna gasped.

Julia heard Anna's gun go off, and she had shot the blond man square in the shoulders. He fell limply to the ground as Damian elbowed the bigger man in the nose. Julia groaned. "Anna!"

"Sorry!"

Julia turned back to Ryan and aimed at the bald man's knee. She fired. The man screamed and collapsed onto his back. He desperately clung to his knee and hollered in pain.

Ryan looked toward her and she saw a brief grin spread across his face. Something seemed to have changed in him as he fiercely attacked the fourth man. He was small, but stealthy, and he moved quickly with Ryan's maneuvers. Julia had a hard time trying to get a shot off.

She missed and hit a bull in the head and broke a few bottles. "Dammit."

Anna didn't have any better luck, but thankfully, Damian cut across his target's chest and the man fell next to his companion. Both didn't move.

Ryan was still going up against the small man. His movements were quick, but became predictable. Ryan seemed to notice and slashed quickly with his sword, which the man blocked. Ryan managed to somehow shoot the man point blank with his gun.

Julia and Anna ran quickly over to them—Julia barely managing not to jump into Ryan's arms. Anna looked equally relieved, but her focus was on the bald man who tried to limp away.

Ryan kicked the back of the man's knee and he fell to the floor. "You filthy traitor."

The man rolled to his back and looked up at Ryan. A wide grin spread across his face and he spat on Ryan's shoe.

He begun to laugh but Ryan kicked him in the head and knocked the man out. "Let's get him back to the Domus."

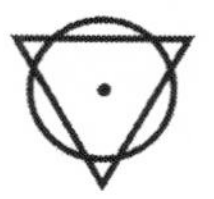

Ryan

Ryan and Damian dropped the bald man hastily down on the table. Neither of them cared about his well being at this point and the loud bang his head made on the table gave Ryan some perverse satisfaction. They were in the part of the Domus that held their interrogation tools. That was the nice way of putting it—in actuality it was a torture chamber.

It was near Ahmose's room and for a good reason. He was the only one allowed to perform such inhumane treatment. Also, it gave him full access to the room and the ability to rest much easier. Ryan didn't know how he could stand it.

Some of the biggest criminals in the world have been brought here to be interrogated. The tools they gathered throughout time were on display along the walls. A metal table with restraints sat in the middle of the room, and next to it sat another metal table with various instruments displayed on it. The room itself was made up of large stone walls and felt dark and damp—it gave the impression of no hope. That helped with the intimidation.

They strapped the man down and pulled the bindings tight. Ryan probably made it a little too tight but he couldn't care less. He glanced back at Julia and felt the urge to make her leave.

There was no reason for her to be around this man.

Ahmose put smelling salts under the bald man's nose and after a minute they began to work. He blinked and glanced around the room in wonder. Ryan watched with amusement as he tried to sit up and pull at his bindings, unable to move or escape.

He struggled to break free, but the restraints would not give an inch. Ryan wanted to laugh and pull the straps tighter, but instead he stood back. This man would endure much more pain than that.

"Let me go," he demanded.

"How about," Ryan said tapped his finger on his chin, "no?"

"You cannot treat an Immortal like this. Let me go!"

"Immortals aren't supposed to attack each other either, but hey, looks like none of us are following the rules," Ryan hissed.

"Enough," Ahmose spoke. "The council has allowed us to interrogate you in any way we deem necessary."

The man's eyes widened and began to look around the room. "They would never allow it."

"Oh they allowed it ol' buddy boy." Ryan laughed.

"What is you name?" Julia finally spoke.

"My word, aren't you a good looking thing." The bastard studied Julia and grinned. "Nice legs, what time do they open?"

Without a thought, Ryan punched the man in the face. "Just answer the question."

The man's nose started to bleed. "Why should I?"

"If you don't I will cut off your fingers." Ryan smiled brightly.

"Sven."

"Well, Sven, I take it you understand why you are here?" Ahmose asked.

"Quit with the formalities and ask this traitor who is in charge and why they feel the need to murder their own people." Damian, to Ryan's surprise, sounded disgusted and angry.

Before they came into the interrogation room, Damian had walked Anna to her room. She was shaken up and he insisted he escort her back. She didn't need to be convinced to go to her room instead of here. Ryan had to wait for him at the stairway to bring Sven upstairs. He was not in the mood to carry him alone.

"I'm not going to tell you anything," Sven said harshly.

"Oh, I really doubt that." Ryan grinned. "You do know where you are right? This room has every torture device imaginable. So you can either cooperate or enjoy getting your body deformed."

Without hesitation, Ryan leaned on Sven's knee and an ear splitting cry pierced the silence. Julia's shot did some serious damage to his knee. He pressed on it again, and more screams followed.

"Oh, did I hurt you? I'm so sorry," Ryan grinned.

"You little-"

Ryan smacked the wound and laughed when Sven cried out again. "Calm down, old chum, no need for ungentlemanly language in front of a lady."

"Ryan," Ahmose admonished looking at him sternly, "that is enough!"

Ryan shrugged, took a seat near the wall and stared at Sven intensely. He felt like a child getting punished. He even crossed his arms.

"Now then, who is your leader?" Ahmose asked.

Sven shook his head. "What part of 'I'm not saying anything,' don't you understand?" he panted. His eyes were drenched with tears he tried to hold back.

Grudgingly, Ahmose walked to the table full of instruments. His fingers hovered over the tools until they grasped a hammer with spikes that stuck out of it.

Ryan silently approved of Ahmose's choice.

"Ryan, Damian, will you please remove Julia from the room?"

"What? No way!" she protested. "I'm staying."

"I don't want any of you in here for this," he said firmly. He had begun tying the strings of a leather apron around his waist. "Ryan, I may need you later though."

Julia turned and stormed out of the room followed by Ryan and Damian. Ryan turned back just in time to see Ahmose lift the hammer up over Sven's arm before the door shut.

Simultaneously, a scream sounded inside the room just as the door latched shut.

Damian walked over to the couches and fell onto them. He closed his eyes and looked dead to the world in an instant slumber. Screams obviously didn't bother him when it came to sleeping.

Julia, on the other hand, glared at Ryan with her arms crossed. He stood awkwardly outside of the door and let her stare.

"It's for the best, Julia," Ryan spoke softly.

"Why? Because a woman cannot handle such things?" She was furious.

"It's not like that at all, I promise."

"Then what is it?" She was like a lioness ready to pounce at the sound of any wrong thing he might say.

"Julia, I've helped Ahmose with this type of thing before. He knows everything about torture and interrogation." He felt the need to crawl into a hole and hide from her glare. "I don't want you around it either."

"Both of you are idiots. I've killed people. Lots of people and this isn't any different," she protested. "I want to know what he is saying and I want to help."

More screams were heard and the sound of soft smacks against flesh was unnerving. He could only imagine what was going on in there. The intensity almost drew him to the sound. He wanted to be the one to hurt Sven for what his little cult did to the Immortals. Families would mourn those lost as murdered instead of being able to honor their deaths in battle.

"It is different in every possible way." How could he make her understand? "It changes a person and you are perfect the way you are. You don't need to be tainted by something like that."

"I'll take my chances." She pushed past him and opened the door. Ryan stood still and didn't bother stopping her. She would have to learn this on her own. He heard another smack and closed his eyes at the sound.

Almost as soon as the door shut behind her, it opened again. Her eyes were wide, and she leaned against the wall. Tears threatened to spill over the rim of her lovely blue eyes and he could not stand the look of sadness on her face. Ryan could not help but go to her and pull her to his chest. He whispered, "I told you."

"Blood," she mumbled.

"I know."

"So much blood."

"I know," he whispered.

"His body-"

"Stop thinking about it," he interrupted.

She pulled away and looked up at him. He just put himself

in an awkward position with her, but he could not help it. He wanted nothing more than to comfort her while their world spiraled out of control. No place was safe for them, not even home.

"Ryan, you've done those things?" she asked pushing him away.

Silence took over when he could not speak. She looked so ashamed of him. All he could do was nod. Without thinking, he pulled her back into him. She gave in. "I didn't have a choice."

"It's barbaric."

"I know."

"I'm tired." She buried her face in his chest and her weight got heavy in his arms. "Can I sleep with you tonight? I don't want to be alone."

He tensed up and let go of her. She stood up straight and just stared at him painfully.

"Julia, I told you I don't want you." He backed up.

The pain in her eyes felt like he stabbed himself in the heart.

"Then why did you kiss me?"

He shrugged. "Seemed like a good thing to do before possibly dying."

"You're lying."

"I'm really not. I mean come on, Julia, you know me." He laughed. "How could I possibly fall for anyone? You're cute, don't get me wrong, but your Cato's sister and if you haven't noticed, I don't like commitment."

Cries filled the air again and Damian snorted awake, then quickly fell back asleep.

She fell against the wall and dropped to the ground. As she hugged her knees, he knew his actions hurt her more than he intended. Was he being selfish by saving his feelings and not hers?

The door opened and out walked a bloodied Ahmose. He wiped his hands on a towel that hung at his waist and looked down at Julia as she sobbed quietly. His eyes widened and quickly looked at Ryan. "What happened?"

"She saw what you were doing," he responded.

Ahmose closed his eyes and took a deep breath. "I'm so sorry you saw that, Julia. Ryan was supposed to keep you out of there."

Ryan was in trouble.

"Is he alive?" She raised her head.

Ahmose glared at Ryan. "He is. I had the priests put a spell on the room years ago. No one can die in it."

"That's horrible," she muttered.

"Anyway, I think you all will be glad to hear what I learned." He looked over at Damian. "Damian, wake up!"

Damian woke with a start and fell off the couch. He jumped up quickly and stood next to Ryan. "What's up?"

"He told me a name," Ahmose spoke softly.

Julia stood up slowly, and they all watched Ahmose anxiously. "So? Who is it?"

"They call him the General."

"Well, we already knew that. Got anything new to share?" He wanted to walk in that room and ask the idiot what he knew. Ahmose was building anticipation, for some reason, and he could not stand it anymore.

"That was the only name given, I am afraid." They all groaned in disappointment. Ryan started to head towards the room when Ahmose stopped him. "He did, however, tell me why they are attacking us."

Damian and Ryan turned quickly towards him. Finally, the answer every Immortal wanted to know, and they were the first ones to hear it.

"Go on man! Speak," Ryan practically yelled.

Despite everything that had happened, Ahmose chuckled lightly. Ryan never saw him as the young man that looked back at him. Instead, he thought of Ahmose like an old wise man, complete with beard and wrinkles in his imagination. "Calm down, you might hurt yourself."

Ryan stared blankly at him and blinked slowly. "I'm waiting."

"They are attacking the Immortals because they view us as the enemy." His tone was full of distaste. "The Gods are the enemy to them and they believe the Gods do nothing while we do everything. They see the Gods as cruel and unneeded."

"Okay..." Ryan was confused.

They were all in shock. Ahmose sighed. "They want us to become the Gods."

"Then why are they killing us if they want us to be Gods?" Damian asked.

"According to Sven, the Immortals that were killed at Anna's ceremony were not planned. They only wanted the Warriors dead."

"Why?" Ryan was confused and could not imagine a world without the Gods. They gave them life and made them who they are. Without them, the Immortals would not exist. They depend on the faith of the mortals.

"We are the main source of the Gods power. We do what they ask and stand behind them. We fight for the Gods and protect their will." Ahmose sounded tired. "Other Immortals live in Urbs, away from the Gods influence and have no contact with them. They do not fully understand the bond we all share."

"So, to kill the Gods, you kill their followers and create your own world?" Damian shook his head. "I don't understand how an Immortal can betray them. They are everything."

"That thinking is exactly why they want us all dead," Julia added. She'd been silent for a while and her voice surprised him. Her eyes were heavy and Ryan felt the urge to take her up on her request and fall asleep next to her tonight.

"Exactly," Ahmose agreed. "That is all I have found out. I will continue to interrogate him—you should all get some rest. Ryan, I may need your assistance so please keep yourself available."

With that being said, Ahmose walked back into the interrogation room and locked the door behind him this time.

Julia ignored Ryan and walked away quickly. Damian turned towards him and smacked him upside the head. "If you don't go after that girl I will bring you into that room and smack some sense into you."

"Can't."

"Ryan, you are in all aspects, but biologically, my brother and that girl is in love with you. If you don't see it than you're a fool." He shoved Ryan against the wall. "You're being a selfish prick, now go after her."

That was a twist. He had no idea how to handle an angry Damian.

"But-"

"No."

"But, I-"

"No, now go." Damian pointed towards the door.

Without another word, Ryan slowly walked out of the room in utter shock. This was a new Damian that took command. The world was starting to become far too complicated and confusing.

It didn't take long to catch up to Julia. She walked slowly, her composure sluggish. The dark hallway led to a wide staircase, which led down to the male dormitory hallway. He walked quickly and grabbed her by the arm gently. "You win."

"What?" Her voice was weak and she gazed at him with teary eyes.

He shrugged. "You win." He pulled her against his body and he kissed her gently. Her lips were soft and inviting. He started to crave more.

She didn't move and Ryan almost backed away, he must have read the situation wrong. Then she wrapped her arms around his neck, her body pressed against his as she shoved him against the wall.

Breaking free, he looked down at her grinning. "Didn't peg you as being forceful."

She stood on her toes and pressed her lips hard against his. He felt a surge of excitement pulse throughout his body when she nipped his lip then seductively looked into his eyes. "You have no idea."

He felt his shirt stick to his skin and looked down quickly. His stitches reopened in the fight and her shoving him probably didn't help much. The sting of it made him grimace, but he tried to hold back for her sake.

She followed his eyes down and gasped. He put his finger to her lips and grinned, but she would not ignore it. "I really wish you would let that heal."

"It will. I've just been busy lately." He shrugged. *Why does she want to talk right now?*

"I mean it, Ryan. You're no good to us dead." She looked down at his wound and her hand hovered over it. Instead, she ran her hand down his abdomen. "You're no good to me dead."

Ryan groaned and lifted her up, her legs wrapping around his waist. He turned and pressed her back against the wall, their lips meeting again. He was not in the mood to talk. She was everything to him, and he could not deny it anymore. He had to have her. He craved to be as close to her as possible.

"What the hell is going on?"

Dammit.

Ryan automatically dropped Julia, who landed gracefully on her feet. "Hello, brother." She wiped her lips and sidestepped away from Ryan.

Cato ignored her—his eyes were on Ryan and he looked ready to kill. Ryan had dealt with Cato on many issues before, but nothing like this. This was like he stabbed his family in the back. "Hey, man."

"What is going on?" Cato was up close and in Ryan's comfort zone.

"We were at Moonshine and were attacked." Julia tried to play dumb. "We caught one of the traitors."

"Ahmose is interrogating him," Ryan added.

Cato looked between them. "That is not what I am talking about."

"Oh?" Julia pursed her lips.

Cato's body was tense and his hand was on the dagger that hung on his belt. Ryan really didn't want to get into a brawl right now. "I told you to stay away from her."

"You what?" She seemed like a ticking bomb, ready to explode. "Cato, will you please just butt out of this?"

"I told him to stay away from you and he said 'no problem.'"

"How could I possibly stay away from her when her brother is on my team?" Ryan shrugged. "I mean honestly. You are asking the impossible."

"He also said that he had no interest in you and then went to Emma's that night." Cato crossed his arms. "Which is exactly why I wanted him to stay away from you."

"What the hell, Cato?" Ryan hissed. Did he have to throw in the bit about Emma? He was ruining what Ryan wanted in a few short sentences.

Julia turned towards Ryan and smacked him in the face. "You know what, I don't want to end up like Emma—miserable and in love with someone who pretends to care about me."

Cato grabbed Julia by her arm and led her down the stairs. "Better get that cut looked at, Ryan," Cato called.

Ryan punched the wall and cursed when he saw his hand start to bleed. At this rate he was going to need another blood transfusion.

Chapter XI

Julia

"He said what?" Grace gasped. The girls were in Urbs at the restaurant New Moon for dinner. The night sky was blue-black from the stars shining so bright.

Grace, Julia, and Colette sat on the patio of the restaurant, the waves crashing below them. The deck was wrapped around the restaurant, which allowed for outside seating. It was her favorite place to come eat as a child. Grace kept bringing her after both her parents died.

The beauty of the moon reflected off the water, and she loved how it felt as if she were in a cabin in the woods with a lakeside view.

She would have asked Anna to come, but she needed time with her team. After all, they were basically her family, and she needed advice.

She tapped her feet on the wooden floor of the deck—Julia was tense and wanted to scream at Ryan. Anger built in her as she described what happened. "Cato said Ryan had told him that he has no interest in me and then he slept with Emma that night. After I slapped him I just left. He obviously said it because he freaked out when Cato told me."

Grace sat back from her pasta and looked out at the ocean. "Men have not changed one bit."

"Sounds to me like he just didn't want your brother to know he likes you. I mean honestly, if he keeps changing his mind about how he feels, he is obviously afraid of something." Colette took a drink of her wine and shrugged.

"What could Ryan possibly be afraid of?" Julia laughed. "He isn't afraid of anything. It's like he has a death wish. I don't know how Cato and Damian function with him."

He was like a child who didn't follow the rules, and for some reason, she could not help but envy his fearlessness, even while she hated his lack of self-preservation.

A bird landed on the railing by their table. It was so close she could touch it. The animals here didn't fear anyone. It was a peaceful existence in Urbs. Everyone here lived far away from the trouble of modern influence and unneeded materials.

Mortals think they are making their lives easier with their technology, when in reality their advancement makes it far more complicated. The need to survive is now outweighed by the need to impress others. Technology will be their downfall.

"They said he is becoming reckless? Honestly, just go and talk to him, Julia." Grace is a firm believer in communication. "If he says he doesn't want you then move on."

"I've noticed Aden looking at you, lately," Colette added.

"Something is up with him. He is acting strange," Julia responded. She wanted to avoid the thought of Aden's affections. "He is acting hostile. Besides, Ryan hates him. I couldn't do that."

"And that, my dear, is how you see if a man truly has affection for you. Make him jealous." Colette grinned maliciously. "Besides, what do you owe Ryan? Nothing. He is tossing your feelings around as if they are nothing. Make him suffer a little."

Julia raised an eyebrow and took a sip of her wine. As she set the glass on the table, she stared at the bird pecking the wood railing. Ryan should suffer a little, but she could not do that to anyone, not even to a jerk like him.

"Don't teach her things like that, Colette. That's bad taste."

"You know what else is bad taste? Him giving her a headache from being a bipolar nightmare." Colette had a point. "He needs a taste of his own medicine."

"Just talk to him," Grace said firmly and gave Colette a slight glare. "If the answer you get isn't what you want then move on, my love. There is no need to torture yourself over him."

Julia knew Grace was right, but part of her wanted to see Ryan's reaction if she was around Aden. Why did they get in a fight when Aden mentioned their dinner? That had to mean he cared for her right?

"Anyway," Colette interrupted, "off the subject of boys. Any news on the war front?"

Julia was slightly relieved for the subject change. Her heart could only take so much when it came to Ryan. "Ahmose is continuing the interrogations. Sven revealed what they call themselves at least."

"Which is?" Grace asked.

"According to my brother, after hours of torture he said they call themselves, The Risen."

Grace shook her head and a look of disgust played across her face. "Ridiculous."

"Well, aren't they clever," added Colette sarcastically.

All three women were disgusted at this point. That didn't stop Julia from taking a bite of her garlic bread after she dipped it in her pasta sauce left over on her plate.

"I cannot believe the priests are allowing his torture to continue." She sighed. "Enemy or not, we are not barbaric."

"Julia, he helped murder innocent people. Not to mention he is a traitor and is plotting to kill all of us as well as the Gods." Grace tried to reason with her, but Julia would not relent. It was torture and it was a revolting reality in life. "It has to be done to save us all."

"Whatever."

"Julia," Grace groaned.

"How can you stand by and be okay with it regardless?" Julia grimaced. "We are supposed to be civilized and held to a higher standard and yet we are purposely hurting a fellow being."

"Julia, your father would not agree with you." Grace sighed. "He would realize this is for the greater good."

"My father?" Julia laughed. "He isn't even alive anymore. You would not know what he would do, Grace."

"I didn't mean to offend you, love."

"Well, I think the man needs to be healed and put on trial." They were supposed to give the man a fair chance.

"Julia, please stop." Colette sighed.

"I'm off to talk to Dr. Jekyll, hopefully I don't get Mr. Hyde." She stood up and tossed a few coins on the table. She was not in the mood for this anymore. "See you ladies later."

Before she left, she placed her unfinished bread by the bird. It happily took it in its beak and flew off to nearby trees. The sound of chirping birds filled the air.

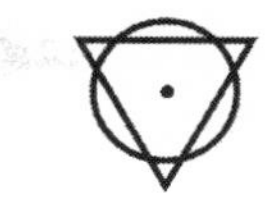

Julia

As Julia walked up the stairs to the Domus, she noticed a figure at the top. He was in dark jeans and a black T-shirt that was blood stained. He had blood all over his hands, face and clothes. Clutched in his hand was a bottle of whiskey. She almost panicked until she realized how drunken Ryan looked.

"Do you purposely try to make yourself look bad?" she asked.

"No, just pure talent." Ryan grinned from behind the bottle. He took a swig and clenched his teeth. "Smooth."

She was desperately trying to remember what is so appealing about him. Then he smiled and her heart melted.

His dark hair fell into his eyes and barely touched his nose. She loved his shaggy hair. Anna made fun of him behind his back. Apparently, he had the "Efron" haircut whoever that was.

He fell back and looked up at the tall columns. She followed his gaze and studied the grandeur of the building. She never saw it as anything but a home, but the craftsmanship was remarkable. The Domus made the White House look like a shack.

"I see Ahmose needed you after all," she observed.

He looked down at his clothes and hands. The dried blood looked eerie and she wondered why he had not washed himself up.

"He sure did," he slurred holding up the bottle, "which is why this is needed."

Perhaps he was not a waste of a human. He obviously felt

remorse for what he was doing and his hard exterior started to chisel away in her mind.

"I would have thought you would enjoy torturing people." She glared. He seemed to like to torture her at least.

Ryan sat up and wiped his hair back. "Are you freaking kidding me right now?"

Instantly she felt guilty. His icy glare made her nervous. He was intoxicated and probably had no control over his actions. She did push that too far. "Sorry."

Laughing, he said, "You know, I may be an asshole, but in what world do you think I would enjoy causing someone an unbelievable amount of suffering?"

"You seemed to enjoy it while you pushed on his gunshot wound."

He cocked his head and took another drink. "That was nothing compared to what I just did, Julia."

"I doubt it," she mumbled.

Ryan laughed. "At this point, you wouldn't be able to see much skin on his body. But apparently in your world that is the equivalent to slightly pushing on a wound."

He had never spoken to her like this. What he did must be a horrible experience. She hated to think of what Ryan had to do, but also how much pain the man was in. It must be excruciating.

"Tell Ahmose you don't want to do it anymore."

"I'm not going to let anyone else do it." He laughed. "I wouldn't wish that on my worst enemy."

"Speaking of enemy," she said trying to change the subject. "Aden said you called me the 'Virgin of the Domus' or something like that."

Ryan looked dumbfounded. "Excuse me?"

Well, she was just making extremely unpleasant conversation with him now, wasn't she?

"We went to dinner, and he said you called me something like that. He also said you told him he shouldn't waste a perfectly good meal on me either."

He clenched his fists till his knuckles turned white. This was definitely not the best conversation to have with a drunk. "Julia, when have I ever said anything like that about anyone?"

"You are a womanizer, Ryan. You don't exactly say the nicest things about the women in your life. Trust me, Cato repeats a lot of what you say."

"Doesn't mean I say things like that about people," he growled. "Every damn woman that comes after me knows how I am. So why does that make me the bad guy? If they can't handle it they shouldn't get involved with me."

He had a point. Everyone knew how he was and yet girls still threw fits about not having their feelings returned. She felt stupid for being upset with him. She knew how he was and yet expected him to be someone else.

"All right then," she mumbled.

Now he seemed to feel bad. His eyes softened. "I would never say anything like that about you. You deserve nothing but the best, Julia, and I truly mean that."

"Thank you." She smiled.

"Now, come have a seat." He patted his legs and winked.

"Let's get you some coffee and sober you up," she said.

"One, I am not drunk—I am in good spirits. Two, I want to drink more." He grinned wide and tipped the bottle to his mouth again.

"Well, if you can't beat them..." She walked over to him and grabbed the whiskey out of his hand. Julia took a large drink, shook her head and laughed.

"Hey, that's mine," he pouted.

"Well if you won't sober up then I will get drunk as well," she declared.

He raised his eyebrows and took the bottle back. "Never took you for a drinker."

"There's a lot you don't know about me."

"Too true." After his turn he handed her the bottle, she took another drink. As she sat down next to him, she could feel his eyes on her. His amusement was apparent.

They sat there for twenty minutes and passed the bottle back and forth. Neither one of them said anything as they drank, and she started to feel the effects. Without meaning to, giggles started to escape from her.

"You okay there, Captain Chuckles?" His pure amusement annoyed her, but she had to admit, it was a rarity to see her this way.

"Are you 'ven drunk?" She laughed and held her hand against her mouth as if it would hide her hysteria.

"Duh, I just don't turn into the giggle monster when I am."

"You'll get there." She grinned and took another drink. "'Dis isn't so bad 'nymore."

"You're cut off, missy."

"No, I likes it lots." She took another drink and found the bottle was empty. She pouted and threw the bottle down the stairs where is landed with a loud crash. Julia turned towards Ryan and grinned widely. He looked delighted and confused at the same time. She leaned in and kissed him hard on the lips. She felt his hesitation before he gently pushed her away.

"What are you doing?" He laughed.

She could not help the anger that filled inside her. She didn't want him to push her away and she felt a sudden need to grab and smack him. "What I want."

"Julia, last I knew, you were pissed at me and you just got done telling me how awful I am."

"And now I'm not." She was trying to annunciate as best she could. "Do you want me or not?" she asked slowly. She could feel her body sway back and fourth, and it was kind of soothing.

He studied her for a minute and looked at the ground between his legs. As he sighed, he ran his fingers through his hair and chuckled to himself. Now she really wanted to smack him.

She cleared her throat, which brought his attention back to her. "What does it matter?"

"'Cus I like you," she stated. "If you don't want me, then goodbye to you, Ryan."

His eyes widened and he blinked repeatedly. Was he really so shocked by her outburst? Probably. After all, she rarely spoke like this—alcohol will do this to a girl though.

"You're not my type, you're far to short for my liking."

"I'm serious."

As she crossed her arms, she felt herself fall back. He caught her and pulled her toward him. She looked up into his eyes and started to giggle again. She couldn't help it, even if there was nothing funny.

"I'm going to tell on you." He smirked.

"I'll beat you up if you do."

He leaned down and pressed his lips to the top of her head. He moved his mouth towards the corner of her eye, and she could feel his warm breath. It gave her the chills, and he wrapped her tightly in his arms. "You may like me, Julia," he whispered, "but you shouldn't."

She pulled back quickly and stared at him. His face was fixed and there was no sign of emotion. Her heart hurt.

As she sat up his arms fell from her. She hugged her knees for comfort. The moon was so bright she had to look at it, as if it had all the answers.

"Oh." Why was he kissing her face like that then?

He put his head in his hands and hid behind them. "I'm sorry."

"Don't be," she whispered.

She heard voices come from the entrance of the Domus. Ryan sat up quickly and hit his head on his hand. "It's Cato and Damian. Your brother is going to kill me if he sees you."

Julia knew it was true and stumbled over to a column by the entrance and crouched down so she could peak around. Cato and Damian came up to Ryan in full battle gear, which was not a normal sight in Urbs. They must be up to something with that many weapons strapped to their bodies. She was close enough to make out what they said, thankfully.

"Thought you were helping Ahmose." Cato crossed his arms, his words dripped with annoyance. Honestly, he needed to get over her and Ryan's moment in the hallway.

"I was, and now I am drunk." He pointed down at the bottom of the stairs. "Its life didn't last long."

"Ryan, seriously? You had to drink the whole bottle? You just bought that." Damian put his hands under Ryan's arms and pulled him up. Ryan staggered a bit and straightened himself. "You really need to figure your life out."

Poor Damian. For as long as she knew him, he did nothing but look out for Ryan. Ryan was lucky to have a friend like that in his life.

"You may be on the downward spiral, Ryan, but don't take us down with you." Cato was being harsh on him and Julia wanted to put her brother in his place. She started to stand up but quickly crouched back down. Why should she stick up for him?

"Ryan, we are on patrol tonight." Damian sighed.

Patrol? She wasn't aware of any patrol.

"Man, I forgot." He really did look ashamed at this point. He definitely was going to explain this one to her. "Just let me go change and I swear I will sober up."

Ryan and Damian exchanged looks and Damian relaxed a bit. "All right, hurry up."

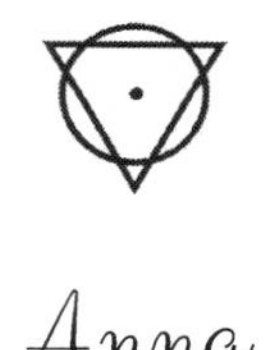

Anna

Anna walked into the Great Temple and looked up at all the statues. There were so many, she didn't even bother to count them all. She had explored the parts of Urbs that were closest to the Domus, all day.

She could not help but think this place was a desperate way to become part of the mortal world. They wanted so much to experience a regular existence, or maybe cling to the lives they once had. All she knew was that it was amazingly beautiful, in its own way.

The statues stared down at her, some looked friendly and others oddly monstrous. What type of Gods did some people believe in? There were Gods with many arms and others that were blue and even demonic looking ones with bulging eyes.

She only believed in one God and she could not find Him in the mix. She looked for hours trying to find His likeness. She was Catholic and felt the need to know more about her God. It was a strange concept knowing they all exist. She was always taught there was only one God, her God.

"You are looking for the wrong image," a voice sounded behind her. Quickly, Anna turned around and saw Colette standing in the doorway. Her long black hair draped over her left shoulder. She looked so different from her portrait.

The woman before her was slightly tanned with beautifully long hair. She was not a normal beauty by modern standards, but her presence was regal and demanded respect. Her portrait made her seem like a cross dresser.

"Who do you think I am looking for?" she asked.

Colette walked in slowly and looked at all the statues with disgust. She reached the middle of the room and pointed at a nearly empty space in the wall. It was big enough to fit a statue, but a small urn sat in the middle with smoke trickling out of it.

"That is the representation of God. Our God," she muttered.

"I don't understand."

"God has no image. We have made Him that way, therefore, he has no image here as well." She stared at the other statues and shook her head.

"Makes sense, I suppose." She could not help, but be disappointed. "Have you ever met Him?"

Colette grinned. "Have you heard of my story, Adrianna?"

Anna nodded her head. "God talked to you."

"If God were a spirit, then would it not be conceivable, that when He spoke to me, He was with me?"

"True," she whispered. Colette had a way of making her feel dumb, and she could not figure out the girl's issue with her. "So, what are you doing here?"

She felt awkward being alone with Colette. It was something she had been trying to avoid since she first met her.

"I wanted to see the progress they have made on rebuilding

and saw you come in here." Colette walked near a statue, her face showing disgust again.

"Why are you looking at the rest of the Gods as if they are evil?"

"No matter how long I live, I will always believe in the one true God. These," she said waving her hand towards the rest of the room, "are false to me still."

Anna did research on Colette—she was the only Immortal in the Domus that Anna knew their past. Joan of Arc was very religious and it would be stupid to think she changed her views. Though knowing what she knew now, Anna had to realize and accept that there were other Gods in the universe. After all these years, how did Colette not come to the same conclusion?

"Has anyone ever met the other Gods?" She was afraid to ask, but Anna desperately wanted to learn everything about her new world.

"Some. From what I understand, these Gods like to live in plain sight among the mortals. They pretend to be mortal and study humanity. That's how they know what is happening in the world. When they see a problem they call on us to fix it."

"I don't understand why they don't just intervene themselves right then." Anna was shocked to hear this. Perhaps she met a god at one time and never knew it. That's pretty freaking weird.

"They have never intervened, Adrianna. The Greeks and Romans had their demi-gods and we have our angels. Every religion has their Warriors, it just so happens it has always been the Immortals."

"So Hercules and the Archangel Michael are real? Do they live in the Domus?" She was somewhat excited.

Colette laughed. "In time you will come to realize who certain people are. It is not my place to give away secrets of other Warriors' lives."

"Why do you hate me, Colette?" Anna blurted out.

Colette was taken aback and raised her eyebrow. Her demeanor changed and she was calmed again instead of resentful. "I don't hate you."

"Really? Because it definitely seems like you do." There was no other way to explain Colette's attitude towards her.

"I don't feel like you earned the right to be here," she said simply.

Anna felt a little hurt by her admission. "How so?"

"You were captured, you panicked in the midst of a fight, and you have no confidence," Colette responded.

"Oh." She looked at the floor. "Here I was thinking it was personal."

"It is somewhat personal, but to no fault of your own." Colette looked ashamed.

"What?"

Colette laughed and crossed her arms. Anna was confused and met the other girl's eyes.

"Adrianna. You are proving me wrong. I hope you know that?" She grinned. "I still don't think you earned this life, but you are starting to. After you helped save dear Julia and the boys, that shows me true courage is somewhere within you."

"I didn't save them, it was a group effort."

"You held your own and didn't run away. You stayed to help and I was actually shocked to hear that." She grabbed Anna's hands and cupped them in hers. "Don't prove my first impression of you to be true. It would be a pleasant surprise to be wrong for once."

Chapter XII

Ryan

Ryan ran upstairs to his room. It was a task in itself not to trip over his feet, given his current state of mind.

He entered his bedroom and shimmied out of his regular clothes. He went into his bathroom and hastily took a shower to wash the blood off himself. After he dried off he put his black fatigues on, followed by his protective vest and helmet.

He walked over to his weapons, decided to grab his silver guns with white handles and a samurai sword. As he slipped the guns in his holsters and the sword in the scabbard on his back, Ryan made his way to the door.

As he opened it, there stood Julia, dressed in full gear and two cups in her hand.

"Where do you think you are going?" she asked.

"Apparently where you think you're going." He walked past her quickly.

She ran to catch up to him, held out a cup, and he took it.

"Coffee."

"Thanks." He drank it quickly and tossed it in the nearest trash bin. "Julia, go to bed."

"I cannot believe you boys have been patrolling," she hissed and completely ignored him while chugging down her coffee. "Why haven't the women been doing this?"

"Mainly because Ahmose believes the Risen is made up completely of men. He doesn't know how they would treat women if they were captured," he said simply, then braced himself for a fit of crude words.

"We are perfectly capable of taking care of ourselves," she spat.

Ryan stopped in his tracks, grabbed her by the arms and stared into her eyes. "I'm not going to allow you to come, Julia."

As she cocked her head to the side leaned in close. "Allow me? So you think you control me?"

Crap. "That's not what I meant."

"Then what exactly did you mean?"

He looked down and avoided her eyes at all cost. "First off, that means you overheard our conversation which means you were around me before Damian and Cato came to get me. Cato won't like that." He looked up. "Second, Ahmose ordered this and if he found out you came, we would all be in deep shit for disobeying a direct order."

She grunted, took off her helmet and tossed her coffee to the floor. She glared up at him. "Fine."

"Julia, I promise it is nothing against you. I know you are as capable as any of us." He agreed with Ahmose though. They didn't have enough information about the Risen to send females in until they knew more about them. This was what needed to be done for everyone's safety.

"I get it. I don't agree with it," she added, "but I get it."

"Go get sober, Julia, you're stumbling in your gear. It's a strange sight."

He managed to get a smile out of her. "Fine. Come see me when you get back? I want to know what happens."

As she walked away from him, he could tell the coffee didn't kick in for her. She swayed, and he suppressed a chuckle. "Light weight," he muttered with a grin.

He turned around and briskly walked to the outside of the Domus.

As he made his way out, Damian and Cato turned around and looked at him.

"Took you long enough," Cato observed.

"Sorry, got coffee. I'm all good now."

"Right."

"Will you two quit bickering like old ladies? We've got work to do," Damian interrupted.

They walked down the stairs together—each took a gun out of their holster and racked the slide. Each man crouched low in a patrolling stance and held their guns up and ready. They walked briskly away from the Domus and searched building after building throughout the city. No one bothered to lock their doors in Urbs. People would never steal from one another here.

They searched candy stores and perfume shops, even the bakery—they found nothing.

Cato stood up straight and lowered his weapon. "We aren't going to find anything. All the teams have been patrolling for two weeks now and there has not even been a hint of where they are hiding," he muttered.

Ryan relaxed. "He's right."

Damian sighed. "Orders are orders, guys."

"It's a waste of time," said Cato.

Ryan agreed. Although the Risen's ideals were idiotic, they didn't seem to be complete morons. After years of experience, he learned to trust his instincts, and his were saying these men knew what they were doing. They would not hide in the open, and they were unable to search the homes of Immortals. There was only one other place any of them were allowed to look.

"What about underground?" he mussed.

"Huh?" Damian turned towards him.

"Has anyone searched the underground tunnels?" he asked.

Damian shook his head. "No, just above."

Ryan laughed. "Seriously? After every uprising in human history that hid out underground, no one thought to give the underground a sweep?"

Cato shrugged. "Guess not."

"All right then." Damian walked to the nearest entrance to the underground, followed by Cato and Ryan. The doors were level to the ground and made of wood like a storm shelter. He lifted up the door and let it fall against the street, Damian gestured to Ryan. "After you, my liege."

Ryan hit him on the helmet and walked down the dark staircase. It was cool below the city. The tunnels were made of large stonewalls and floors, a slight blanket of dust coated the ground.

Darkness engulfed them and they pulled their night-vision goggles down from their helmets. As he turned his on, Ryan saw a few rats chewing on what looked like an old shoe.

Damian tapped Ryan's shoulder and they held their guns up and ready. Ryan took the lead while Cato covered the rear. Damian turned towards the middle passages, when they came up, and found nothing.

They searched for hours under their utopian city until Ryan spotted the symbol of the Gods. It is an upside-down triangle, representing the three sides of life. The topside belonged to the gods—the left represented the Immortals, and the right meant mankind. Entwined with the triangle was a circle, which had a smaller black circle inside it, which represented Earth. It was a simple yet powerful symbol.

Ryan was shocked to see it scratched nearly unrecognizable.

"I think we are getting close," he whispered.

He heard Damian and Cato growl in disgust—they'd obviously caught sight of the symbol. After all, destroying it was unthinkable and punishable by death. Not by the Gods, but by the Council. It was against the law to deface it.

Like the Risen, it showed disrespect to the very beings that gave them life and continued to give them life.

"That is insane," Cato whispered.

Ryan silently agreed. "Come on," he hissed.

They turned right and found another symbol scratched out roughly. Beside it was a different symbol that had a king's crown on top of a circle. Below the circle sat a straight horizontal line.

"What the-"

"Shh," Ryan interrupted. He heard voices and there was a light that crept towards them from up ahead.

They all crouched low and shuffled towards the light. Ryan checked for any sign of traps around the area, and found it was clear. He flipped up the goggles—the others did the same making it easier to see the closer they got to the light source.

They found themselves behind bars that reached from the ceiling to the floor. Looking in, Ryan saw figures dressed in black cloaks. They took them off and hung them near the fireplace—there were at least thirty members.

Surprisingly, the room was well furnished for being underground and almost looked like an actual home.

"What a pointless meeting," a man with short-cropped hair said. He was tall and thin, much too frail to do any real fighting. He must have been a reborn that could not pass the test to join the Warriors.

"At least we know they are sending out patrols now, Max," said a redhead.

Max shrugged. "I suppose. Though why we gave them permission to join at all is ridiculous."

"They renounced their old life, that's the important thing," Red said. "Besides, you didn't allow them, the General did."

"I still don't trust those two," said Max.

"The General does, so deal with it," said the redhead.

"If the patrols started weeks ago, why are we just hearing about this now?" Max growled.

The men continued to argue, and things were getting intense. "We should go. There are too many of them," Cato whispered.

Ryan had to agree. They had found where the Risen were and discovered they had spies in the Domus. They needed to inform Ahmose right away.

Ryan nodded and motioned for them to leave quickly.

"What was that?" he heard Max ask.

The three of them froze and didn't dare to move.

"What was what?" another man asked.

"I saw a flash from behind the bars." His footsteps came closer and Ryan's heart quickened.

He could not tell if they were deep enough in the tunnel to be seen or not.

"Warriors!" Max cried out.

"Run," Ryan ordered.

They three of them ran quickly away from the yelling behind them. The dark surrounded them once more, and he stumbled until he grasped his goggles. As he pulled them down, he saw Cato and Damian run ahead towards the nearest exit.

They climbed up the stairs, pushed the doors open and fell into the early morning. The sun was not visible yet, but the city glowed in the pale first light.

"Don't stop," Ryan called to the other two. They had no idea if the Risen had secret escapes and didn't want to find out.

Citizens started to come out for the beginning of the day and stared at them as they ran by. They probably wondered what a team of Warriors was doing in full battle gear running through the streets in the early morning hours.

After they ran for thirty minutes, Ryan was drenched in sweat, but kept his momentum. Cato and Damian flanked him on either side, and they cut through the city quicker than going through the underground.

As they ran up the steps to the Domus, Ryan noticed Jesse, Caleb and Aden sat on the top steps, smoking their cigarettes. When they reached the top, Aden looked at them utterly amused.

"Eventful night, boys?" He laughed.

"A very informative night," Ryan corrected him.

"Right, no one can find a scrap of evidence." Aden smirked and took a drag of the cigarette. "We spent ten hours looking two days ago."

"Well, I've been saying for years you guys should find a new career. You're not very good at it." Ryan grinned. "Where's Ahmose, we need to talk to him immediately."

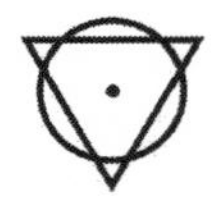

Ryan

The three stooges followed Ryan and his team as they briskly walked towards Ahmose's office.

They were all sweaty and out of breath, but that didn't stop them from nearly jogging.

"What did you find out?" Aden demanded.

Ryan could not believe they would not let up. After his conversation with Julia, his distaste for Aden had grown, and he wanted to break his arm again. He got a little satisfaction knowing that his face was still bruised.

"Go away, Aden, you'll know when everyone else does." Aden grabbed Ryan by the vest and turned him around so they faced each other. Ryan glared at him and ripped himself away from his grasp. "Why are you so concerned?"

Aden shrugged. "Oh, maybe it's because we have put in overtime trying to catch those traitorous punks, even when we didn't have to. We patrolled when other teams were out and found nothing."

"Please, Ryan," Caleb added. "We have been working our butts off trying to find some smidgeon of hope to bringing these guys down."

Ryan sighed and looked at Cato and Damian. They all had a soft spot for Caleb for some reason. Like Damian, Caleb was the buffer of their team, and definitely the level headed one. Caleb was a good guy.

"Fine, just come with us and we will explain everything in

front of Ahmose."

Aden's mood turned from annoyed to excited in an instant and Jesse remained calm as ever. That guy never showed emotion, he was like a robot.

The Domus was a huge square with the center cut out. In the center sat the Garden of Isis, which had no roof, and they decided to cut through it to reach Ahmose quicker. The lower level had very few rooms and was only an empty hallway with staircases the led up to the second level. The outer part of the hallway was stonewalls and the inner had columns that you walked between to enter the garden.

The six of them remained silent as they walked through the grass. The morning dew making Ryan's boots squeak. Needless to say, it was awkward and Cato decided to break the ice. "Nice day, right?"

They all looked at him, Ryan shook his head and Jesse finally spoke up, "Good day to ride."

Cato looked surprised and Damian nearly tripped over himself. Jesse spoke—it was a rare occasion and extremely odd with how casual he was being.

They walked through the flower portions of the garden on a small gravel walkway, overgrown roses were in full bloom. As Ryan swatted the flowers out of his face he heard Damian groan behind him. The flowers whirled around and hit him in the face. Ryan laughed. "Sorry."

"You should come riding with us today, Cato," Aden spoke up. "There's this black stallion that would rival any horse, dead or alive. He's not afraid of his own shadow, either."

Ryan glanced back at Aden, who had a smirk on his face and Damian pushed him forward.

"Let it go," he whispered in Ryan's ear.

There were things Ryan could let go and there were things he could not. Damian knew what pushed his buttons and apparently so did Aden. The willpower it took not to tackle Aden to the ground and stab him was immense.

They finally made it to the end of the Garden of Isis and jogged up the stairs to the third level and took a right towards Ahmose's room. Ryan knocked impatiently on his door.

"Come in."

Ryan opened the door and stopped in his tracks. Ahmose lay on his desk and stared up at the ceiling. The six of them entered and Caleb closed the door behind him.

"What's up?" Ryan asked.

Cato chuckled, and Damian smacked him in the stomach.

"We've searched the east end and downtown as well as the market and baths," Ahmose muttered. "Still, nothing."

Ryan looked up and realized Ahmose had a map of Urbs painted on the ceiling. It was surprisingly exact and Ryan saw many black x's throughout the city that marked places the teams had searched.

Ryan grabbed a knife strapped to his leg and threw it at the Fountain of Olympus. Ahmose slowly turned his head and stared at him.

"They aren't there." Ryan grinned. "We found them."

Ahmose sat up quickly and fell off his desk. As he scrambled up and over to Ryan with a bewildered look on his face—Ahmose grabbed him by the vest and pulled him close. "I swear, Ryan, if you are joking with me-"

"He's serious," Damian interrupted.

Ryan slowly pried away Ahmose's fingers and patted him on the shoulder. "The tunnels, my good man." He grinned wide.

He heard Aden and Jesse whisper among themselves, and

Ahmose held up his hand. Silence fell through the room, and Ahmose paced around as he looked up at the ceiling.

Ryan was concerned for the man's health and sanity, but if Ryan had the fate of all Immortals on his shoulders, he would probably look the same.

"Of course," he muttered to himself. He tapped his mouth and rummaged through the papers littered all over the floor.

Ryan turned and looked at the others, who, like him, seemed concerned. Ryan walked over to Ahmose and hesitantly put his hand on his arm. "Ahmose..."

"It makes perfect sense!" He grinned. "The Jewish uprising, Spartacus, brothels, prohibition."

"We get it," Caleb interrupted.

"They all hid underground. They can evade capture quickly by escaping to the nearest tunnel and spy on anyone anywhere." He grabbed Ryan into a tight hug that made him panic instantly. Ahmose was a stoic figure, not a hugger by any means. Ahmose let him go and looked at Ryan. "How did you know?"

He shrugged. "I tried to figure out why none of our teams could find a scrap of a clue and then it hit me."

"We will send everyone out tonight to find them." With a marker in hand, he stood on his desk and wrote team leader names in random places on the ceiling map. "Zachary over here, and Malakai here."

"By the way," Damian spoke up, "we already found the place."

Ahmose dropped his marker and jumped off his desk. His entire body seemed instantly relaxed when he took a deep breath. "Who did?"

Ryan fearfully raised his hand, along with Cato and Damian. Ahmose looked ready to pounce and Ryan was closest to him. He took a step back and hid behind the other two.

"Let me get this straight." His eyes were glued on them. "You three went into the tunnels and found a group of rebels that not only are a threat to all of our lives, but a threat to humankind as a whole?"

"Uh..." Cato gaped.

"By yourselves?"

"Yeah," Damian muttered.

"Completely outnumbered and without a thought of getting backup?"

"It was on a hunch." Ryan shrugged.

"Were you seen?"

Ryan fumbled with his belt and nudged Damian from behind. He cleared his throat and nudged Damian again, who gave Ryan a dirty look and took a step forward.

"Yes, but we got away. And there's more news," Damian mumbled.

Ahmose sat silently and stared at the three of them as he waited for them to continue. His silence was unnerving. Ahmose was one of the only men that made Ryan nervous.

"They said that they had a spy in the Domus feeding them information," Cato spoke up. "They knew we were sending out patrols and these spies renounced being Warriors."

Ahmose's eyes widened. "You're sure of this?"

Damian nodded. "They were very clear on the matter."

Ahmose turned his back on the six of them and walked to the window. His hands were behind his back as he stared out into the city. "Thank you, gentlemen. Have a good day."

Without another word, they filed out of the office and quietly closed the door behind them. Moments later they heard a crash inside the office. The news must have sent him on a destructive rampage and his office was the victim.

"You found their hiding place?" Aden grabbed his arm and Ryan pulled away.

"What is with you grabbing me? And yes, we found it."

"Show us, let's go after them," he said urgently.

Damian stepped in between the two men and looked at Aden. "No. Not until orders are given to do so."

"Six Warriors can handle them. We've already proven that," Aden urged. "Bring us now."

"What is with you?" Cato asked.

"We don't even need to do anything, just show me," Aden insisted.

Ryan looked at Damian. "Okay, fine. I'll show you."

"No, all of you," Aden pushed. *What was his deal?*

Damian pulled Ryan back. "We are not showing you anything right now, Aden. Not until Ahmose tells us what to do next."

"You're right." Ryan shrugged. "Sorry, Boy Wonder."

"Since when do you listen to your bootlicker?"

Ryan didn't even get the chance to smack Aden because Damian did so before he could. He connected with Aden's jaw and Ryan had to hold him back. "Stop, you are better than this."

Jesse grabbed Aden's elbow and pulled him away. "Let's go."

They walked off while Caleb stayed behind. "Sorry about that."

"You really got the shit end of the stick when you were put on their team, didn't you?" Cato patted him on the shoulder.

"They have their faults but, like you, we have been through a lot together."

"You're a good man, Caleb," Ryan muttered.

"Thanks," Caleb added. "I am glad you found them. There is some hope after all."

Chapter XIII

Julia

Julia stopped brushing her hair when she heard a knock at her bedroom door. She was getting ready for the day and figured Anna had come to ask more questions. Anna loved to hear about all their pasts, and even though it hurt to reminisce she understood the appeal of it all.

As she opened the door she was somewhat shocked to see a tired, but happy Ryan. "Well, hello there."

Ryan walked right past her and into her room. Julia never really had people in her area. She liked her privacy.

Julia's room felt like a little piece of Heaven. The white marble flooring, the pale teal walls and the presence of white furniture flooded one with a sense of peace. She always preferred a clean, fresh look and that is precisely what she accomplished here in her room.

The soft teal walls held paintings of artists from all walks of life. Picasso, Da Vinci and Monet, to name a few, were among the masters displayed in Julia's room. Silky sheer curtains, white of course, tickled across the top of her large bed that sat close to the bay windows.

The ocean breeze whisked through the air, beckoning her to surrender to the waves below. The ocean terrified Julia and yet, when she sat in the warm white sand, her worries seemed to melt away. She feared the unknown and the ocean was, of course, the biggest mystery of all.

She had no weapons displayed in her room. Her armoire quietly held all of her battle gear. Unlike some of her comrades, Julia didn't see the need in surrounding herself with battle every day. Instead, she looked at the joys in life.

"How was last night?" She looked him over, trying to see any wounds.

"It was amazing." He grinned. Her heart fluttered unwillingly. Why did he have to be so handsome?

She took his helmet out of his hands and set it on her dresser. She wanted to know every detail and tried to make sure he knew he was going to stay. As she turned around, she saw him take his vest off slowly and throw it to the floor. Her heart started to pound quickly again.

Julia took a deep breath and picked his vest up. She put it on a hook by the door. "Slob."

He smirked and held his weapons out to her. "I don't know where to put things apparently."

She walked over and gently grabbed his sword and guns out of his hands. As she set them next to his helmet, she took a deep breath. She was alone with Ryan in her room. This was nerve-wracking. Julia instantly felt like a pathetic teenager with a crush.

She turned around and saw him taking his shirt off. Heat

rose to her cheeks and she felt stupid. Of course, this was what he was after. How could she think he would just leave her feelings alone? "What are you doing?"

His eyes looked up from the side of his torso. "Sorry, just checking on it. Sort of overexerted myself today."

Instant embarrassment filled her inside—she walked over to him and examined his wound. His stitches were still intact, but inflamed. "Can you go one day without upsetting this?"

"Doesn't look like it."

She walked over to her dresser and pulled out a first-aid kit. She had a cream the healers gave her that worked wonders. "It's healing at least."

The wound was thankfully starting to close up. She put the cream on it gently, and he stood there calmly. He didn't even flinch when she touched gently around it. She bandaged him up and tenderly rested her hand on his chest. He looked down at her. "Thank you, Doctor."

"Anytime." He smelled like sweat and soap.

He grabbed her by the hand and led her to the bed. He was only in his pants and boots and more exposed then she was used to a man being. He obviously could read her hesitation and laughed. "I'm not trying to seduce you, Julia, I just want to lay down. It was a long night."

She sat next to him—her heart beating fast despite what he said. Her sheer white dress clung to her body and rose up slightly when she sat next to him. Julia nervously tried to pull the dress down until his hand was under her chin, gently forcing her to look at him.

"Your hair has darkened over the years," she blurted out.

He raised an eyebrow and genuinely looked surprised. She could not tell if he was amused or saddened. She would never understand why his past haunted him so much. He was remarkable in his lifetime and it was nothing to be ashamed of or to hide from.

"Lack of sunlight, maybe?" He shrugged.

"Perhaps." She was about to push some boundaries. "Ryan?"

"Yes?"

"I wish you would let me call you by your real nam-"

"No," he interrupted.

She should have seen that one coming. "Why not?"

He dropped his hand on the bed and looked out her window. The sounds of the city waking up could be heard if she listened carefully. "That isn't me anymore, that is someone in the past that died long ago."

"You're wrong."

His eyes met hers and tension filled the room. There was a look in his eyes that put her on edge. "Drop it, please."

"Al-"

"Stop," he interrupted her again with his voice raised. Guilt swept over her. There really was a hidden sadness in him. "What even brought this up?"

She looked down at her hands and faced away from him. This was not how she wanted this to go and she only had herself to blame. "I couldn't help it. I've always admired your history and wish I knew more besides what I've read and from what I've learned over the years."

He grabbed her hand. She didn't want to meet his eyes, but he tilted her face upward and stroked her cheek lightly with his thumb. "I'm so sorry for yelling, Julia. It's just not a conversation I want to have."

She nodded. "I should not have pushed it. I just remember who you were and feel like I want to know the real you."

"You were too young to know who I was." He laughed.

"I am a fully grown woman, thank you very much," she pouted. "It's not my fault I was born a few centuries after you."

With a sigh, he lay down on her bed. His chest was slowly rising, and his eyes were closed. "You, my dear, are stubborn."

She grinned proudly. "I sure am."

"So, are you going to ask me what happened tonight or what?" He opened one eye.

"Oh!" She almost forgot the entire reason he was here. He looked tired and extremely handsome—it was hard to focus. "Yes, what did you guys find?"

He grinned up at her and propped himself on his elbow. "We found them. They were hiding in the underground tunnels and we came up on them."

It was as if a huge weight was lifted from her shoulders. They found the traitors, and it was one step closer to this whole ordeal being finished. "How?"

"Think of uprisings throughout history."

"Of course."

His hand seemed to slide closer to hers, but he stopped himself. Every bit of her was confused. He seemed to like her yet held back. Ryan was not the type to hold back, so was he really not interested?

She slid her hand to meet his and entwined her fingers with his. His eyes gazed painfully at their hands before he pulled away.

"Anyway," he said then cleared his throat. "We found out there are spies in the Domus working for them. I bet its Aden."

Julia rolled her eyes. "Aden is just as loyal as you are. Besides, he fought against them with us at the Great Temple."

"I suppose you're right. It's probably some low ranked Warrior—it would make sense."

"You're letting your hatred for him cloud your judgment," she mumbled.

"I don't hate him." Ryan smirked. "He is still young and extremely obnoxious, but I believe he means well, at least when it comes to being an Immortal anyway. A few hundred more years and I might actually like him, I seriously doubt it though. He wants what I want, and that will always be a rift between us."

"And, what is it that you want?" She cocked her head to the side. "Seems to me you two are more alike than you think."

Ryan pulled her down next to him and they both laughed. She laid flat on her back, while he was still propped up on his elbow. Her heart was going to give out on her from continuously racing then slowing down.

His eyes didn't leave hers when she felt his breath against her skin. She was very aware of his smooth, bare chest and muscles protruding from under the bandages.

"Please don't ever say I am like Aden," he whispered, "I think I may vomit."

His hair narrowly touched his eyebrows, and she pushed it out of the way. This was the first time she could actually study his face. There were small white scars along the right of his jaw that were barely noticeable.

In fact, his neck and chest were covered with the tiny lines, barely even a memory to his skin. She had always thought nothing had ever touched him, that he managed to come away unharmed for the most part. She was wrong. His body had been through a lot and only people that really looked closely could tell.

"Looks like a cat attacked me, doesn't it?"

She nearly jumped from being lost in thought. "Oh, I suppose. There are a lot of them."

"Almost sad they are close to disappearing."

"Why's that?" she asked.

"Makes me look tough." She rolled her eyes. "No, it helps me remember that I really am human. Not some god like my mother believed I could be or invulnerable."

"You act like you are invulnerable." He was not one bit cautious in her mind.

"I know I'm not. I just don't let fear rule my decisions. I never have, and I never will."

She leaned in and kissed him. Yet again, he gently pushed her away, but his eyes remained closed.

"Ryan?"

"Yes?"

"Please don't deny me."

He lay flat on his back and sighed. "Please quit trying to be with me, Julia. I can't force myself to do that to you. I will hurt you and I know it."

"I'm a big girl, I know what I want and right now that's you. So just give in to me and let it happen. We don't have to be together forever, I know that isn't who you are."

"You aren't the type for a one-night stand, Julia."

He was right—she was still pure and had never had any intention of destroying it. She favored the Goddess Artemis for her maidenhood and always felt a connection with her. Ryan made her actually feel something though and the temptation was too much.

She looked him over and noticed his body had no tension in it and his mouth fell slightly open. His eyes remained closed and his breathing steadied. Did he really just fall asleep?

"Seriously?" She laughed and climbed out of the bed. Gently, she took his boots off, put them by her door and grabbed a blanket off her loveseat. She kissed him on the forehead and noticed how remarkable it was to see him at such peace. "Sweet dreams."

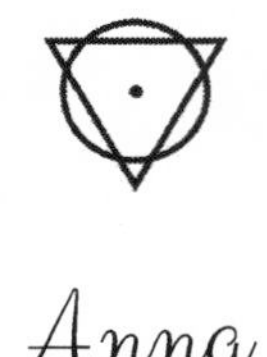

Anna

"How was your dinner?" Damian asked.

Anna shrugged and pushed her empty plate away. "Would have been better if there were some meat involved."

A few nearby tables glanced at her with disapproving looks.

Damian had asked her to go eat dinner this morning while in the training room—she felt reluctant at first, but said yes. Damian had a kind heart and she needed the distraction from all the chaos lately anyway.

The restaurant had an odd name, Silenus. Then again, Urbs was an odd place so it fit rather well. The décor was super weird. Painted fat, little half-goat men were on rocks, playing reed flutes and nymphs danced around in all different colors. There were other magical creatures in the mural that Anna could not recognize, but Damian seemed to know a lot about them and tried to educate her. It was not going so well.

The artwork was mind-blowing. The fur on the animals looked so real, she swore she would feel fur under her fingers if she touched it. Apart from the round-room mural, trees grew up and through the restaurant and Anna felt like they sat in the forest. She half expected a squirrel to run by at any moment.

"Sorry, it's kind of the theme I suppose. Vegetation." She

thought he blushed, but it was hard to tell in the pale candlelight, which happened to be the only light source in the restaurant.

"It was great." She grinned. Although, she still thought a juicy steak would hit the spot. "I still cannot get over this place. Seriously, I think they just built a roof and walls around some trees and bam—restaurant.

He grinned wide and sipped on his wine. He had this certain class about him that made her feel trashy. "It was originally owned by a satyr. He probably could not stand being in an enclosed-"

"I'm sorry, a what?" She coughed as she choked on her wine.

"Oh, I forget they were before your time." He shook his head. "Some are still around but they are going extinct for the most part. Thanks to modern technology and over population. Not to mention people no longer believe in them."

Gods and goddesses, she could handle, but the fact that there are magical creatures out there seemed too far-fetched for her mind. "You're joking."

"Not at all," he said seriously. "They are very good at hiding. Honestly, why would generations and countless amounts of people, who were considered very advanced for their time, make up such things? Especially without witnessing them." She had to admit, he had a point.

"You guys are pretty stuck in the Greek and Roman side of Urbs, aren't you?"

"It's comfortable here." He shrugged.

Their waitress appeared suddenly with their check in hand. Anna felt uncomfortable every time she showed up to the table. The only clothing the blonde wore was a bikini made up of leaves and vines that crawled down her legs and arms. "Ready?"

she asked sweetly.

Damian nodded and took the check. In Anna's experience, any normal man would have his eyes glued on a slightly nude waitress, but not Damian. His eyes remained on Anna with a gentle gaze that made her feel at ease.

It had been four months since Nathan's death and Damian's obvious attraction still confused her. She liked him, but it felt wrong because the love of her life was taken away from her forever.

"Come on," he said interrupting her train of thought. "I want you to see where we are going to race next week."

"Race?"

"You'll see." He held out his arm to her and she took it without hesitation. His old school mannerisms were starting to grow on her.

They walked into the cool night air and she heard music off in the distance—almost like jazz rooms back home. The familiar sound blasted her back into the present and away from nature.

There was a small river that ran throughout the city and they crossed a little bridge going over it. She had to admit, Urbs was a wild place stuck in multiple histories, but it was beautiful.

"Can I ask you a question?"

"You just did," he responded playfully.

"Ha- ha." She nudged him. "Seriously."

"Shoot."

She felt him tense. "How is it that everyone speaks English?"

Immediately his body loosened and shuddered with laughter. She looked up at him with a hurt expression and he bit his lip to stop. "That's your question?"

"What?" She scrunched her eyebrows. Now she felt really dumb.

"Here I thought it was something serious."

"Sorry."

"We don't all speak English," he said simply.

Now she was really confused. "Huh?"

"You ask too many questions, Anna," he stated. With a deep breath he said, "To avoid communication problems, the priests cast a spell on all of us at our ceremony, you don't even realize it. It makes the individual hear others in their own native language. So mortals hear us in their language and I hear them in my own."

"Why not just learn the same language?"

"Some languages are dead and it is easier to just hear what you speak naturally. Don't you think? Besides that would take a fair amount of time." He grinned.

"So you're not hearing English?"

"No."

"What are you hearing then?"

He looked down at her and sighed heavily. "So many questions."

She felt he was starting to grow annoyed with her. "So why does your mouth look like it's speaking English?"

Damian laughed at her again and ran his hand through his hair. They walked on a stone pathway through a park. "All part of the spell is my guess. Mortals hear their own language from us as well. Easier to work with them that way."

"What about words like, awesome and cool? You know, words that languages have no translation for?"

"I am going to assume you are meaning slang, which we have our own. I try not to think about it too much. If you do say something completely unknown, then I hear it in your native tongue and you will just have to explain it."

"Weird." No wonder no one here had accents or trouble understanding her. It really was a logical solution, but she felt like she was not having a real conversation now.

They walked in silence and she enjoyed the scenery. This part of the city was full of nature and it instantly became her favorite spot in Urbs. Statues were mixed in randomly with flowers and bushes. They were not white, but decorated colorfully and with such realism that they looked alive.

One was a mother grasping a child's hand with Native American dresses on. Another had a man wielding a shield and Viking helmet. Her favorite so far was a mother holding her baby. Tears ran down her cheeks as her permanent, loving gaze peered down at her newborn child.

Fountains trickled all around and were lit up by small orbs that floated around them. They reminded her of fireflies.

Anna reached out and touched a flower near the pathway. It was red and so full of life, as was the rest of the park. She had to touch it because it all seemed too perfectly beautiful to be real.

"Breathtaking, isn't it?"

Anna looked at him quickly and pulled back from the flower. She was so deep in thought he'd caught her off guard. "What?"

"The city."

"It's unreal. I've never seen anything like this." She grinned. "It's so clean and free."

"It reminds me of home. A beauty lost in time," he said.

They neared a huge stadium that was shaped in a very long oval. It reached three stories high and was made out of white marble with a red awning to block out the sun or rain.

"Holy sh-" she stopped herself. Was it smart to curse in a God's city?

"Come on." He laughed. There was so much excitement in

his voice, that she allowed him to grab her hand and jogged by his side.

They walked under an arched doorway. Damian let go of her hand to push the heavy wooden doors open. Her breath caught in her chest as she had her first sight of the arena.

It could seat the whole city with ease and she imagined what it would look like full. Thousands of people cheering here would shake Heaven itself.

Soft sand covered the ground and there was a low wall running through the middle of the arena.

The wall had statues decorated in the middle. They must be important people. It also had two markers on each end of the wall. One looked like seven dolphins and the other side had an egg looking thing.

She looked at Damian, who looked like a kid on Christmas. "This is big."

He quickly looked at her with his eyebrows furrowed. "Big? That's it? Come on!"

"It's umm..." She was not good at quick thinking. "A very grand track."

He stood there blinking at her and shook his head. "It's a grander version of the Circus Maximus." His grin returned. "Like I said, races are next week. Ryan, Cato, and I haven't had much time to practice though."

"What sort of race?"

"Chariot, of course."

"Oh, of course." She rolled her eyes.

"We've been undefeated for years now." Damian beamed with pride. She saw him as a real person now instead of the calm, collected man she first met. Damian has these gentlemanly qualities about him that made other men look like losers.

However, in this moment, he was a young man and not a weathered old soul. It was nice to see him like this.

She eyed him curiously and dropped her hands to her sides. She could not hold this in any longer. "When were you chosen?"

Silence gripped the air and she watched Damian as he stared out into the stadium. His expression was unreadable and Anna instantly felt guilty. She was sure he would avoid the question, just like he always did when his previous life came up.

"Why does it matter?" he asked quietly.

"You're super secretive and it drives me nuts," she said simply.

"Well." He rubbed the back of his neck and she saw he hid his amusement. "I'm from Greece. Is that good enough?"

She pouted playfully and put her hands on her hips. Was she seriously flirting with him? Seemed like it. "Not going to tell me more? Please?"

His dirty blond hair fell into his eyes as he looked down at her. Her heart skipped a beat and she felt an urge in her body that had been gone for a while. The way he looked at her would make any girl's knees buckle.

"Why, Anna?" he whispered as he slicked his hair back again.

"I want to know who you are," her voice was soft and genuine.

He tilted his head to the side—a small smile crept onto his lips. "Ryan would kill me if I told you anything."

"Why?"

"We were chosen together. Actually, he was chosen and refused to join unless I was as well. Didn't take much convincing, thankfully, so no one considered me as unworthy." His words dripped with sadness. "Point being, I promised him I would keep our past a secret. It hurts him and he wants it behind him completely."

"Please, Damian?" His mouth parted slightly and she felt victorious. He was giving in and opening up finally.

"You're evil," he said softly.

"Thanks." She walked closer to him. "Please?"

He cleared his throat and took a step back. She didn't expect that, especially since he seemed to like her so much.

"All I can say is that we were born in Greece, in ancient times and Ryan is the greatest friend a man could ask for. He gave me the chance to have this life and I am forever in his debt." He stood his ground. "I am truly sorry, but that is all I can tell you."

"I'm going to find out, Damian. I'm a very resourceful person you know."

Damian took her hand again and cupped it around his. She could feel how worn his hands were and it amazed her how long these hands have been around. "It won't be hard, I am sure. Everyone is aware of who we are, but they rarely bring it up. They may be afraid of the wrath of Ryan so, good luck."

"Why?"

He now cupped her face in his hands. "Enough questions."

She grinned and shrugged. "At least I got something to go off of."

Before she could react, his lips were softly against hers. For a brief second she felt herself give in until Nathan appeared in her mind. She quickly pulled away and the guilt spilled over her again.

She stood there, half in shock and half in shame. Damian quickly tried to apologize, "I'm so sorry, I should have asked."

She watched as he gently kicked the dirt while he retreated

from her. "We better get back," she muttered.

Ryan

Music echoed in the great hall and dancers paraded themselves in front of the guests. He could not breathe from the anger that filled his chest.

Thankfully, he kept his temper at bay and drank from his cup. All the while he watched his father make a fool of himself. Fool was the wrong word. Undignified moron fit the description better.

The banquet held no interest for him but it was his duty to be here. A good son does not disobey his father and he was told to come. Mother was very displeased, but he reassured her that his father was making a huge mistake.

He sat a few spaces away from the new happy couple and he felt the guilt rise in him for his mother. She was alone this night and he feared her obsessing over it. This entire event felt like a betrayal.

He tossed an unfinished fig on to the table and drained the remaining wine in his cup. His father only bought the best wine to get drunk with and tonight he wasted no expense.

A servant came to refill his cup and he held it out for the man.

Just then, the bride's uncle stood up and raised his cup for a toast. Silence filled the room and all eyes were on the man. "Pray to the Gods that this union may bring forth a legitimate heir to the throne."

Silence filled the room as all eyes went to him then back to the uncle.

Anger took over and he threw his cup at the drunken man. "What am I then, a bastard?" he yelled.

To his surprise, his father stood up, his sword in his hand. Instead of turning on his bride's uncle, his sword was held high as he charged towards his son.

Ryan awoke up with a start and saw Julia lying to his left. Her sheer nightgown glimmered in the pale moonlight.

He had no desire to leave her. He wanted to watch her sleep. It was calming and he found himself hoping she would not wake up. Little things she did amused him. The way she smiled slightly and whimpered because of her dreams made his heart flutter. He enjoyed finding new habits about her. This is the first time he had been close to her for a long period of time and he clung to it.

Her habit to kick him periodically somewhat annoyed him. It was cute, however, it was painful nonetheless.

It was early morning and he must have slept all day. He still felt tired after his intensely busy dreams though. He would have to go to the apothecary to get a dreamless sleep remedy and finally get a good night sleep.

He broke his eyes away from her and glanced at the clock on the nightstand behind him. It was four in the morning. He really had slept a long time. As much as he didn't want to, he needed to get out of here. No one would be up and awake right now, but he didn't want to get caught in her room.

He turned back over and found Julia starring at him.

"Leaving?"

He smirked. "Not unless you want me to."

"Done being cranky?" Her expression was blank. She did just wake up, so he tried not to take it as a bad sign.

"Yes," he whispered and tucked a loose strand of hair behind her ear. She closed her eyes at his touch and he suppressed his instinct to kiss her.

"You made my bed stink."

"Sorry, I should have showered and changed before I came over." Her eyes met his. "I'm sorry for getting upset with you."

"Better be," she muttered half asleep.

He kissed her nose and grinned when she scrunched it up.

Her eyes stayed steadily on his and for a moment he thought of telling her how he really felt. He could not bring himself to do it though. "I don't deserve you."

All joking gone from his face, she studied him with what he could only describe as bewilderment.

"Don't ever say that." Her eyes softened. "You've been through more then most and you have the right to only the best and I am a pale shadow of what you deserve."

"Pale," he said caressing her cheek, "perhaps, but you are no shadow, Julia."

The sun began to stretch across the floor and Ryan turned towards the windows.

"The day beckons us." Ryan almost laughed. Why did he just sound old fashioned? Julia didn't laugh at him or seem to mind. Maybe it was his dreams that made him sound from a different time.

"Go take a shower, stinky." She was pretending to be playful, but her eyes betrayed her. Julia's eyes welled up and he felt the urge to stay with her. So he remained at her side and smoothed down her hair.

"I'll stay." It was painful to see her cry.

She closed her eyes and cuddled up against him. His breath caught in his chest and his thoughts would make a priest blush.

She lay in his arms for a few hours yet he did not sleep. He gazed at her and studied her face more. She was so beautiful. Not a trace of makeup was on her and she didn't need it. Most women painted their faces until they looked like someone completely different.

She must be asleep, there was no way she could lay with her eyes closed that long. His urges became hard to suppress. He caressed the side of her face and rested his hand on her neck. He should just give in, even if it was this one time like she said.

He kissed her gently on the lips, trying not to wake her and muttered, "Beautiful."

Her eyes fluttered open and he almost jumped from surprise. He hoped she didn't know what he just did.

Julia raised her hand and pressed it against the side of his face with such tenderness that he could not help but close his eyes.

To his surprise, her lips touched his and he gave in. He tortured himself by staying and he could not handle it anymore. He pressed her down and propped himself on top of her between her legs. Through the haste and confusion he felt her fingernails rake his bare back. His pulse raced through his veins as he hungered for more.

He needed more.

Ryan found she craved for him as much as he craved for her. Undeniable fire and passion filled him as his hands slipped into her lush blonde hair.

They clung to each other as the barrier of denial melted away from his mind. He needed her, wanted her, and his body craved to feel her bare skin against his.

Her mouth grew more urgent against his and he gladly returned the intensity. His hips ground into hers as she pulled him closer. He let go of her hair with only one hand to slide it down her leg. He slowly pushed her gown up towards her hips and felt the warm flesh of her thighs.

He had to stop.

He could not stop.

He tried to be gentle with her, but she was not having it. She gripped his hair and crushed her lips against his. He pressed himself against her limber body and felt her full breasts against his chest, her body seemed to melt against his.

The need to touch her, be touched, nearly overwhelmed him.

Ryan looked down at her and breathed heavily. He rolled over and his hands roughly grabbed her body to pull her on top of him. Her legs felt smooth and her gown barely covered her thighs. She started to pull it off and he grabbed her hands.

"No strings attached?"

"What?" she asked breathlessly.

"No hurt feelings? Just this once?"

"Is that what you want?" She stroked her hands across the muscles of his chest while he refrained from lifting her gown.

"I want you," he groaned as she lightly scratched her nails down his chest. She leaned down and kissed his neck softly.

"Okay then," she whispered, before she nipped his earlobe with her teeth. A surge of pleasure rushed through him that he could not restrain.

Done with talking, she kissed him fiercely and began to unbuckle his pants. He nuzzled her neck and felt a wave of sensation over his body as she pulled them down. Ryan helped wriggle himself free.

She crawled on top of him and he lifted her up to straddle him. Without hesitation, he ripped the front of her gown open and yanked it off with ease. There she sat on top of him in nothing but her dark blue undergarments.

"You could have just pulled it off." She smirked.

"Sorry," he groaned, his hands skimmed above her waist and to the back of her bra.

A loud knock came from her door and he groaned. "Are you kidding me?"

"Ignore it." She grinned and leaned down to kiss him.

The knocking continued.

"Julia!"

He heard Cato behind the door and Julia quickly jumped off him and hurriedly searched for something to cover herself with. She grabbed a light robe and threw it on.

"Hide," she hissed.

Ryan rolled off the bed and landed on the cold floor. The last thing he needed was Cato finding him in his sister's room, in only his briefs.

He heard her scramble around the room and felt his gear and helmet land on his back. "What the hell?"

"Sorry," she mumbled.

The door opened and he heard multiple sets of feet walk in. "What took you so long?"

"I was sleeping naked. I could have answered the door that way if you'd prefer?" Julia snapped.

"Gross," Cato mumbled.

"The reason we are here," Damian spoke up, "is because we can't find Ryan anywhere. We were supposed to patrol again last night and he never showed up. Any ideas were he is?"

"Why would I know?"

"Just wondering if you saw him anywhere or something? We've looked everywhere and can't find him." Damian sounded confused.

Why did everyone decide to have a meeting right now? Ryan started to hurt in a certain area and the floor was making him cold.

"Well, I haven't seen him."

"Okay, thanks." Cato sounded very annoyed. Ryan could not blame him—he felt instantly horrible about missing patrol, but could not control his sleep.

Light footsteps seemed to have left the room and he almost pushed himself up. "Can I ask you something?"

Go away Damian, Ryan thought.

"Sure." She sighed.

"Why is there a pair of men's boots by your bed?"

Ryan closed his eyes, bit his lip and felt the need to disappear. He turned over and wiggled into his pants and shirt behind the bed. If he was going to be caught he could at least have his clothes on.

Julia said nothing, but he didn't intend to just pop out from under the bed.

"Who's here?" Damian sighed.

"No one."

"Don't lie, please."

"It's none of your business, Damian," Julia snapped. She seemed frustrated. Wonder why?

Damian growled, "Sorry, Julia, but I need to know."

Ryan heard footsteps going around the room and finally towards where he was. He grew nervous. What was he going to say? The footsteps grew nearer.

"It is not your damn business, Damian. Now get out."

The footsteps stopped.

"Fine, but I just want you to know that some people may have other intentions than what you think."

"What does that mean?" she asked.

"It means, that someone may seem to care for you, when in reality, they just want something from you." He sighed. "If you get my drift."

The door finally closed and Ryan peeked over the side of the bed.

"What did he mean by that?" Julia asked. She sat on the edge of her bed opposite of him and would not look at him.

"Couldn't tell you." He climbed over to her and put his arm around her waist, she jerked away from him. "What?"

"Go."

"No," he mumbled.

"You are using me. You don't care about me. Even Damian said so. I am done with it. Please, leave."

"What are you talking about, Julia?"

"You heard him." Her voice cracked. "You just wanted something from me."

Ryan instantly grew angry. He had no intention of using her—he was caught up in the moment and could not control it. "I thought we both agreed this was a one time thing anyways, what does it matter?"

"It doesn't," she mumbled. "Stay away from me."

He jumped off her bed and gathered the rest of his things. "No problem," he growled as he slammed the door behind him.

Chapter XIV

Damian

After going by Emma and Julia's room, Damian wandered around the halls trying to figure out what to do with his day, since Ryan was a no-show.

He trudged into the parlor and saw Ryan leaving from the female hallway. He suddenly became aware of Damian and stopped dead in his tracks.

"Morning."

"Morning." Damian raised his eyebrow. "Cato and I have been looking everywhere for you."

Ryan nodded and plopped down on a couch casually. How he could pull off being so calm after being caught ditching his responsibilities was astounding.

"What did you do last night?"

"Had dinner with Anna." Damian crossed his arms. "Then went on patrol like you were supposed to."

Ryan's eyebrows rose. "How was it?"

"Dinner was okay, but ended extremely terrible." Ryan seemed nonchalant. Damian wanted to shake some sense into him. "Wouldn't know about patrol, Aden's team took over."

Ryan motioned for Damian to sit down across from him and Damian slowly walked over.

"Give it time, Damian. She's been through a lot and lost her boyfriend in the process. Just give it time."

"Why are you ignoring the fact that you missed patrol?"

"Why are you badgering me about it?"

"This is important, Ryan." Damian glared. A small breeze crept in to the room. Ryan crossed his legs and didn't seem bothered one bit.

"And, getting rid of my physical frustration is also important," he mumbled.

If there was one thing Damian hated it was Ryan's lack of maturity. After everything that has happened, not only to him, but the entirety of Urbs, he still remained an uncaring creature.

"So, you decided sleeping with someone was more important then finding out who wants us all to die?"

"Pretty much."

Damian gritted his teeth. "Who was it this time? Obviously not Emma, she was alone this morning."

"Does it really matter?" Ryan laughed.

It didn't. Maybe a shock back in to reality would make him see people will not wait for him to change. "I just came back from Julia's room with Cato."

"Oh?" Ryan didn't look at him. He seemed unusually interested in his fingernails.

"Yes." He tapped his fingers. "Someone was in there with her, too."

"Who?"

"I don't know. He was hiding and she seemed very adamant about me leaving." Not an ounce of emotion on Ryan's face. Damian was on the verge of giving up on him. "Boots were in front of her bed and the sheets were ruffled. Not to mention her ripped night gown was on her lamp."

Ryan sat up straight and stared deeply into his eyes. There was nothing there. He must really not care anymore. How did he change so much over the years after being the liveliest human he had ever known.

"Well, good for him." Was he glaring? What did Damian do that warranted the death glare?

"I'm just warning you." Damian felt nervous. "I think it may be Aden."

He detected a small hint of smile on Ryan's lips and tilted his head to the side. He wanted nothing more then to smack Ryan upside the head.

"Did you confront her?" Ryan smirked.

"Yes, I told her to watch what she does. After the conversation we overheard between him and Caleb I don't think he has her best interests at heart."

"I see." Ryan kicked his feet up on the couch and lay down. Damian could not help it—he chucked a pillow across the room and hit Ryan in the head.

"What the hell?"

"Listen to me, Ryan," he started. "If you lose Julia to that little prick and keep sleeping with random women, I will beat you to a pulp."

Shock spread over Ryan's face. "Excuse me?"

"I'm not finished." Ryan's mouth dropped slightly. "You've lost people you love, well so have I. It was a long time ago and you need to get over it. Julia is amazing and if you mess it up with her and hurt her, I swear to the Gods I will hurt you."

"Finished?" Ryan's face was set in stone.

"I love you, Ryan, but I am sick of watching you destroy yourself. I won't do it anymore. So grow up again and start another family."

"Let's get this very clear, Damian." Instantly he felt like he was back under Ryan's command and fear engulfed him. "I will do what I want with my life. You have absolutely no say in what I do. If you keep bothering me about it I will not hesitate to fight you. You may think we are equals, but we are not. I have accomplished more in my mortal life then you ever have in our Immortal one."

Damian sat in silence. There was nothing left to say. He was being put in his place and he felt a stabbing pain in his heart. Although Ryan was right, he'd never thrown it in Damian's face like this before. It was never a competition between the two of them. What was important was bettering humanity, not feeding an ego.

Ryan's glare sunk into him and he had to look away. He suddenly realized Ryan's gear hidden behind the coffee table. Why hadn't he noticed that before? Why did he have that with him when he didn't patrol last night?

Ryan seemed to sense what Damian looked at and hastily grabbed his things. Once he was out of the room Damian sat back in relief and looked out into the early morning light. "Once a master, always a master."

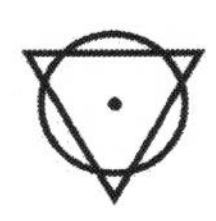

Ryan

"Ready, boys?" Ahmose announced.

Ryan turned around and suppressed a grin. Ahmose looked like an African prince dressed in his formal leopard skin cloak and sandals. His bare chest gleamed in the sun and looked even darker against the short white kilt he wore. *What could he possibly be thinking wearing leopard on a scorching day like this?*

"Remembering the old days or what?" Ryan laughed.

Ahmose adjusted his cloak proudly and stuck out his chin in defiance. "I am honoring it."

Ryan grinned and turned back to his horses. His beautiful white stallions were born and bred in Urbs under his supervision. They had strict diets and were trained by the best men money could buy—Ryan treated his horses like his children. He even named them Athos and Cyrus.

Each horse had green beads braided in parts of their mane as well as a green blanket over their backs. Ryan wore a shirt to match.

His wicker and leather chariot was decorated with green trimming and the wheels had green spokes that gleamed in the sunlight.

Green was Ryan, Damian, and Cato's team color or *prasina* as the Roman's called it.

"All right boys, time to focus." He reached into his pocket, pulled out sugar cubes and gave one to each horse. Athos greedily took his cubes while Cyrus cherished it. "Easy killer."

"And here I thought you didn't spoil these two." Damian came up behind him.

Ryan didn't turn around. He was still unhappy with his

friend, but after a week he tried not to make a big deal over it like a pathetic schoolgirl. "For good luck."

"Look, Ryan, I-"

"Save it," he interrupted.

As he turned around, Ryan instantly felt guilty. How could he possibly be upset with someone that only wanted him to be happy? More importantly, how could someone make him feel like such a jerk?

Damian must be evil. Although, Damian was as maniacal as a box full of kittens.

With sad eyes and a quivering lip Damian said, "Please, forgive me."

With a quick punch to Damian's shoulder, Ryan rolled his eyes and brushed Athos' hair. "You're a drama queen. Yes, I said queen, you big girl."

They laughed and Damian moved next to Cyrus and brushed his hair.

"Did you see Aden's horses? Better then last year," he muttered. "Hope he doesn't run them into the ground."

Aden and Jesse had a tendency to run their horses so hard they collapsed to the ground or broke a leg. Either way, they were always put down and replaced with better stock. It was sickening, but there was nothing Ryan could do about it. Caleb, like always, was the best of the three and has had the same horses for at least three years now.

"They will. They always do," said Ryan.

Athos and Cyrus seemed to agree and nudged Ryan and Damian with their heads. Athos nibbled on Ryan's pocket looking for more sugar cubes.

"Speaking of..." Damian grimaced.

Ryan turned to find Jesse and Aden strutting over to them,

he rolled his eyes. They both wore blue shirts, which was their team color. *Veneta*.

"Ready to lose this year, boys?" Aden boasted.

Ryan continued to brush Athos. "Aden, at the end of the day I'm not you. So everyday I'm a winner."

"So clever," Aden hissed. "You'll be singing a different tune when we take you down."

"I'm not into men."

"Shut up, Ryan," Jesse finally spoke.

Both Ryan and Damian watched Jesse with confusion. Jesse was always so quiet they usually forget he was there.

"Anyway," Aden said, "have you seen our team this year? Only the best from Ireland."

"Oh no, not the Irish." Ryan faked nervousness.

"Just wait and see. Your horses are worn and need to be put down." He gestured to Athos and Cyrus. "At least Cato and Damian had the common sense to get new horses."

As he counted to ten and took deep breaths, Ryan just flashed a wide grin and shrugged. "Like you said, just wait and see."

Jesse put his arm around Aden and led him back to where Caleb waited with their horses.

"Well, I better go see if Cato is ready. His horses are acting a bit skittish," Damian said.

"Great." Athos stomped his feet and snorted. "Calm down boy. We are almost ready."

Damian made his way over to Cato and his team. The horses were skittish and Cato looked stressed. Each of their horses and chariots were decorated the same and each man wore the same green shirt. The only difference was that Damian's horses were black and Cato's were a mix.

Trumpets sounded and the four teams quickly began getting ready. Ryan fastened his helmet and sighed with relief. Some years they were forced to wear leather helmets like in the Roman times and thankfully this year it was modernized and military like.

With one last pat on his horses, he slipped them another sugar cube and stepped up on his chariot. He tied the reins around his waist and fastened his small curved blade to his side. It was a helpful tool to have if you were thrown off and needed to cut yourself free.

He grabbed the reins in his left hand, Ryan held his whip in the other and his horses lurched forward.

Each team lined up at the starting gate with their teammates by their sides. Cato and Damian flanked Ryan and were led to the very right.

Ryan glanced down to see that Aden and his crew were at the very left. The white and red teams were the only things separating them—Ryan knew it would come down to his and Aden's group.

Red and White were usually made up of locals that tried their hand at racing. Mainly younger generations that had little to no experience. It was not difficult to beat them and they were somewhat of a nuisance and in the way.

Ryan and Aden's teams usually are the repeat finalists and it was hilarious to watch everyone else try out for the race, but this year they were too busy to enjoy the spectacle.

Screams from the crowd roared so loud that Ryan could not hear a single word the referee was saying to them. It's not like there were really rules anyways. Once the referee seemed satisfied, he jumped onto his horse and waited for the race to begin.

Ryan watched the magistrates box to see the handkerchief drop to indicate the start. The magistrates box held the Council of Command, Ahmose, and a few prominent members of Urbs. *The high society separated from the regular classes, not much has changed in history.*

A council member stood up and held out his arm with the handkerchief in his hand. The man tried to say something, but was easily drowned out by the crowd. He let go and the small cloth fluttered towards the dirt. It barely touched the surface when all twelve riders snapped their horses into action.

Ryan tried to take the inside quickly and veered left towards the middle of the pack. Cato and Damian fell behind his flanks. The first left turn around the *spina* was coming up and he saw Jesse about to grab the lead around it.

Ryan snapped his whip in the air, causing his horses to shoot into action. He had to gain the lead and then get his horses at a steady speed so he could block those behind him.

First turn went to Jesse.

"Dammit!" Ryan yelled.

Ryan stuck right behind Jesse and tried to maneuver around him. He would not give an inch.

As Cato pulled up next to Ryan, Aden pulled up on the other side of Cato. With one quick lurch towards Cato's chariot, Aden made Cato's horses back off and fall behind.

"You want to play that way? All right," Ryan yelled. Whether or not Aden heard him, Ryan struck his whip in the air once more and Athos and Cyrus pulled ahead of him.

Coming up on the next turn, Ryan pushed his horses' in-between Jesse's chariot and the *spina*. He made a sharp left turn and pushed Jesse towards the outer wall where the crowd screamed in terror, afraid of a crash.

Finally he was in the lead and glanced back to see Jesse pulled up behind the white team.

First lap down and the egg shaped marker popped up indicating the first lap was done.

Six more laps to go.

He came up on the next turn and Ryan pulled into the inside as sharp as he could.

In the distance he saw the dolphin marker up that helped the other side of the arena know which lap they were on.

In the corner of his eye he saw two brown horses with blue plumes at his side.

Crap.

Aden was nearly neck and neck with him.

Damn Irish.

Coming up on the next turn, Aden's chariot pushed into his and threw him off sideways. He pulled on the reins and corrected his horses to meet his direction before the wheels skid out of place and rolled him over.

Inches away from the wall, his horses lurched forward and avoided a collision with another horse.

The crowd roared and the second lap was over.

Ryan fell behind Aden, Damian, and a red team member.

Two eggs were up and he came towards the next turn. Ryan made Athos and Cyrus quickly cut off the red member. The man's horses panicked and headed towards the outer wall while the red member yelled at Ryan with his fist in the air.

Damian let Ryan come up beside him and knew they would work as a team to beat Aden. One of them being the winner was better then Aden getting the win, so it really didn't matter who did it.

Two dolphins up, Ryan and Damian made the turn with

ease and blocked off the rest of the riders from passing.

Three laps down, three eggs up.

Two white team riders must have collided. Medics frantically pulled them off the track as their horses were being run out through the starting gate.

At the next turn, they made sure to keep a steady pace and concentrated on making sure the other riders didn't pass them. Ryan didn't want to wear the horses out before the race was close to over.

As they came up on lap five, Ryan saw Jesse and a red member yelling at each other up ahead. Their chariots were somehow stuck together and they could not get them apart. Jesse ended up punching the other man, who dropped to the ground quickly.

The crowd cheered in glee.

With five dolphins up, Ryan looked over at Damian and they nodded to each other. Both men snapped their whips as they turned and their horses jumped into gear.

Damian pulled ahead—Ryan urged Athos and Cyrus to catch up. Aden came up on the next turn when Damian and Ryan pulled up on the rear.

Six laps down and Aden's horses foamed at the mouth. New horses had their limits and these poor boys were at theirs. Pity filled inside him for the beasts. They were not going to last.

They all turned in some confusion but straightened out finally. They had to get the inside turn.

No luck.

Aden managed to keep them out of the way and Ryan snapped his whip again.

Now on their seventh lap, Ryan was desperately trying to think of a way to get past Aden. He looked at Damian who made a cutting signal.

Brilliant idea, Ryan agreed silently.

Aden got the inside turn and Ryan pulled back. Damian snapped his whip in the air and caught up with the tired horses on their right. With a slight jerk, Damian forced his horses towards Aden's and instantly Aden's horses stopped. To them, stopping seemed better then being run into the low wall where Zeus sported a lightning bolt.

It worked. Ryan pulled ahead quickly as Damian corrected himself and pulled up behind him.

With his last turn, Ryan allowed Damian to come up to his side. He wanted to share this win with him, Cato was nowhere to be found and they passed the finish line with ease.

The crowd roared and Ryan threw his fist up in the air in triumph. He needed this. He needed a win after the nonsense he had been though lately.

Beside him, Damian hollered and jumped in his chariot in excitement. Both of them pulled their horses to a halt and untied themselves from their reins. As they jumped off their chariots, Ryan gave Damian a quick hug and they threw their fists in the air. It felt good to be happy and he could not stop grinning.

The crowd screamed in approval.

Ryan took off his helmet and tossed it into the crowd, who tried desperately to catch it. Sweat dripped down his face and he marched over to his horses. They deserved extra sugar cubes for this.

"Good job, boys." He grinned.

Suddenly, he lurched forward from a shove and turned to find Aden fuming. Ryan steadied himself and leaned on Cyrus casually. He was not about to let Aden ruin this moment and it was even sweeter seeing him so upset.

"You cheated."

Ryan held out his hands and laughed. "Aden, you lost fair and square, but if it makes you feel better, go ahead and hit me. Free shot."

Aden's fist balled up and Ryan could not wipe the grin off his face. Aden was making himself look like a fool in front of the entire city and Ryan could not be more pleased with himself.

The crowd seemed to realize what was going on and started to talk amongst themselves. Some people continued to scream from the win, while others watched in anticipation for what was going on.

Aden seemed to realize they were being watched and made a beeline towards the stables. His horses remained behind and collapsed to the ground. Ryan walked over to the poor beasts and stroked their manes. "I'm so sorry."

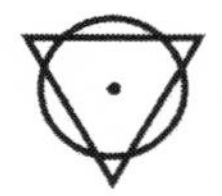

As they rode their horses through the triumphant arch, Cato caught up with them and they went to the city square in front of the Great Temple.

"Good job, guys," said Cato. "Sorry I fell behind. Aden screwed me over."

"It's okay, we did the same to him." Damian smirked.

They pulled up next to the Great Temple—the crowd seemed to find itself there before they did. It was a huge gathering filled with drinking, music, and food.

Vendors from around Urbs set up tents to sell their goods

in one area. It was big party to get drunk and eat whatever type of food you wanted to, all in one area. This time of year was Ryan's favorite.

They jumped out of their chariots and men grabbed their horses to lead them back to the stables. The three of them immediately found themselves flocked with women.

"Hello, ladies." Ryan grinned.

The group of giggling girls ran their hands all over them. He felt like a celebrity getting mobbed by adorning fans. Being the winner came with its advantages. The attention and free drinks called his name and he was going to answer.

Emma quickly found her way over to Ryan. Her long blonde hair flowed behind her. She wrapped her arms around his waist and he felt extremely awkward. "Good job, babe."

Ryan left his arms at his sides and smiled awkwardly at her. "Err, thanks, Emma."

Her grip tightened and she kissed his cheek lightly. Ryan casually tried to shimmy his way out of her grip, but it just tightened.

He looked to Damian for help to pry the piranha off until he saw Julia staring directly at him and his heart seemed to stop. She walked towards him with a blank look on her face and he finally managed to get out of Emma's grasp.

Julia stood next to Emma, a small smirk on her lips. "A fine performance," she said.

Two blondes stood in front of him and both looked like they were ready to kill each other. It was like the start of a terrible blonde joke.

"How about we celebrate?" Emma grabbed his hand.

"An excellent idea," Julia responded.

"I meant just me and Ryan." Emma rolled her eyes and tried

to block Julia out of the conversation. Ryan pulled his hand away smoothly and felt like he was going to have a heart attack. This was beyond awkward.

With ease, Julia slid in next to Ryan and whispered in his ear. "You're never going to change, are you?"

Ryan looked down at her. "Probably not, sorry."

"Don't be." She kissed his cheek lightly. "I'm glad I don't have to put up with your nonsense."

At that, Ryan grinned. "I wouldn't want you anyways. I prefer attractive women."

Julia slapped him so hard his vision went blank for a second. *I deserved that.*

"So, what sort of celebration were you thinking?" He focused on Emma now.

She walked up slowly and put her hands on his chest. Just by the look in her eyes he could tell what she wanted.

"Perhaps, a one on one session." She ran her hands down his sides. "Maybe you can teach me how to ride properly. I am terrible on horseback."

Cato stood nearby and lightly pushed a brunette towards Ryan, who instantly wrapped her arm around his waist. She giggled and the smell of alcohol lingered on her.

"Come on, Ryan, let's show these girl's a good time," Cato said.

Ryan patted Cato on the back and Emma's eyes shot daggers. "How about we get drunk and see where the night takes us, ladies."

"Sounds good to me." The brunette giggled.

Emma wrapped her arm around Ryan's other side and decided to join the party. This could not be any more complicated then it already was. Honestly though, what man would deny the company of two women?

Cato followed next to Damian with his arm around two girls who both seemed to want to keep their hands firmly on his buttocks. Ryan may have had the bad reputation, but Cato was exactly like Ryan was with women, he was just more silent about it.

Ryan loved the party at the end of the race. Women flanked the victors and Ryan could just pick out a few birds to bring back to his coup. Emma was damaging this plan though with her dirty glares to other women and he needed to make it clear he was not hers.

"So how does it feel to be undefeated for over five hundred years?" Emma boasted.

"We have an unfair advantage." Ryan smirked. "We were around when it was invented."

They found themselves under a tent that served beer and wine. Everyone in it seemed overly intoxicated, a few brawls broke out here and there, but ended quickly. He felt like he was mortal again.

Damian found an empty table. They all sat around it and people continuously came up to them to shake hands and buy them a round of drinks. Ryan found himself unable to keep control of his senses with the endless amount of alcohol that entered his body.

Cato sat next to him with a redhead on his lap and seemed deeply concentrated on kissing her neck. Ryan rolled his eyes and noticed Damian had girls around him. When they tried to touch his leg he pulled away from them, clearly uninterested. They didn't seem happy about it, but stayed to be a part of the party.

"Another round, gentlemen? On the house!" An older man

in his forties walked up to them with filled shot glasses.

Ryan quickly grabbed one after the other and took five shots in a row. The old man laughed and patted him hard on the back. "That-a-boy."

Damian shook his head at him. Ryan shrugged. "Time to get drunk ladies and gents."

He twirled his finger in the air and called for another round. This went on for a few hours until Ryan could no longer taste the bitterness of tequila and his vision begun to waiver.

"Well, boys, me and Miss…" Cato turned to the girl.

"Kate."

"Miss Kate and I regrettably must go and..." He laughed. "Oh, whatever. You guys have a good night."

As they left, Ryan and Damian sat awkwardly with a group of women that didn't look pleased. Emma found it upon herself to sit on Ryan's lap and started to play with his hair. He closed his eyes and started to fall asleep, it felt so good.

"Let's go to my room," she whispered in his ear. He patted her on the leg. "Sorry love, but I'm trying a different flower tonight."

She stood up from his lap. "Are you serious, Ryan?"

"Of course I am." He took a drink of his beer and sat back in his chair. "If I can't find someone else I'll be sure to show up though."

Her mouth gapped open and she looked on the verge of tears. In the corner of his eye he saw Damian shake his head at him. It was rather harsh. Emma stormed out of the tent and Ryan downed the rest of his beer trying not to care.

He grabbed the brunette, sat her on his lap, and the giggles started once more. Another dark haired girl sat on the other side of him and he smirked. "That's better."

Ryan pulled the brunette into a deep kiss as they explored each other's mouths. The other girl seemed jealous and pulled him away from her. She began to kiss him with such intensity he knew she was trying to compete with the other girl.

Her hand worked its way up his thigh and she grabbed in between his legs. He groaned and almost pushed the other girl off his lap until she started in too.

"Ryan." Damian cleared his throat. In his drunken state he ignored his friend—he was enjoying this a little too much. "Ryan!"

Ryan pulled away from the girls annoyed. "What?"

"Calm down."

Both girls began to kiss his neck and his eyes closed. "Why?"

"Show a little couth."

"Show a little elation," he groaned. Damian glared at him. "Fine."

"Can we go?" Damian looked on the verge of passing out.

"You better look me up." He wrote down his room number and he handed it to both of the females. Damian was more important than two random women. "Goodnight, ladies."

With that, he picked up Damian as best he could and they both swayed and tripped out of the tent and into the busy street.

"What was that about?" he asked Damian. "Why are you babying me?"

"The city almost witnessed you having sex." Damian groaned. "Anna didn't even say anything to me."

Ryan adjusted his friend and tried to keep both of them up. "I didn't even see her." What brought that up?

"Exactly!"

"Maybe she didn't go?"

"That's even worse!"

"Okay, maybe she could not find you in the massive crowd of people?" He highly enjoyed a drunk Damian, but when women were involved it was just annoying.

They stumbled over to the horse and buggies that waited for drunks to pay their way home. Ryan found an open one and dropped Damian into it. He tried to hand the hooded man a few coins. "To the Domus, please."

"No charge, sir," he said. "You boys won me plenty of winnings today."

"Thanks."

"So why aren't you two still celebrating?" The horse lunged forward. "I would think you'd be out till dawn."

"I think he celebrated enough for the two of us," Ryan replied, patting a passed out Damian on the back.

Damian groaned.

"He isn't going to puke is he?"

"Takes more than that." Ryan smirked. "At least I think."

The shots had melted into his system slowly. He suddenly felt stupid for getting drunk. He forced his speech not to slur.

"So, how is it that you win every year might I ask?"

Ryan laughed. "Partly dumb luck."

"And the other parts?"

"Horrible competition and lack of experience, I suppose."

"That'll do it."

The driver turned in the opposite direction of the Domus. "Excuse me?"

"Yes, sir?"

"Where are you going?"

"I have orders for you," the man chuckled. "Glad I was the one to get you."

The buggy came to a halt and Ryan reached for his sword

but it was not there and neither was his racing knife. Where was it?

He tried to pick Damian up and get them out of there until the driver barreled into them both. Damian fell out of Ryan's grasp and landed hard on the stone road.

Ryan ended up losing his balance and fell on top of him and Damian grunted. At least Ryan knew he was still alive.

He tried to get to his feet until he was hit in the back of the head. Automatically he turned around fast, swung at the driver and connected with his jaw. "What the hell are you doing?"

"General's orders," the man replied.

Two hooded men came out of the park area where they were stopped and secured Ryan's arms behind his back. They bent him over and started to tie his wrists with a rope. "Gonna have to buy me dinner first, boys."

"Ass," one of the men muttered.

"Can we not talk about my ass while you have me bent over? Thanks."

"What did you say you little-"

"Quit it and just get him tied up," the driver groaned.

Before they bound him, Ryan kicked backwards into one of their knees and a loud crack followed. The man screamed out in pain. The driver pulled out a dagger and put it under his throat. He could feel a small amount of blood trickle down his neck.

"Cheater," Ryan mumbled.

He was in no condition to fight much longer. The adrenaline he had was succumbing to the alcohol in his body and took his mind hostage. He felt a sharp pain on the back of his head and fell into darkness. No dreams came tonight.

Chapter XV

Julia

Julia sat in the library next to a fire and read a book about torture tactics. It was a horrifying book, but she wanted to familiarize herself with it. There was a possibility it would become handy one day. Whips with spikes, crucifixion, implementation—it was terrifying to think it happened to humans. It was completely barbaric.

She had a hard time finding much on the subject. The large library was easy to get lost in with its maze of bookshelves filled to the tall ceiling. No one ever put a book back in its place so it was a jumbled mess of different genres everywhere.

The library door slammed shut and Julia jumped. Emma walked briskly over to her, her face looked furious and Julia felt instantly amused. She remained reclined on the leather couch and waited for the irate girl to come over.

"May I help you?"

"Have you seen Ryan?" She fussed.

"What's it to you?" Julia was thoroughly enjoying this.

"I don't know where he is."

"Well, he isn't here." She sighed. "Probably left with some drunken girl last night. He likes his options you know."

Emma's jaw tightened and Julia felt guilt and anger at the same time. Emma never did anything to Julia, she was just jealous of her. Not once had they had problems until they saw each other as a threat.

"No one has seen him since the night of the races."

"That was two days ago. It's a week long celebration."

"I'm totally aware of that, Julia," she squeaked. "Whatever, I don't care."

Julia watched as she stomped out of the library and worry filled inside of her. This was not like Ryan. He would not stay gone that long, at least she didn't think he would. Maybe he went to smaller parties instead of the highly public ones this year. Something didn't sit right with her though.

Julia set the book in a random open spot and left the library. She checked the training arena, parlor, and even his room, but all were empty. Of course they were. She walked to Damian's room and knocked. No answer.

The last place to look was Cato's room. Perhaps Ryan and Damian passed out on the floor. It was known to happen.

She rapped on the door and her brother opened it wide, revealing himself dressed in only his boxers. Julia quickly turned away as she briefly saw a naked redhead run towards the bathroom.

"Oh Gods," she squealed quietly.

"Well, hello there, sister." Cato laughed.

"Honestly Cato," she started, "I am sick of seeing your cuddle buddies running naked in your room."

"Where else would they be running naked?"

"Shut up."

"You're the one knocking on my door, sister. I don't plan on these things."

She rolled her eyes and as she turned around to look at her brother, she was thankful he started to put a robe on.

"Cato, have you seen Ryan?" Her brother's expression was grim.

"What does it matter to you?" he asked.

"Perhaps it is because he is missing."

His eyebrows rose. "How do you know he is missing?"

"I looked everywhere for him and can't find him," she said.

"Why were you looking for him, Julia?" he grunted.

"Emma came and asked me where he was. She said no one has seen him since the night of the races."

He looked totally unbothered by the news. "Did you look in the training arena?"

"Yes."

"The library?"

"Yes."

Cato sighed and started to close the door. Julia pushed it open and shoved her brother. "What is your deal? Your best friend is missing and you don't care!" She felt her face turn red and she wanted to shake her brother. She knew in her gut Ryan was missing.

"You didn't look everywhere and he is a big boy. He just won the races and every year he spends days on end with random women," he blurted out. "I'm sorry. I know you like the guy, but it's the truth, that's who he is."

"You're wrong."

"I will talk to you later, Julia." He touched her cheek gently.

"If he doesn't come to dinner I will help you look for him, I promise."

She wanted nothing more then to slap her brother. "Fine, but if he is in trouble it's on you."

"Love you, sis, but I'm begging you to stay away from Ryan. He's my friend, but he isn't good for you." Cato kissed her cheek gently and softly closed the door on her.

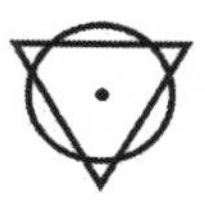

Ryan

A wave of cold water rushed over his body. Ryan gasped for breath as his eyes tried to focus. Someone stood in front of him and chuckled.

"He put up a fight. Not much of one." The man laughed again. "He was easy to get."

"He was drunk and still kicked your ass around a little bit," another man spoke up. "Show some respect at least."

Drops of water fell out of his hair and onto his face. His body ached and he welcomed the cool feeling. As far as he could tell, he had a busted lip and a slow bleeding gash on his eyebrow. Not horrible injuries, but his head killed him.

A stinging pain stabbed into his skull. He tried to move and kick his way free from the chair he was tied to, but it didn't help. He was bound tightly and movement was not an option.

"Stay still, you idiot, she is stitching up your head," the first man spoke. "If it were me I'd let him bleed out."

"Blah, blah, blah, do shut up, Max."

After a moment, Ryan was able to focus on the man—Max.

He was the tall, thin moron in the tunnels. Their eyes glared at each other—Ryan was memorizing his features. He had a name now and Ryan knew what he looked like. *What an idiot for showing his face.*

Each time the needle went into his skin, Ryan gritted his teeth from the pain and many inappropriate words came to mind.

"Has the other one woken up yet?" Max asked.

"No, he is sleeping off the alcohol."

Damian must be here. Ryan panicked inside, but the needle that was stitching him back together made him loose focus.

Snip.

"Finally. Now get out," Max growled.

Ryan heard a woman huff out of annoyance and a door slammed closed. His eyes were in total focus now and he could tell by his surroundings that they were somewhere above ground in an upper class home.

Shelves fully stocked with books surrounded the walls and the floor was made of real wood. He assumed there were windows hidden behind the thick red curtains that reached down to the stained glass littered floor.

This was obviously a library of some sort, but there were high backed chairs in the room. In the middle sat a large throne that towered over the rest. He sat on the opposite side of the room and the only source of light came from tall candles on the floor lining the walls.

He looked to his side. Damian was tied to another chair. He looked fine expect for a small bruise on his cheek. *What's going on?*

Max grabbed under Ryan's jaw and forced his gaze to meet his. "So, this is the almighty Ryan."

"In the flesh," he croaked.

"Bet you never thought you'd end up in this type of situation." Max grinned. "Ryan, Mr. Warrior of the year. Can't see what the fuss is all about."

"Someone obviously wasn't loved as a child."

"I mean, honestly," Max went on, "if you are so great, how did you get caught so easily?"

"Excuse me for not thinking my fellow Immortals would attack me when I was intoxicated." Ryan looked Max up and down. "You don't seem to be a Warrior, you're a little too brittle. Bet your parents were embarrassed when you popped out."

The sound of flesh against flesh rang out as Ryan felt his cheek turn warm and tingle. *What kind of man slaps another man?*

"Enough," the other man spoke. "We were told not to touch them until the General got here."

"A little slap won't do much." Max smirked.

"Yes, especially when it feels like a baby kitten swatting a fly." Ryan grinned. He could taste blood and swallowed it down.

Max's eyes burned with hatred and Ryan's grin grew wider. Max was an easy target and his anger could work in Ryan's favor.

Damian groaned and Ryan's attention went to him. As he pulled on his ropes, Damian seemed to sober up instantly. "What the-"

"Morning, sunshine." Ryan sighed.

"What the hell did you get us into now, Ryan?" Damian groaned.

"These fine gent's kidnapped us and we are evidently going to get the pleasure of meeting the General," Ryan stated. "Horrible name by the way. The General. Must have been a short meeting when you all decided on that one."

"Show some respect you little twit," Max screamed.

"Did you just call me a pregnant goldfish?" Ryan raised his eyebrow and turned to Damian. "Damian, you're the father."

"Ryan," Damian groaned, "shut up."

"Listen to your friend," the other man spoke. "There will be plenty of time to talk when the General gets here."

"Besides that is just a made up rumor. Twit doesn't mean a pregnant goldfish," the other man chimed in. His friend looked at him and rolled his eyes. "What? It doesn't."

Ryan closed his eyes and sat back in his chair, trying to get as comfortable as he could. Julia appeared in his mind. Would he ever get the chance to tell her how he truly felt? She was probably better off without him, but he had a feeling she would want revenge for both of them if they were killed. He didn't want her in harms way.

He should probably quit insulting them so that didn't happen.

That was going to be difficult.

The door creaked open and in walked a tall, extremely muscular man. He wore a long black cloak with the hood pulled over his face. Ryan could not make out who it was.

"Gentlemen," the man said. His movements were smooth as if he were gliding across the floor. Each step was silent, even for his large, muscular build.

"Excuse me for the manner in which you were brought here." His voice was deep and steady. "I'm sure you are aware we have to take certain precautions with men of your status."

"I'm flattered." Ryan tugged on his ropes.

"Again," the General spoke, "precautions. You two have survived longer then almost anyone in creation and there is obviously a reason for it."

"Lack of idiocy?" Damian asked.

Great, while Ryan was trying to watch what he said, Damian finally decided to find some balls.

"Perhaps." The General walked to a table full of sharp instruments. Some looked surgical and others just extremely painful.

His fingers glided gently over the tools and Ryan's chest tightened. He had experience with being tortured and was not looking forward to it again.

"So, why are we here?" Ryan asked.

"I want you to join our ranks," he replied simply. "You would be a valuable asset to our cause. Training those with little experience."

"What like tiny Tim over there?" Ryan glared at Max, who glared back with his fists clenched tightly.

The General chuckled softly and picked up a long curved knife. "Maybe."

"No thanks," Damian replied. "We aren't traitors living an unrealistic dream."

"Oh, but you are." The General walked over to Damian, the knife hanging by his side. "Your dream was to protect mankind, was it not? To be the instruments of the Gods to make the world a better place?"

"Duh," Ryan spat.

"That was good and noble of you back then, but what now?" he asked. "We no longer live in an age were the young rule the world and die early. Leaders today are old and near death. What use are we? We went from being kings and leaders to being pathetic errand boys that have two-hour missions. The only joy you have is killing a pitiful little terrorist that is throwing a tantrum. We are obsolete now. It's time we reclaim our glory."

Ryan was slowly gaining knowledge about the General. One, he was a man and two, he was definitely a Warrior that had experience in the field and has quit. Ryan needed to stretch this out and try to get more information.

"Our whole existence is to serve the Gods. Betraying them is going against our very being," Ryan said. "We are just men, we have no authority to question them."

Ryan did feel useless lately. The General was speaking the truth about that. The older generations had the power now and here they were frozen in their twenties. Powerful leaders no longer died at an early age from charging head first into battle. Long-term missions didn't exist anymore.

The last time any Warrior had to make a life in the mortal world was over a hundred years ago and they were pushing the age limit.

Ryan glanced over at Damian, who looked as if he were just slapped in the face. His expression was grim and his eyes stayed glued to the floor.

"That is your problem, Ryan," the General said. "Your faith runs too deep."

"Yes, it does."

The General sighed and held the knife casually up to Ryan's neck. "I'd prefer if you didn't make me force information out of you. It would be so much easier if you would just join us and give it up freely."

Ryan laughed. "Information? So that's what you really want?"

"What I want is an inside man, someone with extreme skill and the abilities of a leader. You, of all people, have astounding leadership skills and you have proven that since you were a mortal." The knife dug into his neck and Ryan resisted the urge to shallow. "However, if I can't have you join my ranks, I will make you as useful as I possibly can."

"Do whatever you have to, Mr. General. There's no way in hell I will join you or tell you a damn thing." Ryan smirked and leaned back in his chair casually. "On with the show."

"Wait."

Ryan turned to Damian and his friend would not meet his eyes.

"Yes?" the General asked.

"What exactly are you wanting to know?" Damian asked.

Even the General looked taken aback. Ryan's mouth dropped open and Damian's glare still would not reach Ryan's eyes.

"I want to know the Domus' defense system. How much you really know about us. So on and so fourth."

"If we told you would you let us go?" Damian pleaded.

"What the hell are you doing?" Ryan growled.

Damian ignored him and asked again, "Would you?"

The General stood still for a second—the knife gleamed, taunting them with a deadly fate. "Perhaps."

Damian laughed coldly. "Never mind then, old man. We aren't idiots, I can tell you have no intention of letting us go."

Ryan sighed in relief, for a second there he thought he'd lost his best friend. They now knew what the General wanted from them and that was better then nothing. They were going to target the Domus. However, they officially had no chance of getting out of this one.

"Have it your way then." The General sliced a deep gash in Ryan's forearm.

Ryan bit his lip hard and tried to suppress a scream. His breathed deeply and closed his eyes. "What was the point in stitching me up just to cut into me again?" he growled.

The General chuckled and even though he could not see it, Ryan knew he was smiling. "A simple attempt to show good faith. That kindness has certainly run its course."

Another gash opened on his shoulder. Ryan grunted and held back the scream he knew this man craved. The blood dripped from his arms and started to splatter on the floor. This was nothing but a smidgeon of pain he knew he was about to endure.

From behind, he felt a board sliding down the back of his chair and smack against the floor. He could barely turn around to see what they were doing and noticed the board had two holes behind his head. A rope was weaved in and out of the holes with enough slack for his neck to slide in between.

On the back part of the board, a thick stick had the ends of the rope tied tightly around it. *Shit.* Ryan knew this device and was not looking forward to it being used on him.

Someone put the rope around his neck and started to twist the stick around, the rope began to tighten.

"Quit it!" Damian growled. "He isn't the only one here."

No, Damian, just let me suffer. Ryan wanted to say, but words would not form. The rope got tighter and he began to choke. He felt his shoulder slice open and could not scream if he wanted to. There was nothing he could do but take the pain.

"Sorry, Damian, but it seems your deepest punishment is to see your dearest friend suffer. You two have always been close." The General walked back to his table and dropped the bloodied knife. He picked up a hammer-like tool with short spikes sticking out the end.

Ryan could feel his heart about to jump out of his chest. Damian yanked desperately on his ropes and tried to get free. It was no use. The knots were expertly tied and he had no room to wiggle his arms or legs free.

"Don't you dare," Damian said forcefully. Ryan's vision started to blur until the rope lessened. He coughed uncontrollably.

"This is exactly the reaction he wants from you," Ryan managed to say. "Calm down, you've seen me in worse circumstances."

"No, this is bad," Damian hissed. "You're my brother, blood or not."

"Again, he knows that and you're giving him what he wants." Ryan smirked.

Damian leaned his head back on the chair and stared at the ceiling. If it were reversed, Ryan could not bare the sight. Damian was pure good and maybe this was Ryan's punishment from all the bad karma he created from himself.

He turned his attention back to his new favorite crazy person and sighed. "On with it."

"Are you sure you will not reconsider?"

"I've given you my answer."

The General brought the hammer down hard on Ryan's leg and there was no way he could suppress the screams that escaped his mouth. He could feel his flesh being pulled off his leg and the wound quickly drenched his pants with blood.

Max roared with laughter and his friend stood beside him with a smile. The person behind him chuckled quietly as Ryan yelled a few curse words, his breath coming in and out quicker. "Well that sucked."

Damian continued to look at the ceiling and the General brought the hammer down on Ryan's other thigh. Ryan bit his lip so hard he drew blood and scrunched his eyes tightly closed.

A loud grunt escaped his lips as the man pulled the hammer off his leg. He saw spots in front of his eyes.

"Just give me some information, Ryan, and I promise I will end it quickly." The General almost sounded remorseful.

"Going to take more than that, cupcake," he heaved out.

"Very well." He dropped the hammer on the table and the General's hand hovered over the many instruments. He picked up a whip with many leather straps hanging down from it. Each strand contained a spike at the end.

Ryan closed his eyes. Just one strike from this whip could tear flesh to shreds.

"Untie him."

Max and the other man walked briskly to Ryan and untied him. Ryan struggled against them, but it was no use. His legs felt like Jell-O when he put weight on them and his arms stung.

They retied his hands in front of him and he stood there at the mercy of his captor. His legs shook from the pain and he hoped they didn't think he was frightened. Deep down, he somewhat was.

They dragged him to where chains hung from the ceiling, behind his chair. Max yanked his arms up above his head and tied them to one of the chains. He was not going anywhere and he didn't dare to look at Damian. Max ripped his shirt off and he felt the chill of night on his bare skin.

"Don't have any smart ass comments now, do you?" Max grinned.

"Your mom tied me up like this last night. Are you going to get on your knees too?" Max hit him square in the jaw and walked out of sight.

With his arms raised high, Ryan prayed to the Gods silently. Never had he endured this type of pain he inflicted on so many others. The only torture he endured was minimal at best. He prepared himself for the first snap.

He heard a chair scrape the ground and Damian suddenly came into view. His friend's eyes welled up and looked away.

"Watch," the General commanded.

"No." Damian refused to look at him.

"If you don't, I will cut your eyelids off and make you watch."

Damian refused to look at him. "It's okay, Damian. I'll be fine."

It was a lie, but he was glad it was him rather then Damian. Max grabbed Damian's head and forced him to look at Ryan. Ryan didn't look away. He needed reassurance from his friend while he waited for the whip.

"May I, General?" the hooded man that'd twisted the stick finally spoke. "You have no idea how much I would enjoy it."

With momentary hesitation the General replied, "Certainly."

What the hell was this guy's problem?

The man walked by Ryan and he could feel his eyes on him from under the hood. He disappeared behind him and Ryan heard the snap of the whip. The flesh tore off his body as the man pulled it back. Was that him screaming? It seemed unrecognizable and not his own.

Another snap and his body dropped from the pain.

He began to shake uncontrollably. His back was red hot as he hung limply by his wrists, watching the blood pooling below him. Damian yelled something he could not hear clearly. The world disappeared.

Chapter XVI

Julia

It had been a week and there was still no sign of Ryan or Damian, a fact well known to all of Urbs as well as the Domus.

Usually, the weeklong festival after the races celebrated the victors—and the victors were obviously missing. Ryan had never missed the event and his absence became a popular topic throughout Urbs.

Julia was sick with worry. She had spent her nights searching the streets, tunnels, and asking anyone for possible information. No one had any idea where they were and it was a constant thorn in her mind.

Cato was a wreck and started to blame himself for what happened. Julia constantly had to remind him it was not his fault, but he never believed it. He kept saying he should have been there with them or looked harder for them when they first went missing. He was inconsolable.

Ahmose comforted them as much as possible, everyday, by

saying they had been missing longer than this before. His reassurance was not believable due to the worried look that seemed stuck of his face.

As Julia walked along the beach with Grace, she tried to make pleasant conversation and was failing miserably at it. No part of her wanted to be here, she wanted to be out searching, but Ahmose ordered her to take a break.

Thank the Gods for Grace, she was trying to gossip, but Julia had no interest in it.

"...then she just ignored Anna and burst through the doors," Grace finished.

"I cannot believe Colette is still having a problem with Anna. It makes no sense," Julia added. "I thought they were getting along better with one another?"

"Colette has a hard time letting things go, you know that." It was not a pleasant conversation exactly, but she appreciated Grace for trying to keep her mind off everything that was going on. "Maybe it's her race, beliefs, or the fact that Damian likes her?"

Julia's eyes widened. "What?"

Grace laughed and plopped down in the white sand, Julia followed suit.

"Colette likes Damian." Grace smirked.

"There is no way! She has never shown the slightest interest in Damian, or any guy for that matter."

"She hides her feelings very well, I'll give you that." Grace smiled softly. "She only told me after I had a very long, intense conversation with her about her attitude lately."

Julia shook her head and gazed out at the ocean. She loved it out here—it was so peaceful and serene on the surface and chaos underneath.

The water glistened blue under the sun as the face of the ocean slept. Light spray from the water kissed her cheeks and eased the endless heat of the day. A soft breeze whisked its way through her yellow sundress and she closed her eyes. Only the sound of strong waves pounding the rocks could break her momentary serenity.

"He is fine, my dear," Grace interrupted her thoughts.

Apparently she had been silent for a while.

"I hope so," was all she could manage to say.

The women watched as a little white sailboat came into view around a gathering of rocks. Julia watched the man pull in his net in hopes for fish, which had obviously failed. She could hear him cursing at the sea as if Neptune could hear him.

A small smile melted on her lips.

Grace was good company, she didn't need to be constantly entertained and relished in the silence. They sat there for hours until the sun barely peaked over the horizon.

She always loved this time of day. It was like a painting was set out before her. Purple, orange, and pink mixed beautifully together into a masterpiece of nature. Only the divine could create such beauty.

Her mother had always told her the Gods paint the sunset and sunrise everyday. Just the thought of Jupiter or Triglav wearing overalls and holding paintbrushes would make anyone grin.

"Well, my dear, I think I will call it a night." Grace stood up and brushed the sand off her legs. "Please try to get some sleep tonight. You're no use to anyone barely functioning."

"Yeah, okay." Julia forced a smile. She was somewhat relieved for the solitude.

When Grace was out of sight Julia laid back in the sand and

stared up at the night sky. She thought of her mother and father.

If they were alive, would they be proud of her? Would they wonder why she never bore a child throughout all these years? She could not help but think she failed them in some sense.

They lived their lives without fear, without regret, and look where they are now. Ashes. Nothing left of their legacy, but two children that never added to the family name. Her mother always wanted a grandchild, but Julia was too stubborn to settle down.

She wanted battle, she hungered for it and so did Cato. They were made for the fight and parenthood seemed utterly boring. Risky.

Her thoughts went to Ryan. He was somewhere out there and she knew it. She had to believe he was alive and well. She felt guilty because Damian was gone too. How could she forget about him?

At some point she must have fallen asleep. She was startled awake by Ricky, the grounds keeper in the Domus, as he yelled her name and ran towards her. He was a fit, Laotian man that Julia matched up to in height.

On occasion she saw a few Warrior women giggle at his presence and fawn over him. He was a fairly good-looking man, she had to admit, but his comedic nature classified him firmly in the friend zone for her.

He fell down beside her—his breathing was fast and sweat dripped from his brow. "Julia."

"Are you okay?" She almost laughed. He started to cough from exasperation.

"Yep." He coughed. "Been looking… everywhere… for you."

"What is it?" She sat up quickly.

"It's Ryan and Damian," he said quickly.

She clutched his shoulders and stared deeply into his eyes. "This better not be a joke."

"No joke," he choked out.

"Where?"

"Their bodies were hung… outside The Great Temple."

Her heart dropped.

Their bodies.

Hung.

She struggled to get out of the sand and ran towards the stable to grab a horse.

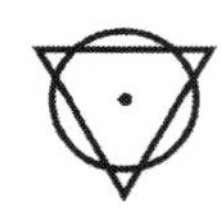

Julia

She rode fiercely down the stone road towards The Great Temple. Julia didn't know whose horse she had—she had just grabbed one and rode bareback.

Ryan, dead.

His body hanging.

Blood.

Lots of blood.

These thoughts played through her mind like a broken record and her heart ached more than she had ever felt before.

It was childish to hope for the best. The hope of Ryan returning to her arms, unharmed and with a stupid drunken story of what had happened to them.

The Gods truly curse me, she thought.

She neared the Great Temple and saw a large crowd had

already formed. They spread apart to let her pass as she drove the horse forward without hesitation. She could hear a few angry shouts at her, she didn't care though, she needed to see him.

As the two bodies came into view, she instantly slipped off the horse and fell to her knees. Her breath was stuck in her chest as she took in the gruesome sight of the men she'd know since her birth.

One of them was a brother-like figure and the other the love of her existence. They both laid motionless at the top of the steps of the Great Temple—at least she thought it was them. They were both shirtless and even from this distance she could see the gashes and bruises on their skin. Blood seemed to stain their entire bodies and it was hard to make out who was who.

Cato stood up from the side of one of the bodies and made his way over to her. He fell to his knees and blocked her view of the two men. She longed to look around him. Cato grabbed her face gently and forced her to look into his teary eyes.

"Julia," he said softly, "go home. You don't need to see this."

"Is it him?" she choked out. If it was Ryan, she had to know.

"Yes."

Her eyes closed and her brother embraced her. She would not cry. She could not. She had to be strong for the civilian's sake. If the Warriors showed weakness how could they possibly believe in them?

She could not breath, she started to panic and Cato held her close. Her head rest on his chest as he smoothed away her hair from her face. It was like being a child again.

"They are alive, Julia," he cooed. "Ahmose is getting a cart to bring them back to the Domus so the healers can work on them."

Her eyes shot open and she tried to pull away, his grip was

tight on her though. "I have to see him."

"I am begging you, go home." He struggled to constrain her.

"Please," she pleaded. "I have to see them."

"Don't get your hopes up, Julia, they are barely with us." Her brother looked on the verge of tears, but he held his feelings back well. "They were hung by their wrists, above the doors, and we barely got them down."

Julia pushed her brother off as hard as she could and ran over to Ryan. It had to be him, his hair was darker and his body was more muscular. However, it was hard to tell through all the blood and open gashes on his body.

She dropped down to him and whispered in his ear, "Ryan?"

He didn't move or show any sign that he heard her. All she could do was cry. There was no containing the feelings that swept over her. He looked ruined. Deformed, almost to the point of being unrecognizable.

She glanced over at Damian, who was obviously in much better condition than Ryan, and clearly saw his chest move up and down. Thank the Gods. He was far less bloody and she could at least recognize him.

Anna curiously came out of the crowd and began to walk up the stairs once she saw Julia. Thankfully, Ahmose pulled up with the cart and prevented anyone from getting closer. Anna stood aside and remained as part of the crowd.

"It was the Risen," Cato said dryly as he walked up behind Julia.

"Why would they do this?" she asked. "What is the point of this?"

Ahmose and Cato gently picked up Damian and briskly, but carefully, went down the steps. They placed him on the straw-bedded cart and ran up the stairs to get Ryan.

"You should really go home, Julia. I will let you know what happens," Cato said gently.

"No, I am staying with him." She followed Ahmose and Cato down the steps as they carried Ryan's limp body to the cart. She had never seen him so lifeless—it was a haunting sight. Small drops of blood made a path from the Great Temple to the cart and she held back her tears as she climbed into the bed of the cart.

"Move aside!" Ahmose yelled at the crowd. He sat in the coach seat and snapped a whip in the air to make the horses lurch forward.

The crowd grew silent. Perhaps out of respect or just out of pure curiosity to find out what was happening, she didn't care.

In the cart, she cradled Ryan's head on her knees and steadied his face in between her hands. Her eyes didn't leave his body. His swollen face was almost beyond recognition. Deep wounds covered his chest with both fresh and dried blood. He must have been tortured for quite some time.

The brutality humans were capable of still amazed her. The ability to beat someone past consciousness was horrifying and for what reason? A message? Some sick twisted game?

No one deserved this.

Chapter XVII

Julia

THEY SAT IN THE waiting room outside the healers quarters. Cato had his head tilted back on his chair next to Julia and Anna was curled up fast asleep on the couch across the room. She had heard what had happened and came straight to the healers quarters.

Caleb had left a couple of hours ago and had given his sympathies to them. She was quite surprised when he asked to be kept in the loop on how they were doing and gave her a hug. They never seemed that close.

Julia continued to stare down at her blood stained hands. Never had she thought she would be covered in Ryan's blood. Cato looked worse. He had carried both bodies to and from the cart and his blue shirt was covered in red.

"You love him, don't you?" Cato spoke up.

Julia removed her eyes from her hands and watched her brother carefully. His eyes were glued to the ceiling.

"Yes." Her voice was barely a whisper.

He closed his eyes and sighed. "Have you slept with him?"

"Cato!"

"Only asking." He shrugged. "Not judging."

Her hands became her focus. She could not look at Cato and talk about this. It was far too awkward.

"No," she muttered. "I mean we slept in the same bed but we just slept."

"That's surprising." Cato chuckled. Even as his friends were on the verge death he could find the amusement in her love life. "I guess Ryan isn't as charming and desirable as he boasts."

"For your information he kept pushing me away," she spat and glared at her brother now.

A mixture of shock and confusion washed over his face. "What?"

"Can we please try to concentrate on them?" she interrupted. "Or have you forgotten your best friends are lying bloody and dying?"

He sat up and from the expression he wore, he was about to get angry with her. Before a fight could ensue, the door opened and out came Ahmose.

She jumped out of her seat, followed by Cato. Ahmose smiled gently. "They are doing well. We lost them for a minute, but they came back to us."

Julia grinned and pushed past him into the healers quarters. The healers were applying a brown salve to the many stitches and smaller scrapes. They paused and looked up at her.

"What is that?"

"For infection," one of them told her. They were dressed in modern-day blue surgical scrubs and were still cleaning the blood off the men's bodies. Both men had oxygen masks on and she was thankful for the steady sound of the beeping monitors.

She walked slowly up to Ryan and with his body cleaned of blood the amount of wounds he had was astonishing. His body looked worse then a Frankenstein movie, his skin just as pale.

Her heart sunk when she realized his hair was gone. It was buzzed down short, but thankfully, not bald. There were a few small rows of stitches on the side of his head and she realized they had to do it. *It's just hair, it will grow back.*

"They lost a lot of blood, but we are replenishing their systems," another healer added.

"Thank you," she whispered.

Cato walked into the room as they finished applying the brown salve. He thanked the dealers as they left the room before he bent over a sleeping Damian. His face was free of wounds and his hair was slicked back in its usual manner.

"I'll find them. I promise," he whispered in Damian's ear.

Julia felt horrible for making it seem as if Cato didn't care about Ryan and Damian. Her brother never loved anyone more than he loved them—they were family. Even if Ryan and him bickered, it went without saying they would die for each other.

Cato stood up straight and stared at them. He seemed to be finally taking in the severity of their mutilated flesh. "This is all my fault."

"No."

"If I had just stayed with them-"

"Then you would be on a table too," she interrupted. "I can barely handle this and to think of it happening to you, I just..."

Tears filled her eyes and she found herself being embraced by her brother again. "I'm sorry."

Ahmose walked in looking exhausted and troubled. His dark skin beaded with sweat and his clothes were stained like

Cato's. He dropped down onto a chair. "I need to talk to you two."

"What is it?" Cato asked.

"They carved a message in Ryan's chest," he said, making Julia cringe.

She looked down at Ryan and saw he was right. There were letters on his body, but from the stitches and brown clay, she could not read it.

The war was beginning. They were finally going to take action and this was the opening act.

"What was the message?" she asked.

"The message said, 'Ahmose.'"

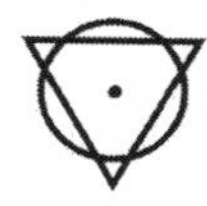

Julia

Julia stared at Ahmose's name carved hastily in Ryan's chest. The message was clear. They were after him now.

"Why would they do this?" she asked.

"I have no idea. If they are threatening me, why would they warn me of it?" Ahmose studied Ryan's chest. She didn't like the way he looked at Ryan. Examining him like a grotesque clue instead of a person.

Gently, she felt the short hair of Ryan's head and sighed. Their bodies were cleaned of blood, but the bruises and wounds remained. She could not imagine the pain they endured and a shiver whisked its way up her spine.

This was not Ryan in front of her. This mutilated man was nearly unrecognizable to the point she even doubted it was him.

It was though. The small scar on his chin made reality set in.

Ahmose walked around Ryan and Damian's bodies, his eyes showed no sign of grief anymore. Instead she only saw anger burning inside the calmest individual she had ever met.

"Are you okay?" her voice was barely a whisper.

Without a word, he fled out of the room, the door crashing behind him. Julia flinched at the sound of the door slamming and choked back tears.

"I'll check on him," Cato mumbled as he left the room.

She grabbed a chair, sat next to Ryan's bed and felt the desire to hold his hand, but the cuts were so extensive even his fingers were a mess.

Silence filled the room and all she could do was think about Ryan. All the heartache he has endured, constantly trying to prove his reputation and above all, his undying loyalty towards the people around him. The complexity of this man lying before her was so deep and so vast—it would be nearly impossible to describe him with a single word.

She could not help it, she needed to see what was done to him. Slowly she pulled back the thin sheet covering his lower body. His thighs had long gashes so deep, she was thankful they didn't hit a major artery. There was meat clever looking marks on his thighs and she remembered something like that in the book she read in the library.

His feet were the most disturbing part. They were perfectly fine, not one scratch on them. It was odd how his entire body was harmed except there.

"Humph."

Julia jumped and quickly covered Ryan with the sheet. Damian stared at her with a somewhat amused expression. She rushed over to him and gently laid her hand against his cheek. "Damian, thank the Gods you're okay."

He studied her for a moment, watching her eyes with intense displeasure. "What were you looking at, exactly?" he croaked.

Flabbergasted, she rubbed the back of her neck. "I was, um, just seeing what all happened."

"Don't worry, that area was spared." He tried to smirk, but the cut on his lip reopened. He winced and lay his head back down. "This is the worst we have ever endured."

Her eyes threatened to tear up again. She grabbed his hand and sat down on his bed. He cringed as the sheets she sat on dragged slightly across his body. Julia instantly felt horrible.

Damian chuckled. "You have the biggest heart, Julia."

"I just don't like seeing you two this way," she said. "I've always looked up to you and here you are, nearing death."

"I'll be fine," he assured her. "How is Ryan?"

Her silence betrayed her and his eyes closed shut. His chest rose faster as his breathing quickened. The heart monitor raced and she turned to call someone. A weak hand thwarted her efforts and she turned back towards him. There was an undeniable sadness in his expression. "Please, don't."

"Okay," she whispered.

"Did he just now die?"

"Oh no! Oh my, I didn't mean he was dead." She glanced over at Ryan. "He hasn't woken up yet. His heartbeat is faint, but it hasn't failed."

"He got the worst of it." He sighed. "Even when he passed out from the pain they continued in on him."

"What did they want?"

"Information." He cringed. "Ryan, of course, was being a

smart ass with them."

Julia glanced at him. "They cut off his hair."

Damian weakly lifted his head then let it fall back against his pillow. "He is going to be furious. I've never seen it short."

He lifted his head again and stared over at Ryan. She could not begin to figure out what was going on in his mind. The heart monitor started to slowly quicken, but his face was set in stone. "It doesn't even look like it's him," he mumbled.

"Julia!" Cato burst through the door—he didn't seem to notice Damian was awake. "Ahmose is gone!"

Chapter XVIII

Ryan

Lights faded in and out.

Everything is numb.

Is this the end?

Is this death?

Chapter XIX

Julia

Weeks passed by and there was still no sign of Ahmose anywhere. Search parties swept the city for days, to no avail. The Immortals were terrified and some even locked themselves inside their homes in fear of the Risen.

Julia was exhausted. Ryan still showed no signs of waking up and she was running low on energy. She led every search party, assigned jobs for the Warriors, and when she had time to herself, remained by Ryan's side.

Cato was no help. His thirst for vengeance blinded him into a rage and he viewed everyone as a possible traitor.

Damian limped next to her, a cane in his right hand. He leaned against the balcony of the parlor and stared out into the ocean. She tore her gaze away from the crashing waves and looked at him with sullen eyes. His body was healing slowly, yet he insisted he felt better everyday.

He wore all black sweats and his hair had begun to get

shaggy. A thick beard filled his face and she smirked. She was not used to his disheveled appearance, but as of late, he didn't seem to care about it. "You look like hell."

Not looking at her, he replied, "Have you seen yourself, lately?"

It was true, her clothes were a dirt-covered mess and her hair matched her disheveled appearance. Showering was not an option the past few days and her gear was starting to smell.

"Any changes with him?" she asked about Ryan.

"No."

Ryan started to look like himself again. His hair grew out a little more, but it was still not very long. His face had begun to heal and thanks to the healers, it would not be very scarred. He did, however, suffer head trauma and there were no signs of him coming around.

When Damian was well enough, he told them what happened when they were captured. They were taken to a home, tortured and interrogated, and after a while they were separated into different rooms. When they were done with him, he could still hear Ryan's screams for hours. When things got silent, they drug Ryan's limp body, by his hair, into Damian's room and continued to carve into him.

He was forced to sit and watch them mutilate Ryan's unconscious body, just for the fun of it. Neither of them would reveal any information. The last thing he remembered was being hit on the head with a bat and then he woke up in the healers quarters.

Julia heard footsteps and watched as Caleb made his way across the room. "Come see the news in Germany."

Julia, followed slowly by Damian, made her way towards the newsroom. She had assigned Caleb to watch the mortal news channels for any sign of anything unusual. With everything going on they could not afford for the mortals to be injured by this personal vendetta.

Emma came out of nowhere and stopped in front of Julia, a scowl set on her face as the two girls glared at each other.

"May I help you?" Julia growled.

"Why have you banned me from seeing Ryan? You are not the leader of this house. You have no say in what anyone can or can't do." Annoyance grew in her stomach.

"You are correct, Emma. I am not the leader," she stated. "Do you see anyone else stepping up though? How about you step in as acting Ahmose? I'm sure so much will get done with you in charge."

She seemed to ignore that part. "He needs me, Julia. He cares about me deeply and you are ruining everything."

Julia, annoyed and frustrated, pushed past Emma and the two boys followed. Damian didn't bother to hide his laugh when Emma squealed in distain. "Mark my words, Julia, I will see him and you will regret it."

"Doubt it," she mumbled.

They reached the newsroom and Caleb opened the door for her and Damian. The room was full of televisions that held every countries' basic cable stations. From ceiling to floor there was nothing but fifty-two inch TV's all around. A single desk sat in the middle of the room. It was a way to keep an eye on the outside world and shamefully Julia had gotten attached to reality TV.

"That girl is insane," Caleb muttered. It was extremely out of character for Caleb to talk bad about anyone and it threw her off.

"Love will do that to you." *Even when not returned*, Julia

thought.

"She talks like she's in a soap opera," said Caleb. "This is the Days of our Lives."

She walked over to the right side of the room and stared at the German news. The Chancellor of Germany was in the middle of denouncing Christianity as a religion.

"...and foremost, we should not believe in a dead God who never answers us. We should not believe in a God that never proves His existence. Instead, we must look towards the future and trust in the those that prove their divinity."

Chaos erupted. Screams of disapproval blared out of the television and they watched as people began to brawl in the street. Women clutched their children trying to protect them from the enraged crowd. A few people were being rounded up into squad cars and whisked away.

The Chancellor calmly spoke back into the microphone and the sound of the crowd was replaced. "If anyone tries to defy the ban of old religions, you will be persecuted and potentially executed for crimes against your country."

"Germany has gone nuts."

"It's not just them, Damian," Caleb replied. "The same thing happened in Turkey, Brazil, and India."

"Have a wonderful day my fellow countrymen and let the real Gods bless us all for eternity."

"This makes no sense whatsoever. Why would they suddenly do this? What could the Risen possibly have done to persuade them to abandon centuries of tradition?" Julia was in utter disbelief. They were doing it. They were actually succeeding in changing all religion. It had to be them.

They all watched as protestors were arrested and thrown into police vehicles. People were being beaten and trampled in the crowd. Julia thought she heard gunshots and then the screen turned black. The news was cut off and silence filled the room.

"Well," Damian grunted.

"This is bad."

"Very bad," said Caleb.

Chapter XX

Anna

Anna paced back and forth in her room. Her new cat, Calypso, watched her intently. Her tail swished over the crumpled up blankets on Anna's bed.

She was feeling lonely without anyone to talk to in the Domus and apparently pets were allowed. Calypso was barely older than a kitten and was roaming the streets when Anna came across her.

Her white fur was caked in so much dry mud, Anna didn't realize her feet were the only black part of her body until she washed her. Calypso had walked up to her with no fear and rubbed against her leg purring loudly. Anna fell instantly in love.

"I should go see him, right?" Anna paused and looked at Calypso for an answer. Calypso laid her head on her front paws and closed her eyes. "Thanks for the help."

Anna flopped down on her bed and stared up at the ceiling.

Her room was a mess. Julia hated coming in here and only stood in the doorway.

Clothes littered the floor and books were spread out all over her desk and couches. Military or not, she was never a neat and tidy person. Calypso didn't seem to mind, in fact, she liked all the potential bed space.

"Why am I being dumb?" She scratched Calypso's head. "It's not like I did anything wrong. I can just go see how he is doing, right?"

Calypso jumped off the bed and curled up on a pile of dirty clothes by her closet. Her backside plopped down facing Anna.

"Well, excuse me." She tossed a pillow in the cat's direction, narrowly missing her. Calypso didn't even flinch.

Anna hopped up and grabbed a pair of black shorts that hung on her desk chair. She changed into them and a blue T-shirt. As she left, she tossed Calypso a cat treat before closing her door.

She walked briskly towards the male dormitories, not paying attention to her surroundings and trying to figure out what to say to him. Her stomach did flips, her heart thumped loudly in her chest, and she felt like she was going to pass out from either excitement or nerves.

Would he slam the door in her face or invite her in?

What would she do if he invited her in?

What was she planning to say?

Before she could answer any of her questions, she arrived at his door. "Oh, balls." Her fist hovered over his door and she bounced on the balls of her feet. To knock, or not to knock, that was the question.

She knocked.

She waited.

Just when she was about to give up, the door opened. There stood Damian, in his underwear, leaning on a cane. His hair was a mess and his body was covered in cuts that were scabbed over. Her mouth dropped and her eyes welled up. It was like he got in a fight with a tiger and lost.

"I know I'm not much to look at, but geez." He smirked.

She shook out her stare. "Oh my God, I'm so sorry. It's just -"

"Shocking?"

"Exactly."

"Looks worse than it feels at this point." He waved her in. "However, it did feel worse than it looked when it happened."

Anna followed him inside. He was another super clean individual. All his furniture was made of dark wood with dark floors to match. It looked gorgeous against the white walls. Books were everywhere and his white bed was the only messy part. "Did I wake you up?"

"Yes, but it's fine."

She instantly felt bad. "I can leave if you want?"

He shook his head and walked over to his white fabric couch, he offered her a seat next to him. "It's fine, I promise."

He sat down after her. "Thanks."

"So, what's up?"

She shifted uncomfortably and noticed him watching her every move. He studied people like he could read them. Maybe he could.

"I just wanted to say I am sorry about the whole kissing thing and sorry that I didn't come see you before now and that I just..." She breathed. "I'm just sorry."

His right eyebrow arched. "Why are you sorry?"

Now she was confused. She had worked herself up for this

and it seemed like it didn't bother him at all. Maybe he was over her already and had moved on. It would make sense, after all he has lived for a long time and must be used to getting over people quickly.

Her expression must have been funny because he chuckled. Her eyebrows scrunched in confusion. "What?"

"You."

"What about me?" Now she was on the defensive.

"Why would you need to be sorry for anything? You can't help how you feel about me." He leaned back and relaxed, which made her relax. "As for not seeing me, well, yeah, you're a jerk."

His grin made her calm down and breathe easier. He was not mad and everything was fine, though part of her wanted him to be upset with her. She wanted to see if he still liked her or not and it seemed like the later.

"I heard how bad it was and I just don't think I could have handled it."

"I don't blame you, I wouldn't want to see you that way either." He laid his head against the backrest.

She caught herself starring at his chest—she could still see his muscles through his battered body. Before she looked further south she jerked her eyes up. He was smiling at her.

"May I help you with something?"

She blushed. "Like?"

"I won't go there," he chuckled.

"Does it hurt?" She reached out to touch his chest.

"Not really."

She placed her hand on his skin and traced the cuts on his body. In the corner of her eye she could see his eyes flutter. His breathing slowed and her heart raced. She had not been this close to a man since Nathan.

"Are you okay?" she whispered.

"Most definitely."

She leaned down and kissed his chest and made her way up. His body tensed and she grinned. "Are you sure?"

"Yes, ma'am."

Face to face now, Anna's lips brushed against his. Those beautiful brown eyes looked into hers and she melted. His hot breath tickled her lips and her skin tingled all over.

"What are you doing?" he groaned. Disappointed, she pulled back, but his arms drew her close again. His cane fell to the floor and no one bothered to pick it up. "Don't."

She could not help it any longer, she pressed her lips against his roughly and rejoiced in the feeling. Tragedy made her realize how much she cared for him and how much she didn't want to let go of him.

Damian pulled her onto his lap and she straddled him as they kissed. His large hands slowly inched up her shirt and she groaned in approval.

Anna pulled her shirt off quickly and he stopped kissing her. His hands gently gripped her bare hips and he stared at the ceiling. She could feel the frustration course through him by his gasp.

"What?" she asked.

"I can't."

"What? Why?"

"I feel like you're doing this out of pity." He closed his eyes. His hands retreated to his sides.

She grabbed his hands and held them in her own. She placed them back on her hips and moved them down lower. As she leaned down, she whispered, "This is definitely something I want. No pity involved."

To her surprise, he picked her up with ease and carried her to his bed. His lips locked on hers and his hands gripped her backside. He gently laid her down on his bed, his body pressed into hers.

"Shit," he groaned in pain. "Probably shouldn't have done that."

"Are you okay?" she panicked.

He propped himself above her and Damian rolled his eyes. He was amused. "Don't worry about me so much."

His lips met hers again and she groaned when his hips pushed into her. She could feel his strength leaving him as his arms began to quiver. Anna pushed him over onto his back and straddled him. He looked up at her totally amused. "No more heavy lifting for you."

His body was still healing and she was perfectly fine doing the work. She leaned down and kissed his neck. His hands felt every curve of her body before she found herself on her back again.

"I'll lift and do what I please." He smirked. He was being forceful and didn't want to give up his dominance. She wrapped her legs around him and tried to flip him back over, but it didn't work. "Don't even try."

"You are stubborn," she groaned.

He sat up and begun to pull off her shorts. "So, what's your point?"

Chapter XXI

Julia

A LOUD KNOCK AT THE door woke Julia up from a deep sleep. It was the first time in days she was able to get some rest and now someone banged on her door. She dropped her head back on her pillow and felt herself fall back asleep.

"Julia!"

She jumped out of bed and fell to the floor. Half asleep and annoyed, she chucked her pillow at the door. She stood up and accidentally kicked the coffee table.

"Damn it." She hopped to the door and opened it annoyed. "What?"

Cato stood there smiling. "Well, don't you look lovely, sister."

"Cato." She yawned. "Of all the days for you to annoy me, you chose this one?"

"Okay, then I guess you don't want to hear the news." He started to walk away and Julia's annoyance grew.

"What, Cato?"

"He's awake."

Julia shoved Cato out of the way and ran down the hallway. She wore only a silk nightgown and she didn't care who saw her. Her heart pounded in her chest and she felt excitement grow inside her. Ryan was finally awake and she wanted to be there with him so badly it hurt.

"Tell Damian!" Cato yelled after her.

Julia quickly turned towards the male dormitories and banged loudly on Damian's door. Why didn't her brother tell Damian? She wanted to be there already. "Damian, wake up!"

She heard noises and whispering behind the door. She didn't have time to wait and she opened the door. Shock spread on her face as she saw Damian put his underwear back on and Anna peeking out from under his sheets.

"S-sorry," she stammered and slammed the door shut. That was embarrassing. It was a relief to see that they finally found each other though. Anna was lucky to have such a man.

After a few minutes Damian came limping out and Anna followed behind him, both fully clothed, thankfully. Anna looked utterly mortified and Julia's continuous smile probably didn't help her embarrassment.

"What's up?" He smirked. His hand entwined with Anna's so casually it seemed they were together forever. She could not remember the last time she had seen him this happy.

"He's awake." Her brother's words echoed from her.

If it was even possible, his face lit up more. All three of them briskly made their way down to the healing room Ryan was in. Julia tried not to get frustrated by how slow Damian moved. She was so excited she could barely stand it.

They burst into the room and Julia found Emma holding

Ryan's hand and sitting beside his bed. Anger flushed her cheeks. This was not what she expected and every bit of her body wanted to grab the girl by her hair and toss her out.

"Hello, Julia," Emma chimed.

"What are you doing?"

"Julia?" Ryan's voice was barely a whisper.

Emma looked back at Ryan who tried to sit up and reach his hand out to Julia.

"Save your strength, sweetie," Emma cooed as she started to pet his head like a dog.

Ryan swatted her off him and sat up as best he could. Julia went to him and wrapped her arms around him. His hand gripped the back of her head as he pulled her closer into him. "I was so worried."

"I bet," he groaned.

Emma stood up in a fury. "Are you two together or something?"

Julia and Ryan both ignored her. Julia didn't care what Emma thought—Ryan wanted her around, not Emma and that felt amazing. No matter what Ryan did to her, her feelings would not go away and everything felt right with him finally awake.

No more worrying about his condition or brain damage. As far as she was concerned, he remembered her and that was all that mattered. The way he clung to her with such intensity felt like he was worried she would disappear.

"I do believe that answers your question, Emma." Damian grinned as Emma huffed out of the room.

Ryan tried to suppress a groan. "What's wrong? What did I do?" Julia looked at his body and tried to find the source of pain.

"Calm down." He smirked. His face was scarred, but she could tell they were fading. The bruises had turned yellow and his body was littered in scabs. He looked so different without his long hair, but she had to admit, it looked handsome. Tougher.

"How is your head?" Damian asked.

"Hurts like hell," he muttered. He tore his eyes away from Julia. "I see you managed better than me."

Damian limped over to Ryan and they embraced. "You had it worse and you know it."

"That would be because I couldn't keep my mouth shut." He smirked. "How long have I been out?"

"Almost three weeks, I'd say," Anna spoke up.

"Whoa." His eyes widened. "Something feels weird."

His hand reached up to his head and he furrowed his eyebrows. Julia bit her lip and Damian shifted uncomfortably. Ryan ran his hand along his short hair and sighed.

"It looks good," Damian assured him.

"Right." He sighed. "This is just a few steps above buzzed."

"It will grow back." Julia grinned. "I think it actually looks better, though."

"Kind of like Channing Tatum," Anna added.

"Who?" the four of them asked simultaneously.

The healer walked into the room and panicked when she saw Ryan. "You just lay your little self down, mister."

"What the-" he mumbled.

She was a stout woman with flaming red hair and a rosy complexion. Ryan tried to bat her away, but she would have none of it. She pushed him down on the bed and pointed her finger at him. "If you sass me again I will strap you down."

Ryan saluted her and rested his ahead against his pillows. The nurse checked his vitals and glanced back at him as she left the room. Her squinted eyes were daring him to defy her.

"Well, she's terrifying," Anna blurted out.

"So, what's been happening? Any news on the Risen front?" Ryan asked.

"Emma didn't tell you? That's shocking." Damian sat down on a nearby chair.

"She said, 'I don't want to upset you because I care about you too much,' whatever the hell that means."

They exchanged glances and Julia felt Emma was somewhat right. Ryan had just woken up and he really should not have to be bothered with it this soon. "Maybe you should just rest for now?"

"Julia, I have been sleeping for almost a month. I don't need any more rest."

"Fine. Ahmose is missing. He went after whoever did this to you and Damian. I have been trying to run the Domus, but everything is breaking out in chaos," Julia explained. "The mortal world is going insane. Countries are banning religions and riots are breaking out."

"So they actually got him, then," Ryan stated.

The three of them stared at Ryan and he shrugged. "I was awake when they carved his name in my chest. They told me if I would not help them they would get the only other person that could."

"Help them with what?" Anna asked.

"They said they needed me for something," he muttered. "Something big. I can't remember..."

He looked drained and his body started to shake. Julia gently put her hand on his arm and it seemed to calm his nerves. Deep down she hoped he would remember. They needed whatever information they could get.

"You just woke up, you've had head trauma. Just rest for a while and we will all figure this out together, okay?"

"Can't do that," he urged.

He started to sit up and Damian grabbed the nurse's call button. "Don't make me do it."

Ryan glared. "Ass."

Ryan

"Go away, woman!"

Ryan threw his pudding at the redheaded healer, named Bridget, and it hit the door. Pudding splattered all around. She would not leave him alone. She hovered over him like he was a newborn and would panic every time his heart rate went mildly up.

"M'dear, you must relax," she cooed.

Ryan picked up a book from his beside table and chucked it at her. "I'm fine, psycho woman." The book slammed against the wall.

"Let me get you something to calm down. Would you like to sleep or just be in a comatose state?" She hurriedly walked to the medicine cabinet. Ryan threw a vile at her. He missed. "Or, perhaps paralyzed all over?"

Just when Ryan prepared to throw a vase full of flowers, Cato and Damian walked into his room. Fury was imprinted on his face and his friends laughed at the sight.

"Easy there, killer," Damian joked.

"Will you please get this woman away from me?" he hissed through his teeth.

"No, no, no, he must be sedated. He is much too upset for

company right now," Bridget chimed in.

Ryan cocked back the vase and Cato quickly grabbed it out of his hand. "It's fine, Bridget, we will make sure he calms down."

Damian nodded in agreement, but Ryan glared at the woman. *Damn, evil woman.*

"Are you sure? I can just give him some pain medication." She walked closer to him.

"We've got this, Bridget. Thank you." Cato grabbed the needle out of her hand and she grudgingly left the room. Once the door was closed, Cato and Damian burst into laughter. "What the hell, Ryan?"

"Redecorating or what?" Damian smirked.

"She is the epitome of evil." Ryan cringed. "Sponge baths, so many sponge baths."

They burst into laughter again.

Damian limped over to his bedside and fell back against the sofa next to it. "Anger issues still in check, I see."

"My sister seems very happy you are feeling better," Cato blurted out. That took Ryan by surprise.

"Isn't everyone?" Ryan joked.

"It must be nice, having such good friends." Cato was fishing for information of some kind it seemed.

Ryan nodded and laid back on his pillow-less bed. "It sure is."

"Anna and I are together now," Damian said. *Damian to the rescue, as always.* "I guess when a guy gets tortured to near death, it puts things in perspective."

"That'll do it. Congratulations." Ryan grinned. *It's about time Damian got a girl in his life.* "Any plans of marriage?"

Damian shook his head. "She was born in a different time, Ryan. You don't just get married to someone you are with anymore."

"Such an odd concept," said Cato.

"Makes sense, I suppose," Ryan agreed. "It's not proper to have many wives anymore so you better see which one is the right one. Enough woman talk, now what's going on with everything?"

Cato sat down next to Damian and crossed his legs. "All of Urbs is afraid to come out of their homes. The Risen has threatened to kill those who oppose them and they are clouded with fear. They are looking to recruit. Urbs has lost faith in our ability to protect them and in some sense that is true."

"Isn't the point of being Immortal to fight for what is good? Why aren't the civilians fighting?"

"Many of them haven't been Warriors for a long time, Ryan. Most are reborns and haven't fought a day in their lives," Damian answered.

"So, what are the Warriors doing about it?" he asked. Cato and Damian exchanged glances—Ryan shifted in his bed to stare at his friends.

"Julia has been sending out teams to monitor the streets for any activity. She's been trying to figure out how to flush them out. We don't have many options, people are afraid to talk." Damian sounded unhappy about this.

"What's wrong?"

Cato rubbed his head and sighed. "There have been many causalities. Nicholas, Mia, Ida's entire team, as well as Ajani and Eetu's teams."

Ryan laid back in his bed and took it all in. So many long time friends gone for selfish ambition, then again, was he really one to talk about selfish ambition?

"Who is out on patrol now?" he asked.

"Julia, Grace, and Colette," Cato muttered. "All the deaths have been weighing on her so she is taking it into her own hands."

Julia looked exhausted when she came to see him a few days prior. Her porcelain skin had turned corpse white and she had dark circles under her eyes. The deaths of their friends would weigh on anyone.

"When are they coming back?" He sighed.

They exchanged looks. "They haven't."

"We've ceased patrolling since their disappearance." Cato sighed.

"How long have they been gone?"

"They left after Julia came to see you." Damian looked at the floor. Cato tapped his foot nervously. Neither one of them would look at Ryan.

"So, you guys just decided not to look for them or something?"

"We didn't want to risk anyone else for now, Ryan, we need a new game plan," Cato insisted.

Julia's plan was on the right track, but to send a few people out at a time was a mistake. Traitors can slip by unnoticed with just a few people. They needed to strike as a group. No escape and no mercy, everyone out to catch them.

The Domus can be locked from within and the servants can remain to reopen it for the Warriors. Besides that, there is a traitor in their midst and he didn't trust them in the Domus alone.

"Get everyone that is left, we are heading out." Ryan sat up. "Arm yourselves heavily. I don't want any more deaths and we need to end this."

"Ryan, you shouldn't be up," Damian insisted. "Lay down and we will lead the patrol."

"Damian, for once in your life will you please not worry about me so much. I can handle it."

Damian and Ryan had a staring match. He knew Damian's worries and knew he was probably right, but he could not sit here and let Julia get killed.

"Fine." Damian sighed. Cato ran out to make the announcement. There were at least one hundred Warriors left and that would have to do.

Ryan yanked the electrodes off his body and swung his legs over the side of his bed. He had not tried to walk yet and he was slightly nervous to try. Given the strength he had to sit up, it was not going to go so well.

He pressed his bare feet against the floor and he stood up straight. His knees buckled and he almost fell, but caught himself on the bed. Damian looked on the verge of helping him, but stood still. He didn't intend to be left behind so he gathered his strength and took a step.

He grinned and yanked out his IV. Blood started to drip out and Damian wrapped his arm with gauze. "Was pulling it out really necessary?"

"Maybe." Ryan grinned. He was just happy to be on his feet again.

One step after another, he walked around the room, a grin spread on Damian's face. "You stubborn shit."

"I was born amazing." He held out his arms in splendor.

Bridget burst in the room and panicked. "Oh, my word, what do you think you are doing?"

She rushed towards the needle Cato had taken out of her hand earlier and Ryan blocked her way. She tried to get around him, but Ryan would not back off. His hands were up defensively and he managed to turn her away from the needle. "Back, get back, crazy woman."

Damian snuck around behind her and grabbed it off the counter.

"Sir, you must be in bed. You are not fully healed yet." *Poor Bridget. She may have just been doing her job, but she is like an annoying fly.*

"This is true, but I'm not going to lay down." Ryan backed her away further from the needle. "So move, devil woman."

"This is for your own good." She sighed. As she turned around to grab the needle, Damian stuck it in her shoulder. "What in the worl-"

Bridget fell on the floor, her eyes closed and a loud snore escaped her lips. At least she was only going to put him to sleep instead of paralyze him.

Ryan sighed in relief. "Never did I think I would rejoice in the sound of a snoring woman."

Chapter XXII

Ryan

RYAN STRAPPED HIS GEAR on with much difficulty. His body hurt all over and his head was pounding. He knew he should not be doing this, it was insane, but there was no alternate option. His strength was gone and just walking posed as a challenge, let alone fighting.

He looked in the mirror and he barely recognized himself. His scabbed up face looked menacing and he started to like his short hair. He wanted revenge for what they did to him. His body was a mutilated mess. Cato told him the healers could make something to diminish the scars.

He hung a shotgun on his back strap, picked up his helmet, and limped out of his room. Everyone was meeting in the training arena and he unquestionably took command of the unit. His gear rubbed against his body and it stung against the scabs. This was going to be one hell of a night.

Damian and Cato waited outside the doors for him. "Almost everyone has shown up," Cato informed him.

"Good." Ryan smirked and took a deep breath. Damian handed him a few pills. "What's this?"

"It will help with the pain." Damian sighed. "I really wish you would stay behind."

"Thanks," Ryan responded sarcastically. He popped the pills and swallowed them dry.

With his helmet tucked under his arm, he pushed the doors open and walked into the training arena—Cato and Damian on his flanks. Everyone was grouped in their teams and dressed in full gear.

The walls of the training arena were nearly bare from all the weapons people had strapped to their bodies. They all looked at him with determination and excitement. It had been a long time since any one of them was involved in a large group hand-to-hand combat.

Ryan felt like he was mortal again. Leading an army into battle was invigorating.

"Thank you all for coming tonight," he started. "I realize we have lost many friends in the past weeks, however, we must not let that cloud our judgment. The Gods saved us to maintain good in the world. If we fail, the world will turn chaotic, not even all of us in Urbs could make it right. The human soul needs faith, it craves it, and it will not survive without it. If it is taken away from the mortals, their souls will be destroyed and their morals will be lost."

"We must not and will not fail, my friends. We must not allow another world war and we will not allow human rights to be tarnished. We have all experienced war, we are experiencing it once again and mark my words, it won't be our last. We will prevail and take down this new evil in the world. Let's turn the tides and find out what we can tonight."

Ryan would not lie to them, he knew what was at stake and refused to sugar coat it. They must realize the cost if they fail. This was just the beginning of a long road ahead of them all. The excitement on their faces turned into determination. Failure was not an option.

"We will span out as far as we can through the city in a line, maintain a visual on one another along each street and do not break the line," he instructed. "We must stay together as a unit, if someone runs into trouble then there are backups by your side. Everyone turn your headset to channel nineteen. Lets find these bastards."

They all put both hands over their hearts and Ryan mimicked it back. This was a first for the Warriors, all of them fighting side by side. They better get used to it because this would not end tonight.

They marched out of the Domus. Ryan and his team remained on top of the steps as they watched a human wall form along the edge of the city. There were not enough of them to completely expand past the city but they managed to cover a lot of ground.

"This is the best idea you have?" Damian asked. "The great and mighty Al-"

"Quit," Ryan interrupted. "The only way to find them is for the Risen to think we sent out just one party. The teams are separated enough they will take the bait and try to attack. Then another team will be near enough to come to aid when they report their location."

"I suppose it will do. Not much else we can do," Cato agreed.

Anna came up behind them dressed in her gear. Ryan made sure she stayed behind to watch the Domus and the servants inside. He doubted they were the spies, but it was better safe then sorry. Anna was one hundred percent trustworthy and the last thing he wanted was for Damian's woman to get killed.

"All ready to go." She stood next to Damian.

"Remember, lock it totally up and let no one inside until Damian, Cato or myself come to the front." Ryan hoped all of them would make it back. "Keep an eye on things, Anna."

She nodded and Damian kissed her gently. He felt somewhat jealous of them, but he had to focus now.

The lines were spread out and waiting for the command. Ryan, Cato, and Damian made their way down the steps to join the center of the line. Everyone looked prepared and ready for a fight. Ryan itched for one, but his body was feeling weaker by the minute.

The three of them put their helmets on and got in place. The other Warriors on his sides were about a football field length away. Ryan spoke into his headset, "All right ladies and gentlemen, roll out."

They marched on.

Ryan put his headset on mute. "Ugh..." He clenched his head.

Damian glanced at him and turned his on mute as well. "You okay?"

"Peachy," he mumbled.

"You should have stayed back, you can't do this."

Ryan glared. "Don't talk so loud, people might hear you."

The Warriors on his side stopped to see why he halted. He waved them on and made himself keep walking.

"I mean it," Damian whispered. "You look terrible, you don't think they will recognize it? You're going to get yourself killed."

"If I do then at least I tried."

"You stick out and so do I. We are perfect targets for the Risen. I'm not in the best shape either, you know." Damian cringed. "Even I'm pushing it."

"Damian, just let it go. I am here and there is no turning back. We can do this."

He had to admit Damian was right. Both of them were the only ones with cuts all over their faces. Not to mention they were smack dab in the middle of the line. He planned it that way. They would stick out and be the ones the Risen would go after.

While they were concentrating on Ryan and Damian, the rest of the Warriors would be ready to attack. No more friends needed to die. He'd rather it be him, than anyone else.

Cato walked over to them, his gun in a held at the ready and pushed his headset on mute. "Will you two shut the hell up?"

Damian shook his head and got in position with his gun. Ryan held his gun in patrol ready position too and took out his knife in case of an ambush.

They walked by the Lokanta restaurant and Ryan was shocked to see the city so empty. Cato and Damian were right. Things must have gotten horrible while he was unconscious—no one dared to come out at night. Graffiti plagued the city with symbols of the Risen and he felt anger build within him. *How did they let it get this bad?*

After hours of searching alleyways and spying into homes and business', they had reached the middle of the city. Nothing had happened and Ryan started to worry more about Julia. There was no sign of the Risen, no sign of her, and the anticipation killed him.

It seemed like tonight was going to be a waste of time. Ryan might as well call it off for tonight. They were three quarters of the way through the city when gunfire sounded in the distance. Ryan looked to his left. "Report."

Silence.

"Report."

"It's the Risen... Cori Candy Shop... four... assistance!" Ryan heard in the headset.

The three of them weren't near there.

"On our way," another voice said.

"Us too," said another.

There was more gunshots in the distance.

"Keep it moving everyone. If you guys can hear me, tell me what is happening," Ryan spoke in his headset.

A reply came, "Two down... One of ours shot in the leg... Taking her to the Domus."

Ryan remained in patrol ready stance as the line pushed forward. Someone was hurt—he tried not to run to their aid.

"Third down... Aja is down," another voice said.

Ryan glanced at Damian who hesitated in his tracks. Aja and Damian were once together, but had mutually split ways, but remained good friends. *Please, no more casualties.*

"Got em'! Moving forward... two wounded... one fatality," a voice said.

"Don't move forward. Bring the bastards back to the Domus so we can identify them," Ryan replied. "Good job."

The line pushed forward. As they reached the end of the city, Ryan's knee gave out and he collapsed to the ground. If it weren't for his gloves, his hands would have been scraped up.

Cato ran to his side and to his surprise, Damian didn't notice and continued on. Ryan muted his headset.

"You okay?"

"Not really," he admitted.

"What's wrong? What hurts?"

"Everything." He smirked. "Help me up, will you?"

He grabbed his weapons—Cato wrapped his arm under Ryan's and heaved him up. "Got it?"

Ryan nodded and Cato let go. They tried to catch up with the line and suddenly Cato stopped abruptly in the middle of an alley. "What?"

A knife flew through the air and dug into Ryan's thigh. He tried not to scream in pain. Instead he bit his lip till he could taste blood. Cato ran over to him and they were back to back. His breathing quickened and his leg throbbed.

Ryan turned his headset off mute. "Damian, get back here."

"So, he lives?" an amused voice to his left said.

Ryan held his gun up and pointed in the direction of the voice. The night made the individual invisible and he tensed. "He does."

"Pity, I hoped you would die slowly, but I suppose the General will be happy to hear you survived."

"Oh, yeah? And why is that?" Ryan could not see anyone. He heard footsteps behind him and from Cato's lack of shooting he figured it was Damian.

"You might be needed after all. Your boss seems increasingly reluctant to help."

Ryan tried to remember why they wanted him in the first place. It was on the tip of his tongue. "If I didn't help the first time I probably won't at all. Move on."

"You two are the only ones that can do it and you know it. The General is very determined."

Realization hit him. He remembered what they wanted.

Ryan felt Damian by his side and his gun still pointed out into darkness. "Come on out and let's all have a nice chat."

Five people in hooded black cloaks with black scabbards walked out of the darkness with guns ready to fire. Ryan breathed deeply. Normally this would not worry him, but now it was a huge obstacle.

All the Warriors could still hear him talking, "Five against three, there's a knife in my leg and you still have your guns on me? I must be terrifying."

"Where's your location, Ryan?" he heard in his ear.

"They only thing that is scary about you is your face. Not going to get anymore women looking like Frankenstein."

Damian stepped in front of Ryan. "Why don't we go to Isis' Palace across the street. Get a bite to eat and have a few drinks, guys?"

One of the hooded figures looked to his right. "I think we beat him stupid."

"On our way," was the response in the headset.

"I rather just kill them, Damian," Ryan spoke up. "I recognize that voice."

The hooded figure clenched his hands around his gun. "Do you, now?"

"Yep," Ryan said. "How's it going, Jesse?"

He heard multiple gasps of shock through his headset. "I knew you were a little traitorous bastard."

Jesse grabbed his hood and pulled it off, revealing his face. "Caught me."

"Pathetic," Ryan spat.

"No, hearing you scream as I cut and burned your skin was pathetic." Jesse laughed.

More sounds of disbelief echoed in the headset. Ryan's grip

on his gun and knife tightened. Damian and Cato tensed up at his sides and everyone stood on guard. Cato spoke, "I was wondering were you've been for the past week."

"Is Aden a part of your little gang?" Ryan asked.

"Not in the least. Loyalty is a flaw in you Warriors."

"You Warriors?" Cato laughed. "Damn glad you no longer classify yourself with us."

"Me too."

"Didn't you fight with us on Anna's ceremony day?" Damian asked.

"Sure did. Quite the performance, wasn't it?" Jesse winked.

There was movement coming from the shadows behind the Risen. Ryan saw Grace and Colette, their hands bound in front of them with gags in their mouths, being pushed forward into the light. Their gear was gone and they had small amounts of dry blood on their faces. At least their black under clothes seemed fully intact, just dirty. It didn't look like they were severely hurt.

"Traitor and woman abuser." Ryan scoffed. "You are literally the biggest piece of-"

"I didn't do it, calm down." Jesse pushed the girls forward. "You can have them. The General only wanted Julia."

Ryan stepped forward towards Jesse and was held back by Damian and Cato. *How could they hurt women? What was the point in only talking Julia? This must be a punishment.*

Grace and Colette made their way over to them, the three of them blocked the females out of harms way. "Take them to the Domus, Damian."

"No, I'm staying."

"No, you're not," he said firmly. He glanced at Damian. Trying to make a point while not taking his eyes off your target was difficult. "Now."

Damian grudgingly complied. He backed away slowly while keeping his gun pointed at the Risen. Colette and Grace had no trouble walking, which was a good sign. They walked in front of Damian as he shuffled away.

"They are out of sight, Ryan," he heard through his headset.

"Where's Julia?"

"She's perfectly safe. Trust me, nothing is going to happen to her."

Ryan laughed. "Trust you? You're joking, right?"

"She's probably in the safest place she could be. That's all I can tell you. So, now what?" Jesse asked.

"Now, I kill you," Ryan replied. "How's that sound?"

"Problematic."

"Sounds spectacular to me." Ryan shrugged. "How about you, Cato?"

"Freaking fantastic," answered Cato.

The two of them started to walk towards Jesse and his crew. Ryan was mentally ready even if he wasn't physically. He didn't care though—he wanted to tear Jesse apart for what he did to Damian and him.

"Sir, there are dozens of Warriors in the city." A man ran up to Jesse from behind the shadows. "We have orders to retreat."

"You're not as stupid as I thought coming out here. Till we meet again." Jesse bowed and then ran off into the darkness.

Ryan started to run after them, but Cato caught up and pulled him back. Ryan tried to fight him off, but his eyesight went blank and he collapsed on the ground. He managed to yell, "Go after them!"

Cato pulled Ryan to his feet and spoke into his headset, "I want four teams in pursuit. Follow them and find out where they are hiding out and report back."

"Let's go," Ryan insisted.

Cato led him in the opposite direction. Ryan started to feel the pain of the knife that was still in his leg and cringed with every step. "You are going back to the Domus and getting rest. You should have never come out here tonight."

"We need to find Julia," he groaned. "We can't just leave her with them."

"There are teams following them right now, if they find their hideout we will personally go and get her. In the meantime, we need you to get your strength."

They made it back to the Domus with no trouble, except the pain in Ryan's leg. Anna and Damian waited by the opened doors. "What happened?"

"They figured out our plan and ran off." Cato groaned from half carrying Ryan. It was a lot quicker getting back to the Domus without having to patrol, but it still took almost an hour.

"Are you okay?" Anna looked at the knife in his leg and winced.

"I'm good, just need to lie down," Ryan assured her.

"All right, go get sleep." Damian patted him on the back and Cato reluctantly continued to half carry Ryan to his room.

"I'm glad you aren't as big as me," he groaned. "Otherwise this would suck."

"You're just taller," Ryan teased. "So shut up."

They made it to his room and Cato dropped him on the bed. He helped Ryan get his gear and boots off and hung up his weapons on the wall. "Want me to send a healer up for that?" He pointed at the knife wound.

"It's fine. I'll stitch it up." Ryan grunted as he rubbed his face in exhaustion.

"Fine, I'll do it." Cato rolled his eyes and went into Ryan's bathroom. He returned with alcohol, a needle, and a thick thread.

"It bothers me how you know where I keep everything."

"I'm sure Damian and I know better than you do." Cato smirked.

Ryan was annoyed how calm Cato was about Julia's disappearance. His flesh and blood was missing and in the hands of the Risen, and he acted as if nothing were wrong.

"She'll be fine, Ryan."

They really could read him like a book.

"How do you know?"

"Do you honestly think Jesse would let anything happen to Julia?" Cato asked.

He handed Ryan a belt that was on the floor and Ryan bit down on it. Cato took ahold of the knife's hilt and yanked it out of his leg. Ryan groaned and laid back on his bed. "Well, good thing you kept it in. It's gushing blood now."

Just what I wanted to hear. "What if he does something to her?"

Cato yanked off Ryan's pants and grabbed the alcohol bottle that sat on the nightstand. Ryan returned the belt to his mouth as Cato poured alcohol over the wound. Ryan gripped his bed sheets. *God dammit*, his mind screamed.

"He wouldn't..." Cato hesitated.

As he sewed Ryan's skin back together, Cato stayed quiet and Ryan grew impatient with him. Neither spoke—there was nothing left to say. Ryan felt like Julia was gone for good and it broke his heart.

When Cato was finished, he swung Ryan's legs onto his bed and tossed his blanket over him. "Get some rest."

"Thanks, Mom."

"Anytime, sugar britches."

"By the way, I remember what they are planning to do," Ryan muttered as his eyes began to close. "We are screwed if they succeed."

"What are they planning?" Cato sounded worried.

"They are wanting to use the Brahmastra."

Ryan

"What the hell is the Brahmastra?" Colette asked. She sat on Ryan's couch next to Grace. Colette, Grace, Anna, Damian, and Cato were all gathered in Ryan's room while he laid in bed. They were treating him like a wounded animal, but honestly he was happy to be lying down.

"It is a Hindu weapon used with the intent of destroying an enemy or army. You must summon it with extreme amounts of mental concentration and be a master of the Gayatri Mantra, to summon it," Ryan answered.

"I still don't get it," Grace spoke up.

"Basically, it's an atomic bomb that targets certain people and the only way you can use it is if you have super human concentration when you meditate the Mantra verse," Cato spoke up.

"So, it's a mental weapon?" Colette asked.

"No, you summon it mentally, but when it appears it turns into a weapon of your choice. It can only be used once in a lifetime," Ryan answered. "Poisonous air, fire, and all the good stuff that kill people in a horrendous way."

"So they are wanting to use this against someone?" Grace asked.

"They want to use it against any Immortal that doesn't follow them. Whoever summons the Brahmastra is going to target them and kill them. There is nothing we can do to stop it."

Cato leaned against the wall and crossed his arms. "It was nice knowing you, guys."

"There is one thing, Ryan," Damian finally spoke up. "The Brahmadanda. Translated it's called the Staff of Brahma."

"It'll be hard to get." Ryan propped himself up.

"Why?" asked Colette.

"It was broken and hidden in three places," Ryan answered. "The Hindu religion created it, but Ahmose changed it up somehow. It's not exactly what the Hindu's had created anymore, but it is about the same."

"Why would you hide the only weapon that could stop the Brahmastra?" Cato laughed.

Ryan shrugged. "My guess is they wanted any knowledge of the Brahmastra's existence to be destroyed. Since the Brahmastra isn't a physical thing, it is easy to forget. The Staff of Brahma is a physical thing and is a reminder of the weapon."

"Well, let's find the pieces." Cato was getting frustrated. "Or are we just going to sit here and wait to die?"

"How do we even know where to look?" Anna spoke up.

"I don't know, Ryan," Damian said sarcastically, "how will we ever find it?"

They all stared at Ryan. He shifted uneasily in his bed. He hated having knowledge of this, but was glad he did. "I know where they are."

"How?" Anna asked.

"I acquired it through a very reliable source."

"Did you sleep with someone you shouldn't have?" Cato asked.

"Most definitely," Damian answered.

"I couldn't help it." Ryan sighed. "It just happened."

"You just happened to sleep with a Queen of India?" Damian rolled his eyes.

He shrugged. "It was payback."

"How did she know?" Anna crossed her legs.

"Her husband is the one who hid it." Ryan shrugged.

"Anyway," Grace interrupted, "how do you know so much about all this?"

Ryan sat up in his bed and pushed the covers aside. He swung his legs over the side of his bed. "There are only two people that can summon the Brahmastra."

They all stared at him, except Damian, who seemed preoccupied with his shoes. Ryan stood up and grabbed water out of his fridge. He drank it empty and tossed another bottle to Cato who held out his hands for one.

"Go on." Colette seemed annoyed.

"Ahmose and I are the only two people alive that can do it." He sat back down on his bed. "That's why they took me. They tried to persuade me to summon it for them. Since I refused, I suppose they hoped Ahmose would."

"Unfortunately," Damian added.

"When I was in India I learned how to summon it and what was needed to destroy it," said Ryan. "So, I made a point to find out how."

"Where are they hidden?" Grace asked.

"Sirenum Scopuli, Shambhala, and the Catacombs of Paris." Ryan cringed. "When the Mayans went extinct, Ahmose removed that piece from their land and placed it in the Catacombs. Archaeologists would go poking around in there and it was no longer safe."

"Nice history lesson, now where do we start?" Cato asked.

"My guess is the Catacombs. Probably the easiest." Ryan stood up and pulled off his shirt and pants. He wore only his underwear and found clean gear in his armoire.

Grace, Colette, and Anna quickly looked away. Ryan chuckled to himself. "You can look, ladies, just don't touch."

"You wish," Grace muttered.

"Okay, so who's going?" Ryan pulled on his black pants, shirt, and socks. He laced up his boots and noticed everyone had their hands raised for the challenge. This was going to be an issue. "We all can't go. Grace and Colette, you two really shouldn't be going anywhere."

"Neither should you two." Grace glanced between Damian and Ryan. "All we got was a busted lip and nose, Ryan."

"Yeah, well, we are the only ones that know anything about all of this." Ryan smiled. "So, too bad. Besides, we need someone we trust watching over Urbs and the Domus."

Grace sighed—Ryan won the argument. "Fine."

"So, Damian, Cato, and I will go," Ryan said finally.

"Me too," Anna chimed.

Ryan thought Damian's neck snapped when he turned to face Anna. "No."

"I am going," she insisted.

"Absolutely not." Damian looked to Ryan, who was contemplating. "She cannot go."

"We may need her, Damian." Ryan sighed.

"Why?" Colette didn't look pleased at all.

"Sirenum Scopuli," said Ryan.

"Okay?" Anna raised her eyebrow in confusion.

"Home of the Sirens," Cato mumbled.

Anna looked confused.

"Sirens, bird women that lure sailors or men to their deaths. Yeah, you are not a man so we would need you, just in case." Ryan saw Damian glaring.

"So you need me to save you from some chicks?" Anna asked. "Yes, pun intended."

"If we are going to the catacombs first, she doesn't need to go yet," Damian insisted.

"There may be a reason we need her in the catacombs too, Damian. I'm almost positive."

Damian still glared at him. "No, Ryan."

"Yes, Damian."

"It's too dangerous, she has no idea what she is up against."

"How else is she supposed to learn?"

"Not like this," Damian insisted.

"Um, hello? Do I have a say in this?" Anna raised her voice—both Damian and Ryan continued to glare at each other. "I am going. That is that. Neither of you are my boss, it's my decision."

Damian stood up quickly and marched towards the door. "Get ready then."

"Meet us in the parlor in one hour," Ryan yelled after Damian before the door slammed shut.

Anna looked nervous and he could not blame her. Damian was right—she had no idea what creatures they were up against. In her mind they were myth and nothing more—this would be a huge shock. "Go get ready, Anna."

Chapter XXIII

Anna

Anna left her room dressed in her gear. Unlike the others, it was brand new, for the most part, and it needed to be broken in. She was glad the black fatigues underneath were somewhat comfortable. She would rather have worn her military gear, but those days were over with.

Her boots squeaked softly with each step as she made on her way to the training arena. Unlike Ryan, her room was not decked out in pointy objects. *What the hell do you bring to the catacombs?*

She pushed the door open and she peaked inside not wanting to interrupt anyone's training session. It was empty. She squeaked her way towards the guns and pulled down an M-4 Carbine. She slung it around her shoulders and grabbed a Colt M45.

Holstering it, she grabbed a few grenades, additional ammo and a few blades. Swords were definitely not her forte and neither were bows. Anna was out of her element and she knew it. Damian knew it too and it made her even more nervous.

Damian walked into the training arena as he was tightening the strap on his vest. He looked up at Anna, both fondness and sadness in his smile. "Ready?"

She nodded. "I think so. Do we need to bring food or money or anything?"

"No." He reached into his back pocket and pulled out a wallet. "Got to love that little invention called credit cards."

Anna grinned. "When do I get one?"

"Ha, never."

Anna pouted, "Not fair."

"Not to be sexist, but never trust a female with a credit card that has no limit." Damian pocketed his wallet.

"Where will we sleep?"

"Just depends on where we are and what's happening." He shrugged. "We might not sleep at all."

Damian grabbed some magazine clips and slid them in his holster pouch. He threw more into a bag, slung it over his shoulder and held out his hand for her. "Ready?"

"One more thing." She grabbed an entrenching tool. "Got to have my E-tool."

Damian smirked and they held hands as they walked out the door towards the parlor.

"I really wish you weren't coming."

"I know."

"I don't think you realize how dangerous these places are." Damian let go of her hand and put his arm around her waist. He pulled her close as they walked down the halls. "Sirens are deadly and the Catacombs are no joke. This is like a suicide mission."

Anna stopped, pulled Damian's chest to hers and kissed

him fiercely. His hands wrapped around the back of her neck and he slid his fingers into her hair. She felt a closeness to him that was familiar. She trusted him as much as she trusted Nathan. This was right.

She pulled away from his lips and she whispered, "Quit worrying. I'm a big girl."

"I can see that." Ryan strutted towards them and put his arms around both of their necks. Anna felt like she was being herded. "I knew you were kinky."

She wanted to hide in a hole.

"Please, shut up," Damian groaned.

"Just saying." Ryan shrugged and Anna felt like she was holding him up. "Pretty sure I saw lip biting."

Yep, kill me, Anna thought.

"You okay?" Damian changed the subject.

"Yeah, why?"

"Because you are putting your weight on us," Damian answered.

"Don't worry about it."

"Ditto," Anna added.

Damian rolled his eyes and Anna grinned. She was worried about Ryan. He may act like everything is fine and a joke, but his eyes gave him away. He was in pain and not just physical.

They reached the parlor and Ryan took his arms off them. Cato was kneeling on the ground with his eyes shut. A small statue the size of a toy solider was in front of him on the coffee table.

Ryan and Damian ignored him, but stayed silent and fumbled with their gear. Damian handed Ryan some ammo out of his bag and tossed the bag on the couch behind Cato.

"What's he doing?" she whispered into Damian's ear.

"Praying."

"For what?"

"He always does this before a mission," he answered.

Damian and Ryan were busy checking each other's gear so Anna walked over to Cato and kneeled next to him. She studied him for a few seconds and felt pity for him.

"Jupiter, watch over my sister. Bring her back unharmed to me and take from me what you will," he muttered. "Take my life, if you must, Jupiter."

With her hand she made the sign of the cross against her chest. "St. Michael the Archangel, defend us in battle—be our defense against wickedness and snares of the devil."

"Almighty Jupiter, bring her out of the clutches of darkness and back into the light."

"Lord, bring Julia back to us, unharmed and well. I pray to you to forgive my sins and seek salvation for our lost loved ones. Amen."

As she finished her prayer, she opened her eyes to find Cato staring at her. His eyes were red and sullen. "Thank you," he whispered.

"All right kids, enough chit-chat, time to go." Ryan clapped his hands together.

Cato looked back at Ryan and Damian. He stood up slowly and pocketed the small statue he asked, "Why don't you pray to Zeus?"

Ryan and Damian exchanged looks. Anna stood up slowly and pretended to adjust her gear. The tone of Cato's voice was a bit alarming. He seemed angry almost.

"I just don't really think about doing it," said Ryan bluntly. "Not like he has done much for me lately."

"We could use it," Cato insisted.

Damian ran his hand through his hair. "Can we not fight about this and get going?"

Cato rolled his eyes and Anna looked between the three. Damian mouthed 'I'll tell you later.'

The four of them stood together facing the balcony. Ryan took out a little purse from his pocket and pulled out a small white rock.

"What's that?" she whispered to Damian.

"It's a crystal, it creates a portal," Damian muttered.

"What do you call it?"

"Umm, a crystal." He smirked. "Never came up with another name, I guess."

"Entrance to the Paris Catacombs," Ryan said aloud.

A black building appeared in a large circle that materialized in the parlor. Anna shook with fear and excitement, it would be the first time being back in the real world since she became Immortal.

She felt nervous about walking into the giant hole and Damian had to pull her along. *This is nuts.*

They walked through the glowing light and were on the streets of Paris. It was nighttime and no one was around. That was odd for Paris, wasn't it a super tourist-filled place?

A simple black building with ropes in front of it sat to the left of a tall, tan stone building. It was easy to miss and Anna was somewhat confused why it would possibly need a roped off walkway. They jogged up to the black looking shack and Ryan picked the lock to the door on the right side of the shack. The door noisily creaked open.

They quickly huddled inside and a small amount of light flooded into the room. There was a board in front of them that informed Anna flash photography was not allowed inside.

Why was this not in French? Oh yeah, that spell crap. Cool, I can read French.

"Guess I brought my camera for nothing." The three men looked back at her confused. "Just kidding."

Cato found out how to turn the lights on and the four of them headed down a white spiral staircase. It had a small railing going down the wall and after a while, Anna started to get dizzy.

"Does this staircase ever freaking end?" She sighed.

"Yeah, when we get to the bottom," Ryan teased.

"How far down is this?" She gasped.

"It's not that far, calm down," Ryan answered.

When they reached the bottom, Anna could hear water gurgling somewhere around them. They walked down a narrow stone corridor with a low ceiling and she looked around waiting for something scary to happen. *What was so terrifying about this place?*

The dark and damp area reminded her of a mine. Small lights followed along the walls and she felt like she was going to get claustrophobic. The stones that made the tunnel looked old and dark. *This must be what a mole feels like in his tunnels.*

"Anna," Ryan said.

"What?"

"I don't know you that well, but please don't get separated from us." She saw him glance back at her. "Bad things happen when you're down here alone."

"I'm not an idiot, Ryan," she said. "I know how to work as a team."

"Didn't mean to insult you, your highness."

"Ryan," Damian said. "Stop."

"I was just saying."

"You are all morons," Cato spoke up.

They took a left and walked until they ran into a locked, barred gate to their left. Ryan turned right down another narrow hallway with large stone walls. There were a few fire extinguishers and she wondered how a fire could possibly start down here. Along the hallway there were barred off rooms on either side. Now she felt like she was in a medieval prison.

She tried to peek into the rooms, but they were too dark to see anything. *Maybe they were just blocked off for tourists' protection or something.* Yep, that was what she was going to go with.

"So, what is the point of this place?" she asked.

"I think they used to quarry stones down here," Damian mumbled.

"Okay, what's so scary about that?"

"You'll see." Ryan chuckled. "Have you never heard of the Paris Catacombs?"

"Nope."

"Your education system baffles me." Ryan sighed.

"Big talk coming from someone that doesn't know who Channing Tatum is," Anna snapped.

Damian sighed. "You two are like cats and dogs."

"She's a feisty one, I give you that, Damian." Ryan patted him on the back.

Anna rolled her eyes. Ryan was being a chauvinistic pig right now. How could Julia possibly stand this man?

"He is just trying to figure you out," Damian whispered in her ear. "Don't take what he says to heart."

"So, he is trying to get to know me by being a giant douche?" She laughed.

"In a nut shell." He smirked.

They walked down a hallway with small uneven stones and came upon a mini castle looking sculpture. What an odd place for such a detailed piece of art. It stuck out like a sore thumb.

The little entrance to the castle was set below it in a half moon shape. Small steps in the middle of it went up towards the front of the castle. It had towers and windows carved into the stones, a perfect little replica. The large brick wall behind the sculpture looked like an avalanche coming to destroy the castle.

"This place is freaking weird," Anna mumbled.

"Just trying to add a little art to liven up the joint." Cato shrugged. "Really odd art, but art, nonetheless."

To her side she saw a cylinder shaped room with a stairway that headed down. A small railing in the middle of the room surrounded a hole in the ground. Inside the hole was bright blue water that sat peacefully undisturbed. *Perhaps this place is not as bad as the boys made it seem.*

Part of her wanted to go down the stairway, but she had a feeling Ryan would yell at her. How these people did this kind of stuff back in the day was amazing. Would she think of doing this? No. Would she be able to do this? Nope.

She noticed the guys were moving forward without her and jogged to catch up.

"What were you doing?" Damian whispered.

"Just looking at that water thing down there."

"Stay together, Anna, it is really easy to get lost in this place." He squeezed her hand and they continued on.

The brick walls were neatly stacked now instead of piled on one another and they entered a tall stone hallway with an arched stone ceiling. She felt like she was walking in a cathedral with such grand high arches.

Between every arch was an empty space with lights that shone on the arches. It made it look almost heavenly. The hallway sloped upward and she held onto the small rail that went up. She was more interested in the architecture then the mission, at this point.

"This is gorgeous," she mumbled. This was an amazing experience. She had never seen anything like this in her life. There was no way Anna could keep her mind straight. How could she?

"See if you think that when we get further in." Ryan smirked and turned to face her. She stuck out her tongue at him. "Keep your woman in check, Damian."

He was such an ass sometimes. Anna honestly could not tell when he was kidding and when he was serious. *Bipolar much?*

They continued to the end of the hallway, taking a left through an opened gate. They entered into a short room with square pillars, which held up the ceiling—Anna could not help but laugh. Jesus this place is so odd. Nothing makes sense or seems to fit in.

Each pillar was painted with what looked like black and white castle keeps along the top. The remaining space on each pillar was decorated like tall windows with the drapes pulled back. The room walls were built in the usual stone stacked way as the rest of place.

"Why does it look like someone spray painted black on the ceiling?" she asked. For some reason, there were black lines along the ceiling going in two different directions, another odd addition to this weird place.

"I know I am probably one of the most intelligent people you know, Anna." Ryan sighed. "But alas, I don't know it all. I have only been here a few times."

"I guess my expectations of you were set too high." She rolled her eyes.

Damian looked at her, obviously amused while Ryan ignored her. The only person that seemed lost in thought was

Cato. He was so different from the other two, he reminded her a lot of Julia. That's probably what is weighing on his mind.

The boys made their way towards an open stone pillared doorway. Instead of the castle keep design, it had white elongated diamonds on a black background decorated on either side of the entrance.

Anna read the sign above the doorway, "Halt, this is the realm of Death."

"Such a warm welcome," Cato mumbled.

It wasn't.

A shiver ran down her spine and they stood in front of the doorway. *Why aren't they moving forward?*

"Anna." Damian turned to her. "This is were it is going to get intense."

"Okay…" She cocked her head.

"If you want to stay here, say so now," he mumbled as he took her hands into his.

"Damian, I really think we are going to need her," Ryan spoke up.

Damian glared at Ryan, but seemed to be mauling something over in his mind. She had no idea what Ryan was talking about. What could she do that they couldn't?

"Fine," Damian said grudgingly.

Anna looked to Ryan and Cato. Ryan popped his neck and knuckles while Cato jumped up and down, pumping himself up like a boxer or something.

"Can you at least give me some sort of hint as to what I am in for?" Anna asked.

"I honestly am not one hundred percent sure myself." His brown eyes gazed at her from under his helmet. "I just know that people like us are very unwanted in places like this. Don't trust your eyes."

Well, that was reassuring.

Ryan led them through the doorway and into a room with neatly made brick pillars that supported the ceiling. *This didn't look terrible.* She looked around waiting for all hell to break loose, but nothing did. She stayed closely behind the boys this time and noticed Ryan was picking a lock on a gated doorway.

"Why is it locked?"

Damian raised his eyebrow. "There has been quite a few locked gates, you just must have been too preoccupied to notice." His smile made her feel warm inside. He was such a calm spirit and she knew he would never hurt her.

As Ryan pulled the barred gate open, he stopped and checked his earpiece. Cato and Damian turned theirs on and Anna stood there awkwardly. She had no idea where they got those.

"Everyone ready?" Ryan asked.

Anna raised her hand and felt like a child. "I don't have a headset."

Ryan rolled his eyes and nudged Damian away from her. As he pulled her closer to him, she panicked momentarily and looked at an amused Damian. Ryan reached into a pocket on her vest and pulled out a headset.

She bit her lip and sighed. "Sorry."

Ryan turned it on and put it on her ear like she was a child. "You should really look and see what are in these pockets, Anna."

"I said sorry," she mumbled.

Ryan leaned in and whispered, "Something may be in there that could save your life and if you died I would never forgive myself for convincing Damian to let you come."

She was taken back by his honesty. "Okay."

"Be careful," he whispered then left her standing confused and dazed.

"What did he say to you?" Damian looked annoyed.

"To be careful." She shrugged. That seemed to be okay with him and he grabbed his gun from his holster.

With Ryan at the lead and Damian pulling up the rear, they walked into the dimly lit hallway. She stopped in her tracks and Damian bumped into her. The walls were covered in human bones.

Leg and arm bones where stacked neatly with the joints sticking out, on top of each other. Human skulls lined the top, bottom and middle of the wall, in between the human appendages. They were perfectly arranged and almost artistic. Anna instantly got nervous.

Her heart beat quickly seeing all the dead, dismembered bones. It was gruesomely beautiful, but it was not normal. *This is not how people should be laid to rest.*

"You okay?" Damian asked.

"Who does this?" Anna cringed.

"Apparently, the French," Cato answered.

"Well, I figured that part out for myself." She smirked when Cato turned and gave her a half smile.

"So, do we know where we are going or what?"

"Ryan thinks he has an idea where Ahmose put the piece," said Damian.

"Thinks?"

"A pretty good guess," Ryan answered.

"What does this piece look like, exactly?" she asked.

"The whole thing forms a human spine."

Anna sighed. "Of course, hide the human spine in a place full of human bones. Perfect."

They walked slowly as the boys searched the walls for the piece of spine. Some parts of the wall broke the continuous skull lines with hearts, crosses and various designs made out of the skulls. *This is a grotesque place.*

"So much disrespect in one place," she muttered.

They entered a small oval room with more skull and appendage-lined walls. In the middle of the room sat a small well-shaped foundation with stairs that wrapped around it, leading up to another area. The well looked unfinished in the front and like the steps around it, led up to the room above.

"I think it is a fountain," Damian whispered.

"Doesn't look like one," she whispered back.

He smiled and they continued on.

"So, you aren't sure exactly where it is and we may be down here for quite some time?" she asked.

"You annoy me."

"Ryan, shut up." Damian pushed him softly.

"I'm just nervous," she muttered, "this place is freaking nuts."

"Yeah," Damian mumbled.

"How many bodies do you think are down here?" she asked.

"I think I read somewhere that there are about six million." Ryan stopped. "Are you able to do this or not, Anna?"

Anna grabbed her gun from her holster. "Don't make me shoot you, Ryan."

He looked her up and down and Anna felt the need to punch him. He shrugged and smacked Damian on the back. "I approve."

Damian looked over at her and his smile was contagious.

Chapter XXIV

Julia

THE COLD TILE FELT unpleasant on her skin.

"Stay," they'd told her.

The door slammed shut and her eyesight finally returned. Julia gasped as she looked around the room. She knew this place—it was her bathroom from when she was a child. Her heart dropped.

Julia had not been to her childhood home since her father had died. She and Cato had sold the house to the city because both parents were gone and they could not bear being here. It was too painful. She'd never bothered to ask who had bought it.

Crawling over to the white fur rug lying in the middle of the room, she embraced the warmth to her body and closed her eyes. Why was she here?

She was too weak to try to escape and she knew no one would be able to find her. They would not feed her or give her anything to drink. Her body felt tired. All she could do was wait and stare around the room.

She was astonished that it looked exactly the same as she left it. When they sold the house, she didn't want any memories brought with her. She left her belongings here for the next owner to do with as they wished.

Hairbrushes, makeups and perfumes she had used more then two hundred years ago sat on top of the sink countertops. She looked to her left and saw her walk in closet and long dresses with intricate embroidery sewn on them, hung side by side. Those were hers.

The tall, wide rack by the closet held old heels that could be in a museum. All of these things were hers and none of them looked aged at all. Even more odd, it was all clean.

Who would go through the trouble of preserving all of my old things?

Opposite the door, across the long room, sat her massive claw foot bathtub under bay windows and a crystal chandelier hung in the middle of the room. The walls were teal except the wall opposite of the closet, which was made entirely with mirrors and the furniture was all white.

Despite her wishes to forget that past, she could not help but realize how much this room mirrored hers at the Domus. Her mother had picked out the colors for her room and it obviously stuck with her.

She heard gunshots in the distance, a very unwelcomed sound in Urbs. She reached and pulled herself up, thanks to the sink countertop. Her legs wobbled from being so weak. She managed to stumble across the room to the windows and looked out into the night.

Warriors were patrolling through the city and she started to bang on the windows with her fists to get their attention. They didn't see or hear her and started running off in the opposite direction. *Why didn't they look?*

"Don't waste your time. The windows are sound resistant."

Julia turned around quickly and saw a large woman with curly red hair and a black dress, pushing a cart into the bathroom. The cart had towels, clothes, and most importantly, food on it.

As she closed the door behind her, she walked up to Julia and bent over the tub. She turned the water on and Julia felt her body tense up.

"Undress," she commanded.

"No."

The woman sighed. "You look terrible and you will feel much better."

"I'd feel better if you let me go," she spat.

"M'dear," the woman cooed. "I will not harm you. In fact, the men that treated you as they did these past few days are being punished for their actions."

"Since when do the Risen care about Warriors?" Julia asked. "The last time one of us was in your care they barely survived the outcome."

The woman grabbed bath beads from on top of the side table next to the tub and poured it in the water. Julia could smell jasmine and her body craved to get in the warm water.

The woman walked back to the cart and pushed it towards Julia. The first thing she noticed was the steak and potatoes and she did everything in her power not to attack the tray and devour it.

"Eat."

"Like I'd trust anything you gave me." Julia scoffed.

The woman sighed, clearly frustrated and grabbed the cutlery. Julia momentarily tensed until she saw the woman cut a piece of steak and pop it in her mouth. "I promise, it is safe, Julia."

With one last hesitant glance, Julia pounced on the food. She stuffed her mouth and noticed the woman look at her with shock. Her manners kicked into gear. She was not an animal, she was a woman with dignity and she picked up a fork and knife.

When she was finished eating, the tub was filled and beckoned her to sink into its comforting depths. The woman slowly walked over to her, as if approaching a rabid dog. Julia sat still and glared at her.

She was stripped of her gear when the men that brought her here. She was left in her black fatigues and boots. When they first started to take her gear off she feared the worst, thankfully they didn't touch her in that manner.

The woman started to lift Julia's shirt off, but she shoved the woman aside. After another large sigh, the woman tried once more and wrapped her arms over Julia's. To her surprise, she was overpowering. "Will you just let me clean you up and quit being a child?"

Julia scrunched her eyebrows and gave in. Her energy was gone and she felt disgusting. What harm could a bath be?

She climbed into the tub, sighed with relief and soaked in the comfort. After the past few days, this felt like a spa to her. The hot water soaked into her skin and melted away her tension. "Who are you?"

"Don't recognize me, do you?"

"Obviously not," Julia grunted.

"I guess after so many years apart from someone you might forget them. Even the woman who raised you while your parents were gone on missions."

Julia nearly jumped out of the tub, but was forced down by the strong redhead. "Maggie?"

"Yes, m'dear."

"Why are you still here? Why are you involved with these barbarians?" She was in shock and felt stupid for not recognizing her old nanny, Maggie.

Maggie grabbed a sponge from her cart and gentle scrubbed Julia's arms. "I never left this home, Julia. It never sold and I kept it up on my own. The city let me and a few other staff members rent it from them."

Julia stared at her. "And?"

"And, I am involved with them because they promised importance again. For more than two hundred years I've been forgotten about and obsolete to the world. With them I feel needed again."

"I am sorry about that." Julia felt awful she'd forgotten her nanny. She was family and she abandoned her without a second thought. Her heart broke for the woman that was like a mother to her. "Come to the Domus, then."

Maggie shook her head and started lathering shampoo in Julia's hair. Her eyes closed from the scalp massage and threatened to fall asleep. This kidnapping experience was not too difficult at all.

"I can't. I've pledge my loyalty." She sounded resentful.

"Mother and Father would be disappointed." Julia looked at her in disbelief. She was the most kind, yet stern, woman she had in her life and she was now Julia's enemy. Would she be able to kill her if she had to? No, she didn't believe so.

"No, they wouldn't be disappointed, Julia," Maggie answered.

"Of course they would. They were two of the most loyal people to the Gods," she protested.

Maggie smiled softly and grabbed Julia's hands, pulling up and helping her out of the tub. Julia felt ten times better. Food in her belly and clean from her bath, she was revitalized.

Maggie wrapped a large towel around Julia's body and helped her dry off.

"I'm very glad they didn't harm you, Julia," she muttered. "They are bitter people."

"I could tell," Julia growled. "Damian and Ryan took the brunt of their bitterness."

Maggie ignored her comment and handed her clothes off the cart. "Sorry it's not your color. They insist on dreariness I suppose."

It was a black dress and shoes with undergarments to match. Julia preferred light colored clothing—her gear was the only black she owned. She stepped into the dress and pulled it up. Maggie zipped the back up and Julia was somewhat annoyed. It was a sleeveless cocktail dress and the bust was very low cut. It clung to her body showing off all her curves and her heart dropped. This was much too sexy for her.

Maggie styled her hair into a tight bun and applied a small amount of eye makeup to her face. Julia almost felt like a child with Maggie and her heart ached for the past.

When Maggie was done she stood back and clasped her hands together. "Gorgeous, just like your mother."

Julia reluctantly slipped her feet into the black heels and turned to face Maggie. "Now what?"

"Now you meet the General."

Panic rose in her. She was about to meet the leader of the biggest threat to mankind and she was dressed like a female escort, not a Warrior. How insulting.

Julia followed Maggie to the door and they walked into the hallway. She gave one last glance towards her old bathroom and sighed. Would she ever see it again? Did she even want to?

The dim lights reflected off the marble floors and illuminated the white walls eerily. The long hallway was decorated with portraits of famous Warriors and it reminded her of the Domus. Julia followed behind Maggie along the long red rug that lay in the middle of the hallway and led them away from her bathroom.

They reached the double staircase that led down to the entrance of the home and descended on the right side. She remembered drawing on the white walls as a child and her mother scolding her. Mother felt so guilty about her outburst that she added a few clouds to the wall drawings to make Julia stop crying.

Julia skimmed her hand along the black banister and was amazed the black chandelier still hung from the ceiling and was lit by candles instead of electricity. Maggie really did take care of this place.

She saw two men dressed in black from head to toe. They seemed to be guarding the tall wooden front door and she instantly tensed up. She accepted the hospitality from Maggie—however, being so near these traitors her instinct was to kill everyone.

"Breathe, m'dear," Maggie whispered.

She inhaled.

When they reached the bottom, Maggie led her to the right and towards the library. More portraits lined the hallways and more traitors stood guard around the house. She could feel their gaze linger on her. Fists balled and ready to fight, she maintained a look of indifference in front of them.

They reached the library doors and two men stepped aside. Maggie opened the door and held her arm out for her to enter. "You're not coming?"

"No, angel." Maggie smiled.

Julia was not happy about that, but confidently strutted inside and stopped in the middle of the room. Books lined the walls from ceiling to floor. There used to be desks and old artifacts in here. Now there was a massive throne surrounded by smaller chairs sitting at the far end of the room, away from the door. A man sat in the massive gothic throne and Julia dug her nails into the palms of her hands.

She looked to her left and saw an area that held multiple forms of torture implements. Her heart dropped. This must be where Ryan and Damian were hurt and she must be next. Panic filled her chest and she could not move.

She thoroughly studied the man in black sitting on the throne. She could tell he was extremely muscular and tall. His black hood shadowed his face and a long sword was propped against the throne. If only she could see his face.

Julia crossed her arms and glared at the man. He must be the General and she was not going to give him the satisfaction of intimidating her. There were two men on each side of him. One of the men walked forward, removed his hood and revealed his face.

"Hello, Julia." Aden grinned.

"You bastard." She cringed.

"Just had a meeting with your brother and his team. Poor Ryan got a knife in his leg. They didn't see me of course, only Jesse here." Aden smirked and Jesse pulled his hood off so she could see who was under it. "Ryan isn't looking too good after what I did to him when the races were over. I was hoping he would die when we strung him and Damian up."

She briskly walked up to Aden and he met her half way with a smug look on his face. She cocked her arm back and swung at him, he caught it before she could connect. She spun around and thrust her elbow towards his face, connecting with his nose. Aden instantly let go of her and his hands flew up to his nose.

"Dammit, woman," he groaned.

Blood dripped on the floor and Julia's fist connected with the side of his head. "I'm going to kill you."

She kicked the back of his leg, when it buckled she sent a right hook at him and he fell to the ground.

"Enough," a strong voice boomed behind her.

She turned and faced the General, who now towered over Aden. He grabbed Aden by his collar and yanked him up and pushed him back towards the throne. She felt somewhat satisfied that his hands were bloodied from trying to stop his nose from bleeding.

Julia turned her attention back to the man in the hood and tried to see his face, but still nothing could be seen. She felt his eyes on her though. He faced her, his head moved up and down slowly and she felt annoyance build in her. "Beautiful, just like your mother."

"How would you know?" Julia asked. The anger in her voice was apparent.

"This house is full of your family's portraits," he said simply. "Not mention the high praise Aden seems to have mustered for you."

"Well, I don't think very highly of him," she spat.

"That is very apparent." The General chuckled.

His voice seemed familiar, she could not pinpoint how she

knew it and her mind raced. His cloak whisked along the floor as he walked around Julia. She felt instantly uncomfortable being surveyed like this. He was studying her and part of her felt self-conscious.

All she could see was his throat and mouth, his chin was strong and his neck was thick. This was a strong man. His presence made her feel weak and miniscule.

"What?" she blurted out.

She saw a smirk under the hood. "You are nervous."

"No." She sighed and crossed her arms again. "I'm not."

"Your breathing has quickened and you are biting her lip."

"Perhaps I am out of breath from beating your crony."

The General chuckled—she had not expected a man like this to find anything humorous. "Silly girl."

"What is it that you want with me exactly?" She was sick of the games. Sick of waiting to know what her fate would be and if she would ever see her loved ones again.

"I want you to join us," he said bluntly.

Julia laughed. "You can't be serious?"

The General stood still and she could only assume he was starring at her. "Of course I am."

"Never." She looked at Aden and the other bastards. "I am not going to destroy everyone and everything I know, just because you are throwing a fit about the Gods. Real Warriors do not betray one another."

"Either you do it willingly or forcefully. It is your choice."

"How can you force me to obey you?" Julia laughed. "You are delusional."

The General ignored her, walked over to Aden and held out his hand. With Aden's free hand he dug in his pocket and pulled out a vile of grey liquid. The General came back to her and held it up. "This little bottle contains a liquid that will erase your memory. No one will be familiar to you. I will mold your mind into what I want. You will know what I want you to know, remember what I want you to remember, and be who I want you to be."

"Why didn't you just use that on Ryan if you wanted him to do what you want?" Julia was hiding her extreme panic at this point.

"If I erased his mind, Ryan would not be able to remember how to summon the weapon. There would be a chance he could, but it would be very doubtful." The General stood very close to her now. Her breath caught in her throat.

"What weapon?"

"You'll find out." He smelled of jasmine and firewood. It was a familiar smell.

"I won't join you," she said again.

Two men came up behind her and secured her arms behind her back. She struggled against them, but it was no use. Aden came beside her, forced her head back and the General popped the stopper off the vile. "Yes, you will, Julia."

Chapter XXV

Ryan

Skulls and bones. More skulls and more bones. Would it ever end?

Ryan kicked a rock and sighed. "Okay, can we eat?"

Damian looked at him oddly and Anna cringed in disgust. Cato nodded and tossed Ryan a granola bar. "Here."

"How can you possibly eat down here?" Anna's face scrunched.

"Its just bones." Ryan shrugged. "It's not like it is rotting flesh."

"Gross," Anna mumbled.

Not a thing had happened since they'd been down here. He was utterly surprised by this. When Ahmose had hidden it, he told Ryan it was an extreme challenge. He barely made it out himself.

Damian smacked Ryan upside the helmet. "Quit pulling on my vest."

Ryan, with a mouth full of granola, smacked Damian back. "I didn't pull on your vest."

"Ouch!" Anna jumped to the side and rubbed the back of her neck.

"Are you okay?" Damian inspected her neck. "How did you get cut?"

"I was just standing there and I felt it."

"Ahh!" Cato jumped to the side and patted his body down. "Something is tugging my pants."

Ryan raised an eyebrow. They were all going insane. He chewed on his granola bar and watched as Damian babied Anna and Cato kept walking in circles, apparently trying to deter anything from grabbing his pants. This was almost comical.

He finished his snack and his companions settled down. Whatever was going on with them seemed to have stopped. "You guys done being crazy?"

They all turned towards him and glared. Ryan shrugged and paced around the area. They were not down here very long, but something was unnerving.

He stopped in his tracks and gasped for breath. He could not breathe. It felt as if someone or something had their hands around his throat and were squeezing tight. He swung his arms to no avail and Damian quickly came to his side.

"What's happening?" he panicked.

Ryan pointed at his throat and gripped his throat like he was choking himself. Damian understood and ran over to Anna. What the hell is he doing?

Ryan's body slammed against the skull wall and he heard a few nasty cracks. His eyesight faded and he could barely make out Anna standing in front of him. His body grew weak and he could hardly hold up his arms now as he slid down the wall towards the ground.

His eyesight started to come back into focus and he noticed Anna held a small cross necklace in her hand. He pushed himself off the wall and his finger accidentally slid into an eye socket. He lunged towards a bewildered Anna and hugged her tight. "Thank the Gods we brought a Catholic."

Anna laughed nervously and Ryan let go. "Guess that means evil spirits are down here."

"You okay?" Damian asked.

"Yeah, just drained." His body weakened further from his wounds and his head throbbed. He hated feeling weak. This was ridiculous.

"Do you need a minute?"

"Nope." Yes he did, but he would not admit it.

"Let's find the piece and get the hell out of here." Cato shivered. "Weird shit is starting to happen and I'd rather not get my ass grabbed again."

"What?" Damian laughed.

"Yeah, ass grabbing ghosts." Cato frowned.

"Okay, from what I remember, Ahmose said it was in an oval shaped structure." Ryan looked around and saw nothing. "We need to keep moving."

The three of them started to walk on.

Wait.

Three.

Ryan looked around and Anna was gone. Damian seemed to notice. He turned and jogged back from where they came. Cato and Ryan followed close behind, their guns ready. He was more than sure a gun would be utterly useless against spirits, but it made him feel better. *Where the hell did that girl go?*

"Anna?" Damian was frantic and Ryan felt the pain of guilt

in his stomach. It was his fault she was here and he should not have allowed it. Damian was panicked, if anything happened to her... "Anna!"

"Get out," a voice whispered in Ryan's ear.

Ryan jumped. What was that?

"Ahh!" Cato screamed and Ryan turned to him.

He clawed at his helmet desperately trying to reach for something. If it weren't for his gloves he would have split his nails apart. Ryan ran over to him and pulled his arms down, and away from his head. "What's wrong?"

"They are everywhere!" Cato screamed. He fought against Ryan's restraint—it was difficult to watch him go through some sort of mental breakdown.

Ryan panicked and smacked Cato in the face. "Whatever you are seeing isn't real. Snap out of it."

Cato blinked warily at him. "Who are you?"

Ryan was momentarily in awe, but shook out of it. *What the hell was he seeing?*

Ryan smacked him again trying to get him to refocus and Cato went into defensive mode. He tackled Ryan to the ground and hammered his fists down on Ryan's face. Surprise could not describe what Ryan was feeling right now. All he could do was put his arms up and block the blows aimed at him.

He finally got out of the initial shock and used his elbows to push himself up. Cato slid down from sitting on his chest and started to punch Ryan's gut. Ryan caught his right arm when he swung at him. He shifted his legs to the right and trapped Cato's foot under him. As he thrust his hips up, Cato toppled over and Ryan rolled out of the way.

Cato scurried towards Ryan, his eyes filled with rage and worry. *What the hell was he seeing?*

Cato tried to tackle Ryan again, but he held his ground. He managed to get Cato in a headlock and squeezed tight so he could not get loose. That didn't stop him from hitting Ryan in his side though.

"Damian, where the fuck are you?" Ryan yelled between gasps. He could not hold on any longer, Cato was doing damage to his side and it is not like he could snap Cato's neck to make him stop.

Damian pulled Cato's arms behind his back and thrust his knee into his back. Cato fell to the ground with Damian on top. Ryan fell to the ground and grasped his side. *Holy shit, that kid could hit.*

Damian and Ryan glanced nervously at each other. What were they supposed to do? Damian leaned down towards Cato's face and spoke, "Cato, that is Ryan. I don't know what you see, but it is Ryan. I promise you. Calm down."

Cato looked between them, sweat beaded on his face. "What is going on?" He was so confused. It was painful to watch.

"Something down here is messing with you." Damian removed his knee from Cato's back. "Just breathe."

Cato's eyes went from wide and frightened to calm. His body relaxed and Damian climbed off him. "You okay now?'

"Yes," he muttered.

Ryan sat against the wall and clutched his side. He needed to rest for a bit. He had fought with Cato before, but never like that. Cato was fighting for his life and Ryan could do nothing, but subdue him.

"Sorry," Cato muttered.

Ryan laughed and winced as he did. "If I piss blood, I'm going to return back the favor."

"We need to find Anna." Damian looked torn. "Can you

move?"

Sure can't. "Yeah, just help me up."

Cato and Damian pulled him up and he fought against grasping his side. *Damn, he did a number on me.*

Cato pulled a rag out of his pocket and handed it to Ryan. "Here, your lip is bleeding."

He wiped the blood off his lip and pocketed the rag. "Thanks."

A loud scream echoed down the hallway.

Damian took off towards the screams and Ryan tried to keep up. After the beat down he just endured, keeping up was problematic. Cato was so surprised he fell behind Ryan. He was in a one-track mind and all caution was thrown out the window. "Damian, wait."

Damian disappeared and Ryan had to stop. His ribs felt a sharp pain and struggled to breath. Cato stayed beside him, he was thankful for that, but Cato seemed winded as well.

"What the hell is he thinking?"

"He isn't," Ryan groaned. *Suck it up*, he mentally told himself.

Another scream.

Ryan and Cato ran until they were back in the tall stone arch hallway and descended the walkway. "Where the hell are they? We couldn't have passed them."

"Damian, are you there?" Cato spoke into the headset. There was no answer. "Anna?"

The headset was silent. Ryan didn't know what to do. The only option was to keep searching for them. Not only did they have to find Anna, but Damian now too. *Why didn't he stay with us?*

"Okay, split up or what?" Cato asked.

"Definitely not."

They stood in the hallway trying to gather their thoughts when Ryan heard the barred gate leading back into the catacombs squeak shut. He ran back up to the gate and tried to shake it open to no avail. "Dammit!"

"It's separating us or something."

"No shit," Ryan spat.

"Don't get pissed off at me, Ryan. It's not my fault we are down here."

"It's not mine either, Cato."

"Maybe you should take your time and think shit through, like when you were mortal. You know, when you were actually good at this kind of stuff."

Ryan's mouth dropped. "Waging war and small group missions are completely different."

"Yeah, it should be easier," Cato growled.

"If you've got something to say then say it, Cato. Don't hold back."

Cato punched the wall and leaned against it. He looked tired and Ryan felt the air between them grow thicker. "You are supposed to be the leader. You are one of the most well known men in the history of warfare and here we are, losing to a pathetic group of rebels. You would think thousands of years of experience would make you greater, but it hasn't. You've grown weak."

"Not only that but you have messed with my sister's heart to the point of her wanting revenge. Now the enemy has captured her and they are doing Gods know what to her. If anything happens to her I will kill you, Ryan."

He had no words. Cato was right. He had become weak. He was not the same man he once was and that was a conscious choice he made. He could not do the things he used to do, be the way he was and still remain part of a team.

He was born a leader, but that was not what being Immortal was about. They work in teams, everyone equal and just as important as the next person. Why did everyone expect him to be how he once was when it cannot and should not be him anymore?

"Cato, I am sorry. I can't be who you want me to be, what everyone expects me to be. I am not that person anymore."

"Maybe you should be that person." Cato sighed. "That's who we need."

"Maybe you're right," he mumbled. "And, for the record, I didn't mess with your sister's heart. I love your sister, Cato."

Cato's jaw dropped. "You what?"

"I love her." He shrugged. "I tried to stay away because you are right, I am no good for her. I tried so hard and I slipped up sometimes, but I promise you I won't hurt her ever again. When we get her back I will be everything she deserves, if it is what she wants. If not, I will respectfully stay away. I give you my word."

Screams came from behind the bars. It had to be Anna. Ryan tried desperately to kick the gate down, but it would not budge.

More screams. This time it was Damian.

Cato pushed Ryan aside and shot at the gate's lock. As it gave way, they pushed through the gate and headed towards the screams. *What the hell is happening?*

Damian and Anna were nowhere to be found. In his frustration, Ryan kicked a skull and its face crumbled in. "Dammit."

Cato leaned against the wall and pulled out his water bottle from his pack. He took a drink then sprayed water down his shirt. Ryan closed his eyes. He was trying to hear any sign of life down here other then Cato and himself.

Nothing.

"I don't understand," Ryan said to himself. He was annoyed. He hated spirits. He hated that he could not be what they needed and he was failing everyone.

"Let's just keep going, find the piece of the Brahma's Staff and do what we can."

Cato was right—they could not just stay and search endlessly. If it came down to it, they would have to leave Damian and Anna to save everyone else. Ryan had no idea when they would use the weapon against the Immortals so they needed to be prepared soon.

They continued on and were back by the fountain. As they made their way up the stairs to go deeper into the catacombs, Ryan's legs were knocked out from under him. His back landed on the wall of the fountain and pain shot through his body.

"Balls," he groaned and rolled over onto his stomach. He pushed himself up and hunched over breathing. "I really hate these damn spirits down here."

Cato started making his way back up the stairs and held onto his now bloody nose. "Yeah, bastards knocked me down the steps."

Ryan looked around. "Why are they so aggressive? The mortals don't even realize they are here."

Cato shrugged. "You have that affect on people, even dead ones."

"Hey, morons." Ryan looked around. "What the hell is your problem?"

Ryan was shoved against the wall and a cut appeared on Cato's cheek. "That's it, Ryan, make them even more mad." He held a rag to his nose and cheek.

"Damn the Immortals," a voice hissed.

"That's not nice."

"Ryan, do shut up."

A man appeared in a mist form and grasped Ryan's throat. His ragged clothes hung from his mutilated body. Half his face had been blown away, possibly by gunfire, and he snarled at Ryan.

"You are not welcome," he hissed.

"I know a great surgeon that could really help out with that half face thing you have going on," Ryan wheezed. The spirit squeezed harder and Ryan swung at him to no avail. He was lifted into the air and his feet dangled above the ground.

"Leave."

Cato yanked on Ryan's arm and somehow got him out of the spirits grasp. The spirit disappeared and they scrambled up and out of the room. "We need Anna."

Ryan agreed. He was not a fan of getting choked repeatedly.

They made their way down the halls and as they turned a corner, Ryan saw five skeletons around Anna and Damian. Some had one leg or arm and one unfortunate one had no legs at all and it made its way around by pulling itself along the ground.

There was a hole in the middle of the skeleton wall and Ryan realized they must have come from there.

Damian lay on the ground unconscious and Anna was being pulled by her feet into the skeleton hole. Her helmet was lying on the ground and her knife was in her hand desperately trying to stop them. She sliced at the no legged skeleton and cut its arm off.

Ryan and Cato went back around the corner, out of sight. "Okay, that's new."

"Shoot them down. Break them into piece. I don't want

those creepy bastards coming back around." Ryan cocked his nine-millimeter. "Ready?"

Cato nodded and they peaked around the corner, Anna's legs were out of sight and she continued to swing her knife at them. Ryan closed his eyes and took a deep breath. He could not let anything happen to Anna.

Ryan and Cato walked into view and fired. Bones shattered into pieces and Anna covered her face from the flying debris. She tried to pull herself out of the hole, but couldn't. There must be something on the other side keeping her in place.

"Hold on, Anna!" Ryan yelled.

"Easier said than done!"

A few skeletons were persistent and made their way to Ryan and Cato. They swung their arms and connected with Ryan's cheek as he was changing his clip. Their fingers clawed his face and he felt the instant sting. "Screw that." He tossed the gun aside, grabbed another from his holster and shattered the bones to pieces.

He ran over to Anna when the path had cleared and grabbed her hands. Her head and arms were all he could see. Panic rose in his chest.

"Ryan," she cried, "get me out!"

He pulled on her arm with every ounce of strength he had left and Cato came up behind him. Both of them grabbed hold of one arm and she started to reappear. He felt her arm pop and she screamed in pain.

Ryan let go of her arm and grabbed her around the waist. He didn't want to inflict any more damage. "I've got you, Anna."

Her sobs made him angry and he yanked on her harder. Women should never cry and this was because of him. Her being here, in this situation, was his fault. He pulled as hard as he could until she was free.

She fell on top of Ryan and he held onto her tightly. His nerves got the better of him and he froze up. "You okay?"

She shook her head and he sat her and himself up. Anna gripped her shoulder and bit her lip trying hard not to cry out loud.

"It's dislocated," she whimpered.

"I'll fix it." Cato crawled over to her.

Ryan tore his eyes from her and crawled over to Damian. His helmet was off and he had a large bump on his forehead. Ryan smacked him in the face. "Get up."

Nothing.

One more smack and Damian's eyes fluttered open. He groaned and sat up as he rubbed his cheek. "Uncalled for."

"Very called for." Ryan smirked and helped his friend up.

Damian buckled his helmet back on and turned quickly when he heard Anna scream. He scrambled to her side. "What happened? Are you okay?"

His hand caressed her face and Ryan felt jealous of what they had. Damian had no need to hide his feelings. They were open and happy with one another. He wished for that in his life.

"I'm okay." Her gaze went to Ryan. "Thank you."

Damian looked between them, but before he could ask, Cato interrupted, "Okay, spine finding time."

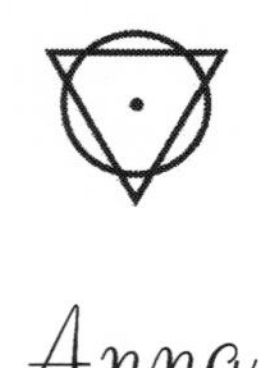

Anna

They were finally all back together again. Anna's arm throbbed, but she was glad she didn't get pulled into whatever hole those skeletons were trying to drag her into. That was single-handedly the most terrifying experience of her life and Ryan, of all people, saved her.

They walked through the skeleton halls and she watched Ryan as he walked. How was he able to function after all his body had been through? An insane amount of torture, getting stabbed in the leg, and now he saved her from getting buried for life. He was a machine and she had nothing but respect for him.

She felt Damian's eyes on her and she looked at him. "What?"

"Why are you starring at him?" he asked.

"Just amazed."

Damian rolled his eyes. "Great."

Anna held out her arm, hitting his chest and he stopped walking. "What's your problem?"

"They all go for Ryan." He shrugged. "I knew at some point you probably would too."

She smacked him hard in the face and walked to catch up with Cato and Ryan. Jealousy was annoying and she was not in the mood, especially not after what just happened.

She heard Damian jog up next to her. "What was that for?"

"The fact that you think I have something for him is insane and insulting." She looked forward. "I was only admiring how strong he is. Going through everything he has been through and still able to do what he does. It's insane. I was in no way, shape or form checking him out."

Damian sighed and grabbed her hand. Even through their gloves she could feel his warmth. "I'm sorry."

He looked so lost and troubled. She kissed him softly on the lips. "Besides, I don't think anyone could handle his personality.

Especially not me."

Damian laughed and Ryan spoke up, "It's not the personality that makes them come back." He looked back at them and winked.

"You're nasty." She chuckled.

"And proud of it."

Cato and Damian shook their heads and Anna saw a smirk on their lips. She felt secure. These three men proved they would never give up on each other or her. *This is what a family is like.*

They entered a room with an interesting centerpiece. It was a large keg shaped structure made out of skulls and bones that reached from the ceiling to the ground. She walked around it in awe.

"Whoa."

"Whoa, is right." Ryan looked around the structure. "I think this is what Ahmose was talking about. It's oval. Sort of."

The four of them searched all over the structure. There was no spine shaped bone anywhere on it and Anna could see Ryan's frustration. He walked over to Damian and whispered something in his ear. Damian shook his head and his expression was grim. They both looked at her and back to each other.

"No," Damian whispered.

"Come on, nothing is going to happen I promise."

"No, end of discussion."

She walked up to the two of them and they stopped arguing. "What?"

"Nothing," Damian snapped at her. *What the hell?*

"We could really use your assistance, but your boy toy is adamant about you being safe."

"What is it? At least let me make my own decisions." She wanted to glare at Damian. She was not a child and didn't need protecting all the damn time.

They exchanged looks and Ryan walked up to her cautiously. "How do you feel about being bait?

"No." She stared blankly. *Is he serious?*

"This isn't an option." Ryan was firm.

"She said no, Ryan." Damian glared.

"You believe in your God, right?" Ryan ignored him. "Fully and whole-heartedly believe."

She nodded. Where is this going?

"That's why."

"I don't get it."

"Most everyone down here did too. Which is why they want you to join them and why your cross scares them," he answered. "They see you as one of them and fear the wrath of God."

"So, they want me to join," she confirmed. "That's why they were pulling me into that hole?"

"Our best guess," Damian added. "Places like this don't like Immortals. We escaped death and there are good spirits and bad spirits down here. The bad ones resent us. A Catholic Immortal would be a prize."

"What does that have to do with me being bait?"

The three exchanged looks again and Damian spoke, "We are going to have to bring these remains to life."

"Why?"

"Again, this is a guess," Ryan added, "but we think the piece is inside of the structure and we can't get to it unless the bones are removed."

"Then remove them or blow it up," she answered.

Ryan sighed. "Ahmose said that in order to get the piece a person must earn it. This is the only way of earning it."

"So, more skeletons?" she inquired.

They nodded.

"And, you want me to stand here and let them get me?" She crossed her arms.

"Pretty much, yeah," Cato answered.

"What if that doesn't work?" she asked.

As if they rehearsed it, Damian, Cato, and Ryan all shrugged at the same time.

"We were going to go with the piss them off method." Ryan shrugged.

"Oh, good plan." She rolled her eyes. This is stupid. This is idiotic. This is down right dumb.

"So is that a yes?" Ryan grinned. What is with this guy? Be safe and don't get hurt. Be bait. What a bipolar nightmare.

"Whatever." She sighed.

Damian walked over to her and tucked her cross under her gear and out of sight. "Doubt they will come if they see it."

"All right boys, let's go hide." Ryan clapped his hands together.

Damian kissed Anna softly on the lips and he gently pulled on her ponytail. "You've got this."

She nodded and stood in place. The boys were out of sight and she looked around nervously just waiting for the nightmare to reappear. Nothing happened.

One hour went by and no sign of the guys, so she continued to wait. *What did I think was going to happen? That they would just appear quickly?* She leaned against the keg of skulls and kicked at the dirt on the ground. *This is boring.*

Another hour went by and she sat on the ground. She found small rocks and threw them at the skulls. They kept bouncing off until finally she made a rock go in one of the skull's eye sockets. *Score.*

Her ponytail was gently tugged and she laughed. "Come up with another plan, I take it?"

Anna turned around to look at Damian and screamed. An arm pulled itself up her body and had grabbed ahold of her hair. She smacked it away and it landed with a soft thud across the room. The arm crawled back towards her slowly and she heard a loud rattling behind her. She slowly turned to watch skulls falling out of place from the skull keg and they rolled on the floor gathering around her. She jumped out of the way as one grabbed for her and she landed on another. A loud crunch came from under her foot and she shivered in disgust.

She closed her eyes. This can't be real. This is just a hallucination.

As she opened her eyes, a gasp escaped her lips. The skeleton walls had transformed. They were no longer bones, but fresh body parts and decapitated heads piled on top of each other. Blood dripped out of the limbs and heads, down to the ground and her heart stopped. The heads looked terrified, mutilated or at ease, and she could see the bones sticking out of the skin on the arms and legs.

She could not help it—she threw up on the ground and wiped her hand on the back of her glove. As she looked up she saw ghosts walk out of the human carnage walls and turn into solid zombie like creatures. Her scream caught in her throat.

Their clothes were torn and hung off their destroyed bodies. Most limped towards her with scowls on their face's and her heart felt like it stopped.

One zombie guy smiled at her menacingly and she finally screamed. This was terrifying and she knew they wanted her dead.

She backed into the keg bone structure. A few more zombies came out that had burns all over their bodies. *This cannot be real. I must be having a mental breakdown.*

The heads on the ground knocked her feet out from under her and she fell down hard on top of a few of them. Pain shot up her back and she scrambled away from the heads and back against the keg.

The zombies were closer now and their tortured hands reached out for her. The smiling one grabbed her vest and pulled her up towards his face. A hole in his head oozed blood. His clothes were rags, barely hanging on his body. His neck made a disgusting crack when he cocked his head to the side.

Bile came up her throat and she held back her scream. Her mind could not process what was happening. *Damian was right, this is out of my element!*

"Stay with us." His voice was raspy and snakelike and his smile never faded. Adrenaline finally started to pump through her and she rammed her right elbow down on the zombie's arm that had ahold of her. Anna about threw up again when the arm came off and fell to the floor. It searched around and grabbed her foot. The Addams's Family popped in her mind.

She kicked the arm away and lacking one of his limbs didn't seem to faze the zombie guy at all. His smile remained and he reached out to her with his other hand. "Stay."

Anna felt the keg structure begin to move and the bloodied limbs grabbed and entrapped her against it, forming a cocoon around her body. Her hands were trapped by her sides and her legs squeezed tightly together as the arms began to pull her in slowly.

Anna could not breathe or move her arms. She clawed at her pants trying desperately to reach for a knife or gun, but she could not reach anything. *This is it, I'm going to die.*

Bullets whizzed around her, breaking her entrapment on one side and she had enough give to pull away from the arms. Damian, Cato, and Ryan ran towards the zombies with their guns blazing. Her body froze up and all she could manage to do was watch the well-oiled machine at work.

Damian was grabbed by a zombie and without hesitation, ducked as Ryan decapitated it in one swift motion. Cato was pulled against the wall by the arms and he tried to yank out of their grasp.

Damian pulled his gun and shot so close to Cato's body that Anna's heart skipped, but Cato didn't flinch. He was able to pull away from the hands and help Ryan cut down more zombies.

She was pulled to the ground and a zombie crawled on top of her. Half of its face was missing and she could see the inside of his head. It dug its bony fingers into her side and she screamed. It cut through her shirt and she could feel her skin being torn away.

Anna reached down and un-holstered her gun. She shot directly into the zombies face and bits of flesh and blood showered her body.

It fell on top of her and she shoved it off. Shakily, trying to stand, another zombie grabbed her foot. This one was strong. It dragged her body towards the keg and pushed her towards the gapping hole in it.

With all her strength she held onto the edges of the hole and pushed away from it. Her hands dug into the flesh of a dismembered head and she cringed. The zombie filled her ears with malicious doom-laden laughter. "You will be mine."

She looked at her captor and stared into its empty eyes. His smile was rotten and his nose was pointed. He must have been in his thirties when he died.

She turned away from the disgusting face and saw Cato get tackled to the ground by a woman in a long ragged dress. His arms were pinned to his side. Ryan sliced her in half with his sword. Damian was trying to kick off an arm that grasped his ankle and fell over a man's head.

She turned back to push herself out of the hole when she saw a small stick lying in the middle of the keg structure. There was nothing around it except a spider that claimed it with its web.

Before she could process anything, the zombie gave her one final shove and she was entrapped in darkness.

Ryan

Ryan threw a right hook in the dead girl's face and he jumped around in disgust when the skin came off on his glove. "Gross." He shook his hand ferociously.

Damian laughed and shot the woman in the head. She fell with a small thunk and disappeared. The undead all started to disappear and leave without a fight. The walls became bones once more and it looked as if nothing had happened.

"Uh, okay?" Damian was confused.

"That was weird," Ryan agreed.

Ryan looked around and there was no sign of Anna anywhere. Last he saw, she was almost being pushed into the bone centerpiece in the middle of the room and now it was whole again. They all walked around the room and there was no sign of her. He heard no screaming and no gunfire—he could tell

Damian was getting nervous.

"Where could she have gone?" Damian jogged into another area and came back looking defeated.

"Anna!" Ryan yelled.

Ryan was hesitant to put his ear near the walls, given what just happened—however, he listened intently for any sign of life within them. Damian and Cato did the same.

All was quiet and Ryan's heart began to race. He should have kept an eye on her. He never should have used her as bait. He should have figured out another way. They lost Anna and whatever possibility they had of getting the piece.

Damian continued to move around the walls and listen for any sign of life. His eyes blazed with worry and determination. "Damian, I am sorry. I shouldn't have made her do this. This is all my fault."

Damian stood straight and his shoulders were hunched. He would not face Ryan, but instead looked to the ground in defeat.

"Yes, it is your fault. She was not ready for this and you knew it. Yet you still allowed her to come." His back slid down the wall and he sat on the ground with his hands draped over his knees. "Her blood is on your hands, Ryan."

He had nothing to say. No smart remark and no words of comfort for his dearest friend. When he looked at Damian now, all he saw was hatred in his eyes. After all of the women Damian had been with throughout the years, this one got to him the most. They always broke his heart and now it was Ryan's fault for this one.

"I'm sorry," he whispered.

Damian glared at him, his eyes were ablaze and he ground his teeth. Ryan took a step back, shocked by his expression. This was not the look of anger. This was hatred. Damian stood up slowly and grabbed Ryan by the vest. He was admittedly nervous when Damian laughed.

"You're sorry?" He slammed Ryan hard against the skull and bone centerpiece. "Everyone I have ever loved is dead because of you, Ryan."

"What?" Ryan was confused.

"Everyone!" he screamed. "It's because of you I am Immortal. Everyone that mattered is long dead and here I am, still living in your shadow. Every woman, then and now, fawns over you while I stand in the corner and look after your sorry ass. Now, the one person I found that is Immortal too, who prefers me to you, and makes me feel something for once, is gone because of you. Dead, because of you."

"I didn't mean to-"

"You never mean to, Ryan," he interrupted. "Mr. Carefree Ryan, doing what he wants when he wants with no regard to anyone else. Does anyone even matter to you? Me? Cato? Julia?"

"Damian, calm down." Cato tried to pull Damian off Ryan, but Damian yanked his arm out of his grasp.

"Don't act like you don't feel the same way, Cato," Damian growled. Ryan had never seen him like this. Ever. "You are a disease, Ryan. You destroy everyone and everything around you. I am done with you."

If ever Ryan felt his heart break it was now. His entire life he had Damian and now Damian hated him. Admittedly he would be lost without his friend. *I cannot lose him*. "Damian, please."

Damian punched Ryan in the jaw and he fell to the ground. The taste of blood filled his mouth and he rubbed his jaw. "You won't talk your way out of this one. You are dead to me."

Ryan sat up and against the keg structure and hung his head low. Nothing he could say or do would fix this. *It's my fault that Anna is gone. Damian's right—I ruin everything around me.*

He would not look up, could not face the truth that his one and true friend despised him. *I have no one now. Julia is gone and Cato has never been that close to me. He was family, but not in the way Damian was. Damian is my brother, blood or not.*

Cato awkwardly cleared his throat. "Now what?"

"We need to figure out how to get the piece. We still have the human race to save." Damian's voice was pained. "Or are you too self-absorbed to continue, Ryan?"

Ryan leaned his head back against the bones and closed his eyes. The best thing for him to do was ignore Damian right now. His fuse was short and fighting one another would help nothing. How could he possibly fix this? How were they going to get the piece?

Ryan drifted to a memory from when they were mortal.

He was running towards a grassy area in the court. He had just received news that his two friends were in a brawl and no one was bothering to stop it.

He saw two sides of men cheer for who they supported and Ryan was instantly infuriated. Egging on this behavior was un-excusable, especially from his generals. Damian was in a headlock and Ryan felt embarrassed by their behavior. The men drew their swords.

He jogged over to the two men and pushed them apart. His anger was apparent. Damian was huffing, his face red and body shaking with anger. His hands were clenched around his sword, ready to use it. The other man was prepared to fight, as well.

Ryan knew he said other words to both of them but he could not remember exactly what. Something about if he caught them fighting again he would kill the one who started it.

Both men looked at Ryan then to each other. They knew they'd crossed a line. They knew Ryan would make good with his threat. Ryan walked up to Damian and didn't bother to lower his voice. These words he remembered very well and regrets it with all his heart to this day. "Without me, you're nothing."

Ryan put his head in his hands and sighed. Even then he was cruel to the one person that cared for him the most. No wonder Damian felt second to him—he even said it.

Cato looked at Damian, who was pacing around the room and back to Ryan. Cato came and sat by him and held out a granola bar. He was not in the mood for food, but he needed the distraction. "Thanks."

Damian went off down a hallway and Cato turned to Ryan. "He will come around. He always does."

"I doubt it. This time is different." Ryan sighed and unwrapped the bar.

"Ryan, I hate to admit this, but you have become a totally different person over the years." Cato smirked

"Admit it? You practically yelled it at me awhile ago."

Cato shrugged. "Don't tell him I told you this, but Damian said you used to be the biggest asshole ever. It was your way or no way. You were not afraid to kill anyone for making you mad and you never ever let anyone talk back to you."

"What part of that is supposed to make me feel better, exactly?" Ryan could not help but laugh.

"You work in a team now. You help others, not just yourself and honestly, old Ryan would have killed Damian for the way he just talked to you."

"I suppose you're right." Cato was trying to make him feel better? What a day.

"You're still an asshole though." Cato smirked and Ryan

grinned as well. "He will come around, Ryan. You two are just like bickering brothers right now and he is just upset. Family always forgives each other."

"Can't say I blame him." Damian came back into view. "He lost his girl because of me."

Cato rolled his eyes. "She knew what she was getting into, Ryan. It's no ones fault."

Ryan felt a soft vibration on his back. It grew harder and he turned to look at the bones. Nothing moved. He must have imagined it.

He turned back around and Cato eyed him warily. "What?"

"Thought I felt something."

A loud crack came from behind him and a small shovel appeared out of the keg. He scrambled to get up when a small hand reached out of the wall and grasped Ryan's shirt. He panicked for a second, but panic quickly turned to relief. It was a female arm with all it's skin and veins working properly. "Anna?"

"Ryan?" her voice was muffled.

"Damian!" Ryan yelled.

Damian was there in no time and shoved Ryan out of the way. He grabbed onto Anna's hand and pulled. Ryan heard her cry out and Damian let go.

"Just stand back," her muffled voice shouted and they did what they were told.

The bone structure opened like French doors and Anna crawled out on her hands and knees. She rolled onto her back and the doorway slammed shut.

Damian was at her side at once. She laid there laughing to herself. He looked worried, but she seemed either amused or suffering from hysteria. She sat up and Damian wrapped his arms around her.

"I'm fine," she said softly.

Damian's eyes looked on the brink of tears and Ryan was lost for words. Damian was in love with Anna on such a deep level he never knew was possible for him. Ryan felt jealous, happy, and sad at once.

Anna put her necklace back on around her neck. Ryan smirked. "Didn't care for it did they?"

She shook her head. "Took me a while, but I remembered you saying they were afraid of God's wrath. They also didn't like me using my E-tool to dig out of that big ass thing."

Ryan smiled, but when Damian glanced briefly at him, it faded. Damian helped her stand up and she took her helmet off. Ryan was glad she was okay but he knew it didn't change anything between him and Damian.

"You scared me." Damian grabbed her face gently. Ryan looked away. It was a private moment and Cato went back to eating his granola bar.

Ryan walked away from the three of them and he'd never felt more alone in his life.

He felt a tap on his shoulder and he turned to face Anna who grinned from ear to ear. "I have something for you."

"What's that?" he asked quietly.

His tone seemed to throw her off, but she held a foot long spine in her hand and Ryan carefully picked it up. He was speechless and without thinking, grabbed her into a tight hug and swung her around. She giggled and he could not contain his smile.

His smile faded when he saw Damian's icy glare and he set Anna gently down. Damian led her to the other side of the room and Ryan turned to Cato.

"You two have been through enough shit, he will get over

it," Cato said with a full mouth of granola.

"I'm not counting on it," Ryan mumbled. He dropped down next to Cato again. "He has never said anything like that to me."

"After two thousand years it was bound to happen." Cato smirked. "Besides, he got his lady back and I have a feeling she will put him in his place. She's a tough one."

Damian and Anna walked up to them hand in hand. She looked rather pleased with herself and Damian still looked uneasy. "Let's get out of here before anything else happens."

Chapter XXVI

Ryan

THEY STEPPED THROUGH THE glowing orb and back to the Domus. Ryan was relieved to be back and away from the dead people. "I'll be right back, guys."

Ryan ran to his room and closed the door behind him. He pulled back the rug in front of his bed and stuck his knife between the floorboards. They pulled up with ease and underneath was his floor vault. He locked the piece inside and covered it back up.

His mind raced and he had no idea what his life was turning into. He used to be so carefree. No woman to be in love with, his best friend was always there, and the Immortals were not threatened. Becoming Immortal took the stress of his life away and now it returned at full force.

He momentarily wished he died when he'd been tortured. At least it would have been an honorable death. *Don't think that way*, he told himself.

He ran back into the parlor and stopped as he entered. Everyone looked at him with different expressions. Damian looked panicked and nervous, Cato seemed furious, and Anna was worried. “What?”

Ryan glanced at the other side of the room and saw Julia standing there. She was dressed in a tight, short black dress with heels to match. Her long flowing hair was pulled back into a tight bun and she was not herself.

Beside her stood Aden, who looked as if he had just become the richest man in the world. He wore black pants and shirt to match Julia’s new wardrobe. They held each other’s hands and he felt his face get warm.

“Hello, Ryan.” She smiled sweetly. She seemed completely unfazed by what she was doing to him.

“What the hell is this?” he growled.

“Ryan, that is no way to talk in front of a lady.” Aden grinned and kissed Julia softly on the lips. “What have you four been up to?”

Ryan froze. Time seemed to stop and he felt his body shaking with anger. Never in his life had he wanted to kill someone more then he wanted to kill Aden right now.

Julia looked between them and looked confused. “Is something wrong, Ryan?”

If you loved

INFINITE,

Don't miss out on book two of THE INFINITE SERIES,

OBSCURE.

Prologue

RYAN KISSED JULIA PASSIONATELY as they laid on his bed. The cool ocean breeze tickled his bare skin and gave him chills up his spine. Julia shivered beneath him. Before he could offer her a blanket she pulled his body to her.

He closed his eyes once more and when he opened them Ryan stood in the middle of a throne room. Tapestries hung along the walls and torches were the only source of light. A large table overflowing with food sat on a raised platform to the side of the room. Julia walked towards him dressed in a blue tunic and a heavily jeweled stole.

She walked up to him sensually and he almost fell to his knees to worship the goddess before him, but her hands did not reach out to him. It was like she looked straight through him to someone else. Could she not see him? Was he invisible?

Ryan moved his mouth to speak, but his voice was absent of sound. Julia looked hungry, almost lustful and he felt his body warm up to the thought of her body against his.

She walked straight to him and he held out his hands to her, but she did not stop. As she grew closer, her arms outstretched towards him. When her hands should have touched his, her hands went directly through him.

Was he dead? A ghost she could not see?

She walked right through him. Quickly he turned to find her embracing Aden. He was dressed in a loose fitting, white toga and sandals with a cocky glint in his eye. Ryan saw right through his façade, but Julia soaked up his attention. Aden pulled her into a tight embrace and kissed her.

Ryan tried to scream again, but the noise did not exist in this terrible daydream. He'd tried to escape reality, yet the present still lingered in his brain. There was no blocking the truth.

Julia walked towards him with a dagger in her hand. She thrust the dagger into his heart and twisted it. Her eyes gleamed with excitement.

Acknowledgements

First and foremost I want to thank my grandmother Doris for her unwavering belief in my book and everything she did to make it a reality. I love you!

Also, I would like to thank my coworkers for putting up with my constant rambling of my publishing process and story. Sorry guys! I know it was annoying.

Special thanks goes out to Elizabeth, Drake, and Brianna for their support and input.

A very special thanks goes out to the people that helped me with this process; Beth, Krista, Michelle, Jennifer and Stacy. I literally could not have done this without you and I apologize for my ridiculous and endless amount of questions!

About the Author

Nicole Corine Dyer is an author from Kansas with a Degree in Liberal Arts. After having her two children, she finally gained the courage to write her first novel. She continues to write the next installments of The Infinite Series and fulfill her dreams as a writer.

Contact Nicole
Website: www.nicolecorinedyer.com

Made in the USA
Columbia, SC
13 August 2020

16316154R00195